I0702405

Carpe F*cking Diem

K.D. Miller

Copyright © 2023 by K. D. Miller

All rights reserved. No part of this publication may be reproduced, distributed or transmitted in any form or by any means, including photocopying, recording, or other electronic or mechanical methods, without the prior written permission of the publisher, except in the case of brief quotations embodied in critical reviews and certain other noncommercial uses permitted by copyright law. For permission requests, write to the publisher, addressed "Attention: Permissions Coordinator," at the address below.

K. D. Miller
P.O. Box 14430
New Bern, NC 28561
www.kdmillerbooks.com

Publisher's Note: This is a work of fiction. Names, characters, places, and incidents are a product of the author's imagination. Locales and public names are sometimes used for atmospheric purposes. Any resemblance to actual people, living or dead, or to businesses, companies, events, institutions, or locales is completely coincidental.

Book Layout ©2017 BookDesignTemplates.com

Carpe F*cking Diem/ K. D. Miller -- 1st ed.
ISBN 979-8-9887609-0-0

To anyone traveling down your own road of grief and healing.
It's ok if the path isn't always smooth or easy.
Keep going.

"'We are drawn to stories," he says in a soft voice, "and every scar has one.'"

—MARIE LU

A note to my readers

This book is intended for ADULTS. It deals with some heavy
topics involving loss, trauma, and the after-effects of those
things. It also has lots of scenes involving...*mowing the lawn,* to
use my favorite euphemism. These lawn-mowing scenes are not
for the youngins, so if that might be you, please gently close this
book or your e-reader, grab a snack, and maybe check out one of
my YA books instead.

For everyone else in the adult age bracket:
buckle up, be a good girl, and remember
to carpe f*cking diem!

-X-

K.D. Miller

Contents

CHAPTER 1

Lincoln

"Oh alright, no problem, I'll just go fuck myself then!" she calls out to the runner who just plowed into her—and kept going like a complete jerk. Her sweet, southern drawl is so at odds with the words she's spoken that I actually huff out a laugh, my alarm quickly transforming into amusement, my lips curling upward.

I'd been planning to lie low this morning and not draw any extra attention to myself, wearing the standard celebrity-in-hiding disguise—the very stealthy combination of a ballcap and sunglasses—but as I rush towards her, that plan goes out the window.

It isn't that I don't enjoy meeting fans, I honestly do for the most part, minus the odd or disturbing encounter here and there (I once had a woman knit me a thong with her face on it...), but I just hoped for a little break. Being an actor is strange sometimes. I love the art of it and all of the opportunities this particular career path has given me, all the things I've gotten to see and experience, all the people I've gotten to meet, all the good I've gotten to do—but being in the public eye, constantly scrutinized and bombarded...well, it can get overwhelming.

But to be honest, the plan not to speak to anyone had gone out the window the moment I'd spotted her. I'd been searching for a coffee shop in the quaint downtown area, in desperate need of some caffeine, when I saw her just up the street. She was looking through a stack of paper with a small smile on her lips and I stutter-stepped—actually fucking *stutter-stepped*. I am well aware of how absolutely cliché and ridiculous that is, but I couldn't help it. She was *stunning*. I was immediately drawn to her, feeling like if I didn't speak to her that instant I might die. I've never put much stock into love at first sight, and have been a bit cynical about the entire notion of love in general lately, but in that moment, I wondered...

Then I promptly kicked myself mentally and told myself it was just jetlag messing with my head.

Her honey blonde hair was in one of those braids to one side that's messy but somehow perfect at the same time, with a few strands curling against her temples, framing her face. She was tiny, especially compared to my six-foot-two frame, maybe topping out at five-three, with a slight build, though I wouldn't dare call her delicate. There was something about her that drew my eye, making it utterly impossible for me to pull my gaze away, but I couldn't quite say what. She was gorgeous, that much was obvious even from a distance, but there was something else. Maybe the way she studied whatever was on the pages in her hand, with tenderness and affection. Maybe just the way she held herself, exuding a strong confidence and a quiet strength without seeming to try. Whatever it was, it caught my attention and refused to let go.

That was when the runner brushed past me, though I barely noticed as I tried and failed not to stare at her. I really hoped nobody noticed me, because I was probably looking creepy as all hell, actually. The guy neared her and I knew what was going to happen a heartbeat before it did, not even enough time to call out a warning. He ran right into her and I winced at the contact. She cried out in surprise, rather than pain thankfully, and spun, papers flying across the sidewalk. She managed to catch herself on the light post before she fell completely. The guy stumbled for a second but quickly righted himself—and *kept going*, jogging backward and giving her an apologetic look while tapping his watch, apparently worried about his run time.

Now, she kneels down, calling the guy a fucking prick under her breath in a slightly *less* sweet southern drawl, again making my lips twitch in amusement. She reaches for her strewn papers and though I have half a mind to chase the runner down, before I know it, I'm kneeling beside her.

"Here let me help you." I actually hold my breath as I glance to her left hand. *No ring. Please no ring...*I let out a quiet sigh of relief when I see nothing on her finger. Of course, that doesn't mean she's single, but still, it helps my chances.

"Thanks," she says as we both make small piles. "Can you believe that guy?"

"No," I say honestly. "I thought the south was the land of impeccable manners. All *yes sirs* and *no ma'ams* and all of that." She turns her face upward and hits me with a smile that would have dropped me to my knees if I wasn't already on them. It should be on toothpaste commercials. Her eyes are a beautiful hazel with bright flecks of green and gold flashing bright in the morning sun. Tan skin kissed by the sun, high cheekbones, full lips, and one of those adorable noses that upturns slightly at the end, the faintest smattering of freckles along the bridge.

"Not from around here huh?"

"No ma'am," I say with a grin and hers widens, nose scrunching a bit. We both straighten and I hand her my stack of papers to add to her own. My gaze dips for the briefest moment. *Fuck me.* Slim but athletic, curves making me think things I shouldn't be thinking. She has what looks like a plain silver band on a chain around her neck. A wedding band? It's thick, looking like it would be a man's ring. Maybe it belonged to her father? The more obvious answer is a spouse, but she looks so long, early thirties maybe, that the idea of her being a widow just sits oddly in my mind.

"Are you alright?"

"Oh yeah, I'm fine..." She trails off and her eyes narrow a bit as she studies my face, still half covered in my disguise. I can see her wheels turning. Slight recognition flares in her eyes, quickly squashed as she tosses the idea that who she *thinks* she's looking at could possibly actually be standing here. *Might as well get it over with then*, I think. With an inward sigh, I take off my sunglasses and hang them on the collar of my t-shirt, smiling widely.

Now her eyes flare wide, mouth falling open in shock. "Are you...holy shit...oh my God you *are*! You're Lincoln Ashmore. Holyshitholyshitholyshit. Wait—is this real? Am I hallucinating?"

"No hallucinations," I say with a smile, though I'm honestly a bit disheartened that she recognizes me. People always act differently once they realize who I am. It's like once they clock me as a celebrity, they can't just *talk* to me. Not always, of course, but most of the time it's gushing or fawning or freaking out—all of which are flattering in their own way, but I don't always *want* to talk about my movies or career or love life. I enjoy talking about those things, to an extent and under certain circumstances, but sometimes I just want to have a normal conversation about normal things, to be treated like a normal guy...to flirt shamelessly with a beautiful woman and not have her think I'm just playing the movie star, or wonder if she's only responding in kind because of it.

"I love you," she blurts before scrunching her nose. "Well, *that's* a strange thing to say to someone you just met." She flashes me an easy smile and I immediately feel relaxed, though my heart starts racing. "Let's try the less Stage Five Clinger version: I love your *work*." *Well, maybe a normal conversation is possible after all.*

"Well, thank you." I glance down at the papers. "I, uh, love your work too?" She looks down, as if she's forgotten what she's holding, and huffs out a laugh.

"I volunteer at the library on Wednesday mornings when the preschool classes walk over for Story Hour. We read a book and then the kids draw a scene from it." She holds up the stack up so he could see the picture more clearly. A mouse with a glass of milk. My lips curl upward. I used to read that one to my niece, Sami, all the time. "I combine them all into a book for each class at the end of the year..." She trails off, staring at me again. She shakes herself after a few seconds, looking embarrassed. "Sorry, I'm still in a bit of shock here. This is totally surreal. I gotta ask the obvious question: why in the hell is *the* Lincoln Ashmore, AKA Captain Ultra himself, in Sandlapper Cove?"

"Well, I'm not *technically* supposed to tell anyone who isn't involved in production yet...but you look trustworthy enough." She arches a brow and smirks. She seems so relaxed despite talking to, as she put it, Captain Ultra himself. "I'm working on a new movie. We start filming here in about a month actually."

I told myself that I came to the small coastal town early to scope out all the locations and get familiar with the area, but honestly, it was mostly just my gnawing need to escape the grind of Hollywood for a little while that made me decide to come down so early. I've been getting restless lately at home, feeling like L.A. just isn't where I'm supposed to be, like the universe has been trying it's absolute damndest to get me out of there. Plus, Audrey has been trying to get in touch with me again, despite being blocked on everything imaginable and all my *true* friends refusing to speak to her. She even showed up at my gate a week ago—thank God I changed the code as soon as we broke up.

So, yeah, a little pre-filming vacation on the southern coast had sounded like just what the doctor ordered.

"I'd heard rumors that film maker types had been poking around and that something was shooting at the Mandrake again soon, but I never would have imagined it would be something Captain Ultra-level." Her lips curl upward, flashing those pearly whites again.

We're using several locations in the area—a lighthouse, some of the beaches and marshes, a few other historic buildings—but the biggest chunk is taking place at Mandrake Manor. It's a massive colonial style mansion sitting on acres upon acres of manicured grounds, elaborate gardens, and a small, private lake, all nestled right in the heart of downtown Sandlapper Cove. The governor had built it in the early days of the states as a vacation home or something along those lines and it was rich with history.

I'd actually taken a tour of it early this morning, and as soon as I'd stepped foot inside, I knew it was the exact right place for the film. Despite *Shadowlands* being a teen drama, I'm not exactly known for romantic or dramatic roles, but I'm excited for the challenge and to change things up a bit. Whether fans will accept me as anything other than Captain Ultra these days is still up in the air.

"Well, the rumors are true," I shrug.

"The town is going to go nuts." She tucks one of those loose locks of hair behind her ear and looks at me. No, not looks, *studies*. Her eyes sparkle with intelligence and insight that I can't explain. She seems to see right to the heart of me like no one else ever has. I shake myself inwardly. *Get a fucking grip, man.* She grins and shakes her head again. "Jesus, I can't believe I'm standing here talking to you right now."

"And I can't believe I'm here talking to..." I let the sentence hang, arching my brows and silently asking her name.

"Oh fuck, sorry, I'm an idiot. I'm Savannah Riley. Savvy," she adds quickly. "Also, I realize I've now said both *shit* and *fuck* in front of you multiple times. I really do cuss like a sailor. It is a fundamental part of my DNA and I hope it doesn't offend you." She doesn't say it apologetically, merely shrugs as if to say *it is what it is, get used to it.* Again, it makes me like her even more.

I hold out my hand and a tiny jolt goes through when she places hers in it. *Get a freaking grip, Ashmore. You're acting like a fifteen year old on his first date.*

"It's nice to *fucking* meet you, Savvy. I'm Link." She looks like she's trying to hold back a huge grin and it makes mine widen.

"Nice to meet you, Link."

Not wanting the conversation to end, I gesture for her to feel free to walk wherever she was headed before the incident. Her brows fly up in surprise, but she shrugs and we start to stroll leisurely down the sidewalk.

"It's beautiful here," I say, taking in the town as we walk. I honestly hadn't paid that much attention between the Mandrake and my quest for coffee, but now I really study it as we walk.

It's mid-morning on a Wednesday, so the streets aren't very crowded, but there are plenty of people roaming about. A restaurant halfway down a side street seems to be a popular destination for breakfast, with a steady stream of patrons going in and out. She catches me staring.

"That's The Lighthouse Cafe. Phenomenal pancakes and the best grits in town." I make a mental note to give it a try. Businesses are getting morning deliveries, a group of children walks toward a park, and there are a handful of motivated individuals out for their morning runs and bike rides.

Gigantic oaks line many of the streets, Spanish moss hanging from their branches and swaying lazily in the breeze, the branches themselves curving outwards towards each other, creating a gorgeous living archway over the roads on many of the streets. I can smell the bite of salt in the air from the ocean not far off mixed with the flowers blooming on every corner. It really is a beautiful town.

"So, I just got here last night and all I've seen so far is the Mandrake. What should be on my agenda for the rest of the day?"

"Well, I guess that depends on what you're in the mood for. Honey Bears over on Crown Street has the best homemade ice cream. Literally like heaven in your mouth. We've got a handful of pretty good restaurants if you're hungry—The Lighthouse for Breakfast and Ruby's is a must-go for lunch or dinner—but if you like seafood, the absolute best ones are out on the islands. Some of the old churches are really pretty. Umm, the ghost tours are fun, but those don't go until after dark." Her brow furrows in thought. "Oh! If you like history, Fort Tyndall is really cool." Her eyes light up at that one and it makes me take note.

"That sounds like a winner to me."

"It's not actually here in Sandlapper, it's on the other side of Bowman's Island. So, about forty-five minutes away or so."

I eye her for a long moment and she holds my gaze. I really don't want to say goodbye to her. I know it's ridiculous, know that nothing can come of it and that she might not even be available, but I'm a firm believer in the *shoot your shot* mentality. Can she be feeling this strange instant connection like I am? *One way to find out.*

"This might sound a little crazy, but I don't suppose you'd be willing to play tour guide for me?" I ask, maybe sounding a little too hopeful.

Her blonde brows shoot up in surprise. "Seriously?"

"I mean, unless you're busy. I don't want to intrude on your day or keep you from your...boyfriend or anything." I cringe inwardly at how obvious that was. *Jesus Christ, Link. Really?*

"No," she says quickly. "Not at all. I mean, I'm not busy...and I don't have a boyfriend." She tucks her hair back again before running her fingers over the band at her throat. She eyes me again, seeming to deliberate before finally saying, "I'm still not convinced any of this is actually happening, but...I'd love to play tour guide. Do you want to drive or...?"

"Oh, I, uh, don't have a car with me at the moment, actually. I had a driver drop me off for my tour this morning."

"Well, looks like I'll be both tour guide and chauffeur then. I charge double for that." She winks and then giggles. She's so...carefree and easy. It's refreshing. She digs around in her purse and freezes. "Fuck." My brows draw down in confusion and she meets my gaze. "Ok, so this will be slightly awkward, but um..." She slowly pulls up her keys from the bag, looking guilty, and I laugh out loud when I spy the Captain Ultra keychain.

"In my defense, I've been a Captain Ultra and the *League of Heroes* fan since I was a kid...but you might have renewed my interest a bit..."

"A bit?" I ask, holding my hand to my chest in mock hurt. She laughs and I chuckle in response. I'm already feeling more relaxed and free with this woman than I have in almost too long to remember. Even with Audrey it was never just...*easy*. I loved her, but I never felt like I could be completely myself with her. I think with her, I was the person who I figured the world *wanted* me to be, the person I was *expected* to be. Audrey loved traveling and red carpet events and A-Lister galas, but those aren't quite my idea of a good time. They're fun sometimes, but I'm more laid back than all that.

I was mostly happy to oblige, play the role of doting fiancé because I figured love meant putting your partner's wants and needs above your own—and I still believe it is, to an *extent*. But not if you completely lose who you are in the process. Plus, if it's real love, your partner wouldn't allow you to do that, would give enough of themselves up so that it's a compromise, a balance...right? I push the thoughts away, not wanting to go down that particular path of introspection and regret at the moment.

She nods to a blue SUV parked on the street just a few feet away.

"Not exactly a Lambo, but it gets the job done." She grins and I think she's...teasing me? Here I was worried about having a normal conversation and this girl pulls a one-eighty and is actually *teasing* me.

I roll my eyes but smile back. "I have a Tahoe, thank you very much. Not even a *new* Tahoe."

She smirks as she circles to the driver's side, and I ease into the passenger seat. The leather seats are worn and comfortable. I take in the space: semi-clean, a water bottle in one of the cup holders, Aviators in a clip on the visor, a beaded necklace that looks to have been handmade by little fingers hanging over the rearview mirror right beside an air freshener shaped like an old school Nintendo controller. I grin, enjoying this glimpse into her personality.

She slides in, turning to place the papers and her bag in the backseat and I force myself to ignore how close that puts her, how *good* she smells. Whatever the perfume is, it's officially my new favorite. She settles back into her seat and buckles up. She glances over to me and shakes her head again before pulling out into the slow traffic.

"I can't believe I'm actually sitting in a car with you right now. This is so fucking trippy," she says, almost to herself.

"I won't bite, I promise," I tease.

"Unless I ask you to?" she says with a sly grin, but then her eyes widen, as if she can't believe she's just said that. She quickly cuts her eyes back to the road and I laugh out loud, unable to stop myself. Why is this so easy with her? Her cheeks flush ever so slightly and she continues on, changing the subject. "Shouldn't you be more worried that I'm some crazy fan that has nefarious intentions? What if I go all *Misery* on you?"

"I'm an excellent judge of character," I shrug. Honestly, I probably *should* be a bit more worried. Or maybe not worried, exactly, but at least maybe have thought it through for thirty seconds before going off on a road trip with a woman I just met. *Oh well.* Something is telling him that this is...right. I want to laugh at how ridiculous it sounds, even in my own head, but my dad has always told me to trust my gut. No matter what it was, he was confident that my gut would always steer me right. And, to his credit, the times I *hadn't* listened to it had all ended not so great. *Alright, dad, I'm listening.*

She points things out as we head away from downtown: restaurants and parks, stores to check out and where to go for the best cup of coffee. Not five minutes later, she pulls into a gas station and parks near the door.

"Ok, so fun fact about me: it is physically impossible for me to be in the car for more than fifteen minutes without snacks, so if we're going all the way to the Fort, I'm definitely going to need cheeseballs. Want anything?"

I frown, a bit confused. "Um, am I not invited inside?"

"Oh, sorry, of course you are. I just figured you get bombarded when you go...well, basically *anywhere*, and you might want a break from it. So, I'm happy to be the snack gopher if you want." She gives me another one of those smiles and my pulse quickens. On top of that, I'm oddly touched by her thoughtfulness.

"That's really considerate, and it is much appreciated, but I'd like to come in if that's alright with you." She shrugs and we head inside. She keeps her distance from me at first, as if terrified of the idea of being seen with me or attacked by fans, but thankfully the store is mostly empty and the older gentleman behind the counter either doesn't recognize me, or if he does, he just doesn't give a shit.

"I'm silently judging your choices by the way," she says matter-of-factly as we browse the shelves. I arch a brow in challenge but grab my favorites and she grins. In a British accent she says, "You have chosen wisely."

I huff out a laugh and grin, "Was that an *Indiana Jones* reference?"

"Ooh, extra points for the Captain," she says, adding a bag of peanut butter M&Ms to my pile. My grin widens and I can't even pretend that this isn't shaping up to be one of the best days I've had in a long while.

Laden down with candy, chips, and drinks, we hit the road once more.

CHAPTER 2

Savannah

This can't be real. There is no way in hell that Lincoln fucking Ashmore is sitting in my car, eating junk, and heading to spend an entire afternoon with me. Maybe I really did hallucinate this whole thing. *Maybe I should call Dr. Forrester.* I keep flip-flopping between freaking the fuck out and remembering that he's just a normal man—a normal man who is obscenely attractive and smells really good and is making it nearly impossible to concentrate on the road. I'm Ten and Two-ing it hardcore right about now to keep myself focused.

The entire thing is so surreal, like it must be a dream. He's a bona fide movie star and I've loved him since I was a teenager...but strangely, despite all that, I feel totally comfortable with him in a way I haven't in a very, very long time. Stabs of pain and guilt flare, but I force them away. I made the conscious decision not long ago to look for the good things, to be positive and live each day to the fullest. At the risk of sounding like one of those inspirational signs you see in people's living rooms, tomorrow really isn't promised, so you shouldn't wait. Don't wait to try new things, don't wait to go on an adventure, don't wait to tell someone how you feel. My motto has become CFD—*carpe fucking diem.* It wasn't a decision I came to lightly, took me *years* to get there, but once I made it, I promised myself I'd stick to it. I don't know why I'm being given this opportunity, but I'm going to take it and enjoy the hell out of it. *I'm carpe-ing the crap out of this fucking diem.*

I know that it isn't going to be anything more than a crazy story that I'll tell one day about the time I showed Lincoln Ashmore around the old Fort, but...I can't help but feel like it's something *more.* There's some weird connection between us that seemed to click into place the minute I met those startling green eyes: deep green, like emeralds, but flecks of gold starburst from the center. I shake myself. *You're just starstruck. Get a grip.*

We laugh and talk a bit, not about anything too deep, and I admittedly try to keep the conversation focused mostly on him so we can't delve into my own life too much. I point out landmarks and, like a true tour guide, be sure to include the local legends that are most likely rooted in fact, but have been heavily embellished over the years. I grin when he laughs at my ridiculously eclectic mix of songs, though he seems to be enjoying it and hums along to most of them in the lulls in conversation.

We both belt out every word to *Ice Ice Baby*, and are still laughing as it morphs into *Tennessee Whiskey.* The laughter quickly fades and we both seem to tense at the same moment. The air in the car seems to shift, to thicken, and a tension surrounds us in a way I've never experienced before, like it's electrified. Stapleton's voice is too sexy, the song too sexy...the man not two feet away from me *far* too sexy. I'm suddenly very aware of just how imposing Lincoln—Link—is in person. He's every bit of six-two or six-three, and as I glance sidelong at his arms, his biceps bulging beneath the sleeves of his t-shirt, I'm reminded of just how good he looks shirtless.

I shift in my seat, suddenly feeling all the tingles and jingles that I haven't felt in far too long, and white-knuckle the steering wheel, goosebumps erupting over my arms. *God, does he notice?* He takes a deep breath and rubs his fingers over his thigh, back and forth, and I watch the movement out of the corner of my eye. Back and forth...back and forth...I swallow hard. Why in the fuck is that...*arousing?* He's just tracing his fingers over his leg, but something about it...I barely stop a shiver. *What the hell is wrong with me? Oh wait, I know. I'm losing my freaking mind. This is finally it, it's officially leaving the building.*

I take a breath as quietly as possible, hoping he can't hear how shallow it is, how shaky, hoping he can't somehow hear how wildly my heart is beating. He seems to tense further, his fingers curling into a fist on his thigh now. Is he feeling it too? *No way...*

I glance his way and he's staring at...my lips? The tension in the car ratchets upward and now it doesn't seem electrified, it seems *combustible.* One tiny spark would send us up in flames. *Maybe that wouldn't be so bad,* I think as those green eyes meet mine. I lick my bottom lip and his jaw clenches. I swear he leans towards me ever so slightly before he jabs a finger at the stereo, pausing the song, and clears his throat. I jerk my head back to the road, wondering what in the fuck just happened. Whatever it was, he definitely felt it too.

After a super tense second of silence, I glance his way again and he flashes me a smile.

"Well, uh...that was...*interesting.*"

A nervous laugh bursts free from my throat and he joins in. I like that he goes right to the heart of it instead of dancing around it. Thankfully, the tension eases and we're back to chatting and cracking jokes.

"Aw man, stupid yellow," I pout when I open my Starburst.

"Give it here, I love the yellows."

I turn to give him a horrified look. "I knew you were too good to be true! Deep down, you're a psychopath. I'm calling every tabloid in existence right now to spread the news."

He chuckles and holds out his hand for the offending candy. "Gimme. They're delicious." He unwraps it and pops it in his mouth, making exaggerated yummy noises that make me snort with laughter. This is so *easy* with him. I don't get it. I'm laughing and sharing and joking around like I've known him for years instead of minutes.

"We somehow keep talking about me, what about you? What do you do?"

I flash him a grin. "Other than chauffeur movie stars around the beautiful South Carolina coast?" The right side of his lips curl and I want to curse whoever gave this man an adorable crooked grin. *That hardly seems sporting for us mere mortals.* "Well, I was a photographer—mostly weddings and families—but I'm taking a bit of a break from it." *An eight-year break.* "Right now, I volunteer at a few places around town a few times a week to occupy my time. Ya know, being a good human and all of that."

"Photography? That's awesome. I've always been interested in it, but don't think I have the eye."

"Well, you're no slouch on the other side of the lens," I say pointedly and he rolls his eyes.

He wasn't just handsome, but photogenic as all hell. Even his paparazzi photos were always good. I remember a few years back when pictures of him very obviously tipsy after a night out went viral—because he still looked so damn good in them. Who the hell looks like a model when they're trashed? Not this girl, that's for sure.

"It's all editing, I promise." I roll my eyes and he chuckles. Switching gears, he says, "So, you're acting remarkably...unphased by all of this." I glance his way and arch a brow. "Not that I'm complaining. You have no idea how refreshing it is, I'm just surprised is all."

"Well, don't get me wrong, I am fan-girling inside *hard core* right now," I say with a smile. "But you're just a person like anyone else." I hike a shoulder. The more we talk, the more I'm reminded of that fact. He's so...normal. Down to earth. Funny, charming, goofy...*He's freaking perfect. Ugh.*

"You are..." He shakes his head as if he can't quite find the right word to describe me. "Thank you," he finally says instead. It makes me sad to realize that he doesn't get this often, to just be treated like a normal guy, to have normal conversations. I decide to rein in all my fan-girling and forget who he is for the day. He's just a guy, that's all.

"You're welcome." His eyes bore into mine for a long moment and I force myself to pull away before I run off the road. "So, um, are you allowed to tell me about the movie that you're filming here?"

We keep up the easy chatting and all too soon, we arrive at Fort Tyndall.

The Fort had been used during the Revolutionary War and was built just off the shoreline, a few hundred yards of beach and a small stretch of trees between the outer stone walls and the ocean.

"This is amazing," Link says, glancing around as we enter the courtyard. "I honestly thought it was going to be like one crumbling brick wall with a plaque that said "Former Location of Fort Tyndall" or something."

I arch a brow at that. "And you were willing to drive an hour and a half round trip with me for that?"

He hikes a shoulder but smiles. "I didn't have anything else to do." He holds my gaze again and that strange feeling of connection from before comes back again. Am I imagining it? Could he possibly be feeling it too? *No fucking way.* He's Lincoln Ashmore for crying out loud. He's beyond gorgeous and could have any perfect Hollywood starlet he wants. Hell, he could have a different woman every day if he felt so inclined—there definitely wouldn't be a shortage of volunteers. He'd been engaged to a freaking supermodel for fuck's sake, though that had admittedly ended badly. I remember feeling sorry for him when it all went down. Being cheated on was bad enough, but being cheated on and having it blasted all over social media and on the cover of every gossip magazine on the planet? I can't even imagine trying to navigate that or what it must have felt like. Violating, I'd imagine.

I can't help smiling back at him before dropping my eyes and tucking my hair behind my ear, my fingers reaching for the band at my throat. His eyes follow the movement and I quickly tuck it beneath my shirt. I could kick myself for not dressing up more today. My hair is in a messy side-braid and I'm wearing old cut-offs and a long-sleeved t-shirt from a local crab shack. My shirt literally says "I got crabs from Captain Tony." While hilarious, I can't believe *this* is what I'm wearing when I meet Lincoln Ashmore. *No, today, he's just Link, remember?* Even still, the universe couldn't have given me a sign to maybe do my hair and makeup this morning since it knew I was going to meet one of my celebrity crushes? *Of course not.* The cruel irony of being a walking miracle? It didn't mean the universe actually *liked* me.

After touring the interior rooms on the first floor, we make our way up the wide stone stairs to the second story. The Fort was built in the shape of a pentagon, high stone walls with bastions at each point surrounding an open courtyard in the middle. We walk out onto one of the bastions and Link runs his hand along a cannon aimed towards the ocean in the distance.

"They used to heat the cannon balls in the giant fireplace in the middle of the courtyard before they shot them. That way, when they hit the ships, they not only destroyed the hulls, but more often than not, caught them on fire."

Link whistles low. "Brutal, but effective."

"We weren't fucking around, as they say."

He chuckles. "This place is pretty awesome."

"I told you. I'm usually right about things." We grin at each other and then I turn to stare out at the waves in the distance, the breeze blowing hair across my face. "I used to come here a lot," I say quietly, "but haven't been here in years." *Not in almost eight years to be exact, not since...*

I close my eyes and take a deep breath in as pain laces my chest, hot and sharp. It's like that sometimes, a quick flare, like the lash of a whip, out of nowhere. Other times, it's just a constant, dull type of ache, one that I always feel but have learned to live with.

"God, I love that smell," I finally say, mostly to myself.

"Is the beach public?"

I force the threatening tears away and smile. "Well, even if it weren't I'm sure Captain Ultra would be allowed," I tease. "But yes, it is. Probably pretty empty today since it's not quite tourist season yet." It's still early spring and though it's warm enough for shorts a little farther inland, it definitely isn't really beach weather yet.

We leave the Fort and walk down the winding path that cuts through the small patch of trees to the beach. It's even cooler here at the water's edge, and the beach is mostly deserted except a few tourists taking pictures despite the chill. We walk through the sand, getting closer to the edge of the water and Link surprises me by picking up several shells on the way, holding them up with a big smile like a kid. He pockets them as two girls approach, their excitement nearly palpable.

"Oh my God, are you Lincoln Ashmore??" the brunette asks, breathless.

Before he can respond, the Blonde adds in a shaky voice, "Would you mind if we took a picture?"

"Of course not," Link says, giving them a warm smile. My lips curl upwards. One thing I've always loved about him as a celebrity is how kind he seemed to be. I've heard nothing but good stories in the news and on social media about him, and that definitely isn't the case for a lot of actors in his position. He spends time at children's hospitals, gives to charity, never turns down autograph or photo requests, makes sure fans are treated well at any event he attends. I'm glad to see that it isn't all just BS spun to the masses by his PR Manager.

"Here, let me," I offer, holding out my hand for the brunette's phone. They look to be in their late teens or very early twenties, and it's clear that they're both losing their minds. I really can't blame them. I'm honestly not quite sure how I kept my relative cool today.

"Thank you so much!" she says, big blue eyes glassy with tears. "Can you take a couple just to be sure?"

"I got you, girl." I give her a smile and start snapping picture after picture, turning the camera this way and that. I switch up some settings on the phone's camera and have them shift positions to get some really great shots. The girls are grinning from ear to ear and it makes me smile even more. I'd almost forgotten how much I love capturing moments of joy like this. Or used to. Or still do I guess. It's complicated.

The girls squeal when they look at a few of the pictures and thank me over and over.

"Can we get an autograph? Oh my God, I can't believe we're really meeting you!"

They rummage through their purses for something for Link to sign, and I wave and wander off a bit to plop down and give them some time with him alone. I put my flip flops beside me and dig my toes into the sand, wiggling them and sighing at the familiar feeling. I watch Link as he signs what look like receipts for the girls, taking the opportunity to really ogle him. He's even more handsome in person than he is on screen and that's really, *really* saying something. Tall with broad shoulders and a lean build, muscles for days but not in an over-the-top way; dark brown, somewhat shaggy hair that I can imagine running my fingers through all too well; chiseled jaw with that perfect perma-five-o'clock-shadow that I love and a cleft in his chin; gorgeous green eyes and a killer smile. All of that combined: he was a full-on panty-eviscerator.

I've always loved him as an actor, going back to his days on *Shadowlands*, the supernatural teen drama that really started his career. Early on, he'd started falling into that typical young

Hollywood trap of boozing and drugs and women, but he straightened up pretty quickly. After *Shadowlands* ended, he'd taken a bit of a break and done a few smaller and indie films, but had made an epic comeback when he landed the role of Captain Ultra in a string of superhero movies that the entire world had fallen in love with. The last *League of Heroes* movie had come out almost five years ago now, but the hype was still very real. I honestly don't think it'll ever end—he'll be the Captain until he's ninety.

I still can't really believe that I actually met him, let alone that I'm spending the day with him and chatting like we're on a date or something. He's so...*normal.*

Link eventually says goodbye to the girls and wanders over, settling down beside me and resting his elbows on his knees. We aren't touching, but we're close enough that I can feel the heat of him, feel myself flush at his nearness. Being in the car earlier was one thing, but now there isn't even a dang center console between us. That tension starts to settle around us again, my pulse quickening, my blood heating. I take a deep breath and hold it for a few seconds to try to calm myself, but all it does is remind me of how good his cologne smells. It's probably something crazy expensive but man, is it worth every penny.

Forcing myself to focus, I tilt my head towards the girls, still fawning over the pictures and talking animatedly to each other as they walk off, looking back over their shoulders ever few seconds until they're finally out of sight.

"I imagine that's very..." I cast about for the right word.

"Overwhelming? It is sometimes."

"I was going to say lonely, actually."

He cuts his eyes to me, giving me a look I can't quite decipher.

"It is," he says quietly. "No one's ever...I mean, most people don't see that side of it. How can you be lonely when you're constantly surrounded by people, right? But that's exactly how it feels sometimes."

"I know that feeling," I say, forcing myself to pull my gaze away from his and stare out into the water. We sit in silence for a few minutes, just enjoying the feel of the sand and the sound of the waves crashing against the shore.

I glance back at him after a few minutes and see that he's staring at the scar on my knee. Another one is peeking out from the edge of my shorts on my right thigh. I'm sure he must have noticed that one as well. My scars are very much a part of me, an integral part, and I got over feeling self-conscious about them years ago, but in this moment, just for a second, I wish I didn't have them. I don't want him to see me scarred, I don't want him to see me as...*broken.* I tense, preparing to answer his inevitable question about them with some version of the truth.

But to my surprise, he doesn't ask about the scar. Instead, he reaches over and ever so lightly grazes my right wrist, over the small tattoo there. I swallow hard, my entire body seeming to light up in reaction to that soft touch. *Get. A. Grip.*

"CFD?" he asks.

I scrunch my nose, always feeling so lame when I explain out loud what it means. To me, it's the opposite of lame, but to everyone else, it probably just sounds like a slightly different version of *YOLO* and that makes me want to puke.

"It's kind of my personal motto. Carpe Fucking Diem." I shrug and he smiles, chuckling lightly.

"I like it. Is that why you agreed to run off with a perfect stranger today?" he teases.

"That, and you aren't too hard on the eyes I suppose," I tease right back.

His smile widens, looking so good it's just unreal. It hits me again that I'm actually sitting here with him. Not because of who he is, though that's a whole other thing, but because he's just a devastatingly handsome man who I'm finding myself laughing with. That's been like Bigfoot for me for a long time: elusive to the point of myth.

"So," he drawls, "why haven't *you* asked for a picture yet?"

My lips quirk. "Honestly, I was trying really hard not to be *that* fan."

"Well, I'm asking for one then." He pulls out his phone.

"What?" I laugh, wrinkling my nose. "Shut up."

"I'm serious. Will you please take a picture with me?" He holds the phone out in front of us for a selfie. I can't help but laugh as he leans in closer to me. I cover my face and he chuckles as he snaps several pictures. "Oh come on."

"Alright, alright," I finally groan, facing the camera and leaning my head towards his. My shoulder rests against his chest and I realize how close we are. I can't deny how good it feels, how...right. *Ugh, again with the crazy, Sav?* I smile at the screen, caught up in the moment. He snaps a few more, but something just behind the phone catches my eye.

"Oh my God," I breathe. "Dolphins!" *No way. No fucking way.*

I scurry up, kicking sand all over the place, and sprint to the edge of the water. I barely even notice when the waves splash against my feet despite the cold. Link joins me a moment later. I stare out, wondering if I really am just losing it.

"I swear I just saw...there! Did you see the fin! Oh there's another! And another!"

We stand together, watching in wonder as a whole pod of dolphins plays in the waves.

"I've never..." I swallow, my throat suddenly thick. "I've never seen them here before. Down at some of the other beaches, but never up here." I can't believe this. I'd had doubts about this weird connection before, but now? Dolphins are like my sign from the universe in all things and seeing them now...Well, I can't ignore it. I just *can't.*

"Whoa," he says quietly, seemingly entranced by the sight.

"Whoa," I nod in agreement, tears stinging my eyes. Link would never understand what this moment means to me, how much it both hurts and heals something deep inside in that moment. I hide the tears as best I can and we watch in silence until the very last dolphin swims out of sight.

***

I let out a low whistle as I ease the car towards the gate at the long driveway leading to the massive beach house. It's big, even by Reid's Island standards, which is really saying something. It's the ritzier of the islands around Sandlapper Cove, where multi-millionaires buy vacation homes that are classified as McMansions. We're talking twenty-room houses with indoor basketball courts and shit. Definitely where one might expect to find a movie star.

"Nice digs, Captain."

"I didn't pick it, but it's definitely nice. The code is...um, hang on I have to find it in my phone. Don't give me that look, I've only been here for a day, remember?" After I put in the code, I ease us forward towards the house.

"You know, you should probably change that code now."

"I'm not worried," he says easily.

I chuckle lightly as I take in the house. It's absolutely gorgeous. Slate blue with a sprawling white staircase leading up to the second story entrance. Porches wrap around each of the three floors, fans spinning lazily over white rockers.

I put the car in park and turn towards Link. I'm honestly not exactly sure what to say or do now. I don't want the day to end, want to just stay in this weird dream for a little while longer, but I know I can't. Just as I'm about to say something witty about the tour ending and tips being appreciated, Link cuts in.

"Do you want to have dinner with me tomorrow?"

"Seriously?" I blurt. He grins and it makes my stomach flutter. *Effin A, are we for real?*

"Yes, seriously. I'd like to take you to dinner tomorrow."

"If you think you owe me for driving you around, it's fine, really..."

"That's not why I'm asking you. Please," he adds, sounding so sincere I can't stop the answer from tumbling out.

"Ok."

His smile kicks up a notch and I can't believe anyone can be so handsome. It should be illegal, honestly.

"I have a couple of meetings during the day, but how does dinner around 6:30 sound?"

"It sounds...unreal, honestly. But yes, 6:30 works fine."

"Great. I'll let you know the details...which I'll need your number to do that I guess." He exhales roughly and runs his hand through his hair. "I'm usually better at this," he mutters. The fact that he's struggling in this for some reason makes it somehow more real and more *sur*real all at once. He's just a normal guy, being nervous to ask a girl out...but the fact that *Lincoln*

Ashmore is nervous to ask *me* out? What the hell kind of parallel universe is this?

"Sure, Casanova." He smiles and waits dutifully while I give him my number. A few seconds later, my phone dings with a new text.

"There you go, now you have mine."

"Seriously, this has got to be a dream," I mutter, shaking my head.

"I was thinking the same thing," he says softly. I cut my eyes to his. "I had a really good time with you, Savvy." He holds my gaze and I can't seem to pull mine away, don't want to. I don't understand what's going on. He finally clears his throat and breaks the connection. "I'll, uh, talk to you later then. And I'll see you tomorrow."

"Right. See you tomorrow," I say, somewhat dazed. He gets out of the car and waves as I make my way around the circular driveway and back out through the gate.

"Holy fuck, holy fuck, holy fuck," I chant as I make my way back home. Though my place is only about fifteen minutes from Link's since I live on the outskirts of town, the drive flies by in the blink of an eye as I replay every second of the day. There's way too much to process: I met a huge movie star; I spent the day with him; I felt such an intense and instant connection with him; I saw dolphins at the Fort...

It's all just too much in such a short period of time. I can already feel myself starting to overthink the entire situation. I do that a lot. One of the many ways my mind tries to compensate for all the fucked up shit I've been through. *Trauma: the gift that keeps on giving.*

I *want* to just accept that I had an amazing day with an amazing guy who also happens to be one of my favorite actors and a ginormous celebrity, but my brain just laughs at my silly wishes and goes into overdrive. It instead decides that these are the facts: he's a megastar who can have any girl he wants. He's stuck in a small town for the foreseeable future and knows he's going to be bored. I'm attractive and was in the right place at the right time. He's just looking for something to kill time, a summer fling with the small-town girl type of thing. Or maybe he's planning to have a new small-town girl every other day, just plow right on through the whole coast, and I'm just first in line.

I shake my head, not believing it even as I have the thought. Despite having only known him for a few hours, I just don't get those vibes from him. Granted, he's an actor—and a good one at that—so he could absolutely play me like a fiddle and be long gone before I knew what hit me, but...my gut is usually right, and it's telling me that's not the case. As batshit crazy as it sounds, I honestly think he *likes* me. And fuck my life, I like him too. I keep telling myself it's just a product of being starstruck, but deep down, I know it's more than that.

"What in the hell am I getting myself into here?" I mutter to Griffey as I fill his food bowl and he dances in excitement, spinning in circles and barking. I smile at the goofball, thankful for him every single day. It had taken a long time before I was ready to get a pet, to have another life in my own. It took almost an entire year of encouragement from Dr. Forrester before I finally even agreed to *consider* it. I wasn't even planning on going to look at the shelter that day, but I found a stray kitten and had to take her in. She was adorable, but I'm allergic to pets of the feline persuasion, so I ended up at Happy Paws that fateful Tuesday morning.

A man was there, obviously distraught, with a purebred Golden Retriever puppy in his arms. He was trying to explain as best he could through tears—and what I think was a bit of a shock—that he'd gotten the puppy for his father, but his father had tragically passed away the evening before. The man couldn't keep the puppy himself and had no one else who could take him. I wasn't trying to eavesdrop, but I couldn't help it and when the puppy looked over his shoulder at me, that was it. Fate, or serendipity, or whatever you want to call it, but one look and I was done for. I just knew he was mine.

"I'll take him," I'd said, walking to the man and laying a reassuring hand on his shoulder. "I'll give him a good home, I promise. And I'm sorry about your father." He'd deflated at that, not in defeat, but it seemed in relief. To know that someone was taking the puppy, or to have someone acknowledge his pain maybe, I'm not sure. But he'd let the tears fall and gave me a watery smile.

"Thank you. He's a good dog. Dad loved him for the week he had him," he'd choked out as he'd handed the puppy to me. "I can't believe he's gone..." I'd shifted the dog so that I could embrace the man and he cried on my shoulder for a few minutes. I didn't mind. I knew the kind of pain he was going through on too many levels to count and sometimes just having someone there while you let yourself break down helps more than anything else.

"What's his name?" I'd asked when the man finally pulled away, wiping his eyes roughly but seeming like a bit of weight had been lifted from his shoulders.

"Oh, uh, dad named him Griff, but you can call him whatever you want. He didn't really have time to learn the name, I'm sure." Another flash of pain in his eyes.

I'd given him a wide smile at that. "Well that's just perfect—Ken Griffey, Jr. was my favorite baseball player growing up."

His face softened. "Must be fate," he said quietly. He'd thanked me again, I gave him the name of a few good grief counseling groups I knew of, and we parted ways—him with the tiniest bit less worry and me with a wiggly ball of fluff in my arms.

Now I scratch behind Griffey's ears before setting his bowl on the floor. He gives me the obligatory kiss before digging into his food like a heathen. I pop some popcorn and head to the couch, grabbing a fluffy blanket on the way. I pull out my phone, about to look at the message from Link, when a FaceTime call comes in.

"Ok...remind me...why I agreed...to do...this stupid race?" Tiff pants into the phone as soon as I answer. She's covered in sweat but still looks like a model. Actually, I take it back: she doesn't sweat, she *glistens* and somehow her auburn hair looks perfect instead of the frizzy mess mine turns into when I workout. I only hate her a *tiny* bit for that.

"Because it's for a noble cause, and despite how much you grumble during training, you do, in fact, love doing these marathons."

"Oh, right. That." She scrunches her nose and rolls her blue eyes, and I can't help but chuckle. "How was your day? Oh what was the name of that one boutique where I saw the bag with the thing on it? You know what I'm talking about. What are you up to right now? Did I go out with a guy name Lance at some point? I feel like yes, but I can't be one hundred percent sure. Want to have dinner tomorrow?"

Tiff is my absolute best friend in the world, has been since college, but has a habit of asking fifty questions at once without waiting for answers to any of them. She's been that way for as long as I've known her, and it used to drive our soccer coach absolutely insane, but I love it—and her. I can honestly say that she saved my life more than once over the years, both literally and figuratively.

"Good, but unusual. The bag was at Tradewinds, down in Southport Shores. I'm eating popcorn and sitting on the couch, waiting for Griffey to demand his share. Yes, you absolutely went out with a guy named Lance and if I do recall he had a "lance in his pants" if your over sharing is to be believed. And I can't tomorrow, but how about this weekend?"

"Oh my God, yessss! Lance in the Pants! You love my over sharing, don't even act like you don't. You have to live vicariously and all of that." She winks. "I should really look him up again...I think he's my friend on SnapChat actually, now that I think about it...And yes to dinner this weekend then—we can go down to Southport Shores, go to Eli's and I can get that bag."

"You have literally hundreds of bags."

"Everyone has their things, Sav. It could be drugs, you know. Be happy that it's purses." I hear Griffey stop rooting around in his bowl and then the sound of his paws skittering across the wood floor as he makes a beeline for me.

"Oh crap," I groan just as he takes a flying leap into my lap, tail wagging like crazy and barking up a storm.

"There's my boy!!! Hey buddy! How are you handsome?! Did you miss Aunt Tiff? Did you? Awww of course you did, I bring you all the good treats don't I buddy?!"

"Griffey, calm down!" I get trampled and grunt when one of his paws lands right in my stomach. I eventually manage to make him to lie down in my lap and hold the phone where he can see Tiff. "There. Geeze. Not like you didn't see her like three days ago or anything."

"Don't you take that tone with my baby," she scolds me. Their relationship cracks me up because Tiff is *so* not a dog person, but she fell in love with the little golden goofball the second she saw him, just like I did.

"Ok, ok, you saw her, now get outta here, you big dufus." I shove Griffey away and he gives me a lick in the face before curling up beside me on the couch with his head resting on my thigh.

"Ok, so why was your day unusual? Did you find dirty underwear in one of the library books again?" She laughs, but then her dark brows draw down. "And, wait—why can't you have dinner with me tomorrow?"

I chuckle. "No to the dirty underwear, though that story was one for the books—no pun intended." I bite my lip and slowly run the band along the chain around my neck, my go-to unbreakable habit. "Well, um...I kind of...met a guy."

"What?!" she screeches so loudly I wince and Griffey raises his head, tilting it in a *is she ok?* gesture. She nearly drops the phone and the picture goes crazy for a second, giving me a glance of the sunroof of her car and then her shoes before she rights it again.

"Ok, calm down, it isn't that big a deal." She gives me the driest look in the history of dry looks and I roll my eyes. "Ok, ok, fine. It's sort of a big deal. But I spent the afternoon with him and he asked me to dinner tomorrow."

"And you said *yes*??" she asks incredulously. Her shock is justified: this isn't the first time I've been asked out in the last few years, but it's most definitely the first time I've accepted.

"Yes."

"Ohmygodohmygodohmygod. I can't believe this. This is amazing, Sav! Tell me about him!"

I don't want to drop the identity bomb on her yet, so I just say, "He's...just a guy. He seems really nice. Really cute. Ridiculously good looking actually, if I'm being honest. But I need you to come over after work tomorrow and help me get ready."

"You mean help you not have a total overthinking meltdown and cancel on him." She's teasing, but I can hear the underlying worry in her voice. She's concerned that it might be too much, even after all this time, that I won't be able to go through with it. I'd be lying if I said I wasn't slightly concerned about that too, but so far, I'm actually feeling...ok.

"Yes, that. Plus, I have no idea how to get ready for a date. Or dinner. Or whatever this is."

"I'll be there at 5:00 sharp."

"Thanks, Tiff."

"Of course. Hey I gotta run in and grab my to-go order from Ruby's, but I'll text you later, ok? Love you."

"Love you too."

"And Savvy?"

"Yep?"

"This is a good thing, I promise."

I nod, giving her a small smile before saying bye. Maybe it *is* a good thing. I'm trying not to read too much into any of it yet, but...well, it feels like it's something big. I tell myself how stupid that is, but whatever. Even if it's nothing more than dinner that he feels he owes me as thanks for showing him around, it's the first step back towards putting myself out there again. So, yes, either way, it's a good thing.

I run my fingers over Griffey's soft ears for a few minutes, lost in thought, when my phone dings

Link: don't suppose I could call you?

I bite my lip to try to stop my smile, and my stomach flutters. God, it's like I'm back in high school again.

Savvy: I suppose I would allow that...

A moment later, the phone rings.

"Hi," I answer with a smile.

"So, I know there are supposedly rules against calling within a certain number of hours after receiving a pretty girl's phone number, but I couldn't help it—and I'm too old to pay attention to rules like that anyway."

"Well, rules are meant to be broken I always say."

He chuckles and the sound sends shivers down my spine. His voice is low and smooth, with the slightest husk to it now. He sounds tired.

"Exactly. So...I had a really good time today."

"Five out of five stars for my tour guide services, huh?"

"And then some. What are you doing now?"

"Sitting on the couch with a devastatingly handsome blonde."

"O-oh?" Does he sound disappointed? I chuckle.

"My dog," I clarify.

"Oh," he says again, sounding relieved. "I love dogs."

"He's spoiled rotten, but he's the absolute best." He really is. Griffey isn't a therapy dog, but he easily could be. It's as if he knows exactly when I'm having a hard day, sometimes even seems to know it before I do. I've fallen asleep crying into his fur on more than one occasion.

"What's his name?" Link asks before yawning.

"Griffey. You sound tired."

"You're joking, right?"

"Um, no. You just yawned. That's usually a sign of being tired," I say slowly, confused.

"No, I mean about the dog's name. Ken Griffey Jr. was my all time favorite player as a kid! I got to meet him a few years back and I totally freaked out, like could barely even talk. It was extremely embarrassing actually." I laugh even as another part of me thinks *you've got to be freaking kidding me*. This is all too good to be true. Before I can let my thoughts spiral out of control, he yawns again.

"I think someone needs to go to bed."

"I do," he sighs. "Jetlag is finally catching up to me."

"Well, off you go then. Sweet dreams." I wince. *Did I really just say sweet dreams?*

There's a smile in his voice when he responds.

"I'll text you tomorrow and let you know the dinner plans."

"About that—"

He interrupts. "I promise it will be fine. Please don't overthink it," he adds softly. I'm struck silent for a moment, wondering how he can see me so clearly somehow. No, he probably just assumes that anyone would be freaking out right about now.

I let out a long sigh. "Alright then. Oh, hey before you pass out, can you send me those pictures you took today? I promise I won't post them on social media or anything like that, I just want them...for me. If that's ok."

"Are you ashamed to be seen with me? I'm hurt," he teases.

"Well, of course that's the reason," I tease right back, rolling my eyes and laughing when Griffey rolls onto his back and sticks his feet straight up in the air. "And I've changed my mind. I'm definitely going to sell them to the tabloids now."

He laughs and it makes my stomach flutter again. He's got a great laugh. *Fuck me, he's got a good everything.*

"I appreciate you being so considerate, but you can post them if you want to."

"I'm not really on social media much these days, so I really do just want them for me. To prove this day actually happened when I wake up tomorrow convinced it was all a dream." Before I can decide to keep him on the phone all night, I say, "Well, I'll let you get some beauty rest. You obviously need it."

"You don't need to sleep a wink then."

"Smooth, Captain. Very smooth," I say, but I'm grinning like an idiot. "Good night."

"Night."

A few seconds after we hang up, he texts me the pictures. They're...cute, actually. Somehow, I don't look like a complete trainwreck next to him, and they make me smile. God, he really is handsome. His smile is so easy and warm—and perfect, of course. White, even teeth that would make any dentist cream in his jeans. He has the slightest hint of a dimple on his left side and it's adorable. How can he be sexy, handsome, and adorable all at once? That hardly seems fair. I quickly save the pictures, somehow convinced they're going to disappear any second.

Before I can think better of it, I have the first season of *Shadowlands* going on Netflix. God, he looks like such a baby in the first episode! Granted, he was nineteen at the time, but still. I'm quickly reminded of why I was so in love with him, with the show in general. I end up binging the entire season, getting completely drawn into that world all over again. I'll have to tell him tomorrow how much I still love it. Would that be weird? Would I sound like a crazy fan girl? I'm too tired to care too much honestly. I wake up Griffey and make my way into my bed. I fall asleep replaying the utter insanity that was my day with Lincoln Ashmore, a smile on my lips.

CHAPTER 3

Lincoln

I have a problem. A big problem. I can't stop thinking about Savvy. I thought about her until the minute jetlag finally pulled me under, replaying every detail of the day over and over. The way she'd laughed, the thoughtfulness she showed both to me and to the young fans who asked for pictures and autographs, the way the sun made the green in her hazel eyes flash like glowing emeralds. The way she'd teared up when she saw the dolphins. I don't know what the story is there, but there is something much more than a simple love for the beautiful creatures. Perhaps, if I'm lucky, she'll tell me one day. I want her to tell me that and so much more, want to know anything and everything about her. I don't understand what's come over me or why I feel so connected and attracted to her. And I don't mean a physical attraction—though *dear God* there's that—but it's an emotional attraction, like she just...*gets* me. Somehow, someway, without even really knowing me, she *gets* me in a way that almost no one else does.

I shake my head, well aware of how fucking crazy that sounds, even as I pull out my phone. I'm about to seem way too overzealous, but hopefully she finds it endearing and not stalker-y. I pull up our text message from the night before, smiling at the photos I sent her, staring at my favorite one for a few extra seconds. It was taken the moment before she finally agreed to take a real picture, so her face is turned towards me, eyes closed and a soft smile on her lips. It's an intimate shot somehow, something about it making my chest clench. I shake myself and type up a message:

Link: Good morning. What are you up to?

My thumb hovers over the send button for a good three minutes before I finally mutter "Just do it, you fucking idiot" and send the message. To my delight, she responds almost immediately and a smile spreads across my face.

Savvy: Morning. I'm walking Griffey to our favorite coffee shop before I drop him at the groomers.

Before I can respond, a second message pops up:

Savvy: Want to meet us?

I'm halfway out the door before I type a reply, asking for the address.

***

The courtyard next to the coffee shop is almost completely hidden from the street by large hedges, dotted here and there with bright pink and purple flowers. The hedges close in the entire space and string lights zig-zag back and forth overhead and within the trees, giving it the feel of some far away oasis or a secret garden. Savannah is sitting at a small café table in the far corner, the only one here at the moment, and I take an extra second to take in the sight before I join her. I honestly want to see if I somehow imagined how beautiful she was yesterday, but nope, she's truly gorgeous in an understated, easy way that makes my pulse race. Her hair is down today, falling in beachy waves over one shoulder, a pair of Aviators perched on top of her head. She's looking at her phone while she stirs her coffee and runs the ring back and forth on the chain around her neck. I noticed her doing it yesterday as well, a worn-in habit she doesn't even seem to notice she's doing. I smile when I spy the golden retriever lying by her feet. He looks almost exactly like the one we had when I was little, though Duke's fur was a shade lighter.

"Well good morning," she says with a smile when I walk up. "Looks like that beauty rest did you some good."

"Har har. Good morning."

She nods to the seat across from her where another cup of coffee is waiting. I could marry her just for that, right here, right now. *God, I need some coffee in the worst way.*

"I did some online stalking and found what's supposedly your go-to coffee order. Not sure how accurate your fanatics are, but I figured it was worth a shot." She hikes a shoulder and I laugh.

"Whatever it is will be perfect so long as it comes from coffee beans and includes lots and lots of caffeine." I take a sip from the steaming cup and my eyes slide shut. "Damn that is *good.*" A wet nose suddenly buries its way under my hand on my knee. "And you must be Griffey." I let him sniff my hand for a few seconds before he gives me the go ahead to pet his head. His tail wags like crazy, thumping against the table, and he nuzzles into my hand. "What a good boy," I say, trying my best not to dip into my doggy-talk voice that probably isn't exceedingly attractive.

"Of course he likes you," she says, shaking her head as if half exasperated, half amused. Is she thrown by how perfectly we seem to fit too? He settles back down on the ground, head resting just beside Savvy's foot and tail thumping against mine every so often.

"This place is nice," I say motioning to the courtyard.

"It really is. We come here almost every day. Hands down best coffee in town—and I figured the garden would give us a bit of...privacy." She glances to the entryway as if she expects photographers or fans to converge on us any second. Thankfully, my identity and presence in the town are still under wraps, so we don't have anything to worry about on that front. For now. It'll come soon enough and then I'm not sure how she'll react. Will it freak her out? Will she even want to hang out with me once that becomes a part of my daily life here? *Stop getting ahead of yourself, Link. Just enjoy the moment.*

"So, what does a movie star like yourself have on his agenda today?"

"Well, I'm checking out a few of the other filming locations with some of the production team, then a conference with my marketing people to figure out scheduling for the next few weeks, and a couple of phone interviews after that."

"Sounds glamourous," she says with a grin before taking a sip of her coffee.

"And yourself?"

"Taking Griffey to get pampered and then I have a couple of appointments." She looks away ever so slightly at that, as if she's embarrassed by the appointments or hoping I don't ask about them. Of course I never would. I know all too well what it's like to have no privacy and to have people pry into every facet of your life. I would never do that to anyone else.

"And then...?" I prompt.

She taps her chin and purses her lips as if deep in thought. "Hmm...did I have something else on my calendar today? I'm not sure..."

Griffey lifts his head and barks at her, as if reminding her of our dinner plans. We both laugh at that, seemingly thinking the same thing. "Ah, that's right, I do believe I have dinner plans with some guy I just met."

"Sounds like a lucky man."

She grins, and then looks down at her coffee cup, tucking a lock of hair behind her ear. We chat a bit more about this and that, and I would be happy to sit here all day with her, but we both have places to be, so we eventually make our way back to the street.

"I'm headed this way," she says, nodding to the left.

"I'm parked that way." I hike a thumb to the right. Thankfully, my rental car arrived this morning, so I don't have to get carted around everywhere.

"Well, then I guess this is where we part ways." She hesitates for a second, biting her lip. I wait, letting her decide if she wants to say whatever it is she's debating on saying. Finally, she says, "About dinner tonight. Are you sure you want to...you know, be seen with me? In public?" She sounds...nervous?

I frown for a moment before I understand what she's really saying. She's worried about the media and I can't blame her for that. I was originally going to take her to one of the seafood places she recommended out on the island, but now my wheels start spinning on a new plan.

"I promise that no paparazzi will be invited to tonight's dinner, ok? Do you trust me?" She eyes me for a long moment but finally nods. "Good. See you tonight."

I give Griffey another good head scratch before we both head off to do what we need to do, but the second I get in the car I wish I could just cancel everything and spend the day with her again.

"Get a grip, man," I tell myself as I start up the truck. I head down the street and count down the minutes until I see her again.

CHAPTER 4

Savannah

I turn this way and that in front of my floor-length mirror while Tiff lounges on the bed, sipping her rum and pineapple and petting Griffey.

"Ugh," I groan before darting back in the closet and yanking the dress off, throwing it in the ever-growing pile of *nopes* for this evening's outfit choice.

"Will you relax? You're exhausting me."

"This isn't funny, you turd," I say as I poke my head out. I'd woken up this morning about ninety percent sure that I'd dreamed the entire day with Link, but a quick look at my photos and text messages ensured it had been real. I'd grinned like a moron when he texted me and had given into the temptation to invite him to have coffee with only the slightest hesitation. I've been excited to see him again all day...but now, I'm also freaking out.

"I don't know what the fuck I'm supposed to wear. Do you know the last time I went on a date was?! And I don't even know if this is technically a date. I mean, it's dinner with a man who seems into me, but like...I don't know. Do people even call dates *dates* anymore? Is "dating" even still a thing? Or is it all just dick pics and hook ups? And I don't know where we're going and of course I didn't ask before and now I'm supposed to be there in…" I glance at my watch and want to puke. "Forty-five minutes and I can't very well ask *now* because he doesn't need to know how much of a fucking mess I am. There are some swanky ass places over on Reid's Island! But what if we're just grabbing crab legs at Captain Tim's?" I'm breathing hard after my rant, and panic feels like it's just on the horizon.

Tiff rolls off the bed and grabs my shoulders, ducking her head to get eye level with me and forcing me to meet her gaze.

"I need you to breathe, ok?" She isn't being her normal sarcastic self at the moment. She knows how dangerously close I am to a full on panic attack and neither of us want that. Even Griffey seems to know that I'm freaking out for real and comes to lean against my legs, demanding pets and letting me know that everything is ok.

I take a few deep breaths with Tiff, long and slow. My heart stops racing and I give her a nod, letting her know I'm ok. I'm trying not to let the overthinking happen, trying not to think about anything deeper than what to wear and going on a date for the first time in what feels like a million years. *Don't think about anything else. Don't go down that road. Don't. Don't. Don't.* I already went through all of this with Dr. Forrester earlier this afternoon, talking about the familiar feelings of guilt and anger that pop up whenever I take a step towards "moving on" in life, and I felt…ok after I left her office. I don't want to slip backwards now.

I know the thoughts aren't rational, I know it's ridiculous to feel the things I feel about something as simple as a dinner date, but that's the great thing about trauma: it doesn't leave you with nice, rational thoughts and feelings. It leaves you a clusterfuck of irrational and messy—and that's ok. It took me a while to understand and accept that it is, in fact, ok to not be ok, to be a total mess sometimes. Another deep breath.

"Ok. I'm ok."

"That's my girl. Ok, so do you want the good news or the bad news?"

"Uh...the good news?"

"The good news is, that bra is making your boobs look amazing." I snort and she smiles at me. "The bad news is that, alas, we must cover them up—unless you want to do the whole show-up-on-his-doorstep-in-nothing-but-a-trench-coat-and-lingerie thing. I fully support it if that's the route you want to go, mind you. I did that once," she adds thoughtfully.

"Oh I remember it clearly: Alex's parents were there visiting and got a full view of you in a thong and pasties when you dropped the coat without checking the room first. Good times."

She winces. "Ok, so not my finest moment exactly. But hey, we still dated for four more months after that and his parents even invited me to Christmas that year, so I still call it a win." She shrugs and then gets serious again. "Ok, so here we go. Step one: wardrobe."

Tiff goes into the closet and, after a few minutes of rummaging around, comes back with a black A-line dress. Not too formal, but not too casual. It could work whether we're hitting The Charleston or Jeb's Oyster Shack.

"Ok, how did you do that so easily?" I ask as I grab the dress and pull it on. I spin in the mirror, checking myself out.

"Perfect," she grins and hands me some sexy, strappy heels that are always a good choice. "And I did that so easily because I'm amazing, obviously."

I put on the shoes and take in the whole look again in the mirror. It doesn't look too bad, actually. I haven't worn the dress in years and though it's not quite as snug as it used to be, it doesn't look too baggy. It's fitted through the top and then flares out a bit at the waist. The straps are thick, like a tank-top and it doesn't dip *too* low, but you can see the top of my scar peeping out between my breasts if you really look. *Will* he really look? I...kind of hope so? Not because I want him to see my scar, but because I want him to check me out. It's been years since I felt like I was seen in that way, and I'd be lying if I said I didn't miss it. Who doesn't like feeling sexy and wanted and as if someone thinks they're beautiful?

"It's fine," Tiff assures me, noticing as I subtly pull the top of the dress up a bit. "Hey, if he has a problem with your scars, then he doesn't deserve to be in your company," she tells me seriously.

"I know, I know," I mutter. I shake myself, knowing that she's right. It took me a long time to be ok with how my body looks now, but I've accepted it and embraced it. Even so, a tiny part of me wonders what Link will think of it.

"Plus, if he's looking there, trust me—he ain't noticing that tiny bit of a scar." She waggles her eyebrows at me and I throw an empty water bottle at her. She ducks and cackles. "What!? I told you that the bra is working wonders with your already great chest. Is it a crime that I'm aware of this fact? Honestly, it would be a crime if I *wasn't* aware of it." My chest isn't large by any means, but I'm definitely not flat-chested either. I'm happily in the middle ground—but push-up bras are still my best friend.

I laugh and relax a bit, though part of me is still a little worried about going out to dinner with him. Not because I don't want to spend time with Link—I absolutely do, was thinking about him practically all day long—but I have this vision of being attacked by paparazzi or people recognizing him and wondering who the fuck I am or why he's with me. What if I end up on the front of some tabloid or something? I guess that's something that's inevitable if this thing actually goes anywhere, but I'm not prepared to really think about it as a possibility yet. I mean, there's no guarantee that this is going to go past this evening. I'm getting ahead of myself. I close my eyes and take yet another deep breath. *Calm down. Just focus on the here and now, be in the moment, each moment.*

CFD.

"So, you still aren't going to give me any details about mystery man, huh?" Tiff pouts.

"I plead the fifth," I snap, sticking out my tongue at her. "Let me figure out if this is even a thing, and then I'll fill you in on everything, I promise."

"Alright, alright, fine. I guess I can give you that—but when you say you'll fill me in on everything, you do mean *everything*, right? I need all the sexy details please. Length, circumference, appearance, skill on a scale from 1-20—half scores are acceptable."

"There is so much wrong with you," I laugh, shaking my head. "I don't plan to know any of those things tonight—don't give me that look! I will be taking my time in that department, jackass. Now, help me with my hair and makeup please."

After twenty more minutes of getting just the right amount of glammed-up, I'm ready to go. On a date. With Lincoln Fucking Ashmore. *What even is my life right now?*

I say bye to Tiff who makes me swear to give her an update as soon as the date is over—even if that's tomorrow morning. I tell her yet again that I'll be home and in bed—alone—by ten and will text her then. I give Griffey a kiss on his adorable little nose and then head towards Link's rental house. He'd wanted to pick me up, but I'd insisted on meeting him. He refused to tell me where we were going, saying he wanted it to be a surprise, so I'm meeting him at his place. I would feel weird not inviting him inside if he came to get me, but that would just lead to too many questions and answers I'm not ready to give quite yet. He'd agreed easily, but I could tell he felt like he wasn't being gentlemanly or something by not picking me up. It was sweet, actually.

I pull up and before I can even hit the buzzer, the gate starts to open. I bite my lip and smile. *He was waiting for me.* He's coming down the steps by the time I pull up to the front of the house. He looks fantastic, though mostly casual, in navy blue golf-type shorts and a white button-down with the sleeves rolled up to his forearms. I'm actually relieved that he's not in a suit. I relax knowing we aren't going anywhere super fancy tonight. My dress is casual enough to match his outfit, even with my sexy heels. He grins and waves as I park the car.

I get out of the car and his steps slow. He takes a minute to look me up and down and my heart speeds up. It isn't a predatory or skeevy look, it's...sensual, like a soft caress against my skin everywhere his eyes travel. His throat bobs as he swallows, and then he shakes his head as his smile widens.

"You look gorgeous," he says, eyes raking over me once more.

I smile, but look away quickly, tucking a lock of hair behind my ear. I'm not exactly used to being complimented by a movie star, and he sounds so damned sincere I'm not sure how to react. Maybe it's all an act, but I hope it isn't. It feels *good.* I'd forgotten what it felt like to be appreciated like this, to feel beautiful and seen. Not stared at, but *seen.* I'm not sure if he looked closely enough at my chest to see the very tip of my scar there, but he doesn't seem to have noticed—or as Tiff pointed out, perhaps was distracted by other things in that area.

I bite my lip and let myself check him out again. His shirt is fitted through his muscular chest and for some reason, his rolled sleeves look criminally sexy. How can someone's forearms be sexy? They're *forearms* for crying out loud! *There is something seriously wrong with me.* I'm suddenly keenly aware of how long it's been since I've been with anyone, in any capacity.

"You don't look so bad yourself," I say, trying not to sound as breathless as I feel. I'm about to go on a date with an obscenely handsome man, a man who gives me butterflies for fuck's sake, and I don't even know where to begin dealing with that. "So, um, where are we headed then?"

"Well, I thought maybe a casual dinner here by the pool would be nice?" He looks at me and seems to be holding his breath. Is he worried I won't like it? That I'm expecting to be treated to an elaborate four-course dinner at a five-star restaurant?

"That sounds absolutely perfect," I tell him honestly, and he seems to relax, his smile widening again as he gives me his arm to lead me up the stairs.

"Then, allow me to show you to your table, Miss." I giggle but take his arm, inhaling sharply when my hand touches his bare forearm. It seems like electricity jumps between us, the attraction so intense from such a simple touch. Does he feel it too? I glance sidelong at him and see the muscle in his jaw ticking beneath the thick stubble. I think I've found his tell.

What is it with us? This connection and tension is insane, unlike anything I've ever felt before. Maybe it's just because it's admittedly been a very, very long time since I've touched anyone like this, been even close to a situation like this, but I don't think it's just that. I think there's just something between us, something intense and instant and...terrifying.

He clears his throat and removes his arm so he can open the door and lead me inside.

"Whoaaaaa," I say as I spin in a circle, taking in the massive two-story entry way. It's absolutely beautiful with a large crystal chandelier hanging in the center, white marble floors, and soft blue accents. Beachy, but in the absolute chicest of ways. "Not too shabby," I say as we make our way through the enormous living room. A massive U-shaped couch faces a gorgeous stone fireplace and giant flatscreen. The entire back wall is made up of glass doors that Link starts sliding back into one another until the entire space is open to the back deck. The view is spectacular, the setting sun glinting off of the waves in the distance. He motions for me to head outside, so I make my way out onto the deck. The top level is covered, with several lounging areas and one dining table, but he's got another smaller table set up next to the pool on the lower level. String lights hang all around the space and a firepit is burning bright on the other side of the pool. Music plays low from speakers that seem to be hidden all around us.

"Wow. This is...impressive." *And romantic as hell.* He pulls my chair out for me, ever the gentleman, and grabs plates from the outdoor kitchen counter.

"So, I'm assuming you're alright with crab cakes since you mentioned them yesterday."

"They're only in my top five favorite foods."

"What can I get you to drink? I have pretty much anything you could possibly want—my manager, Colin, had the place stocked to the nines before I got here." I spy a beer sitting near where he'd grabbed the plates and nod my head towards it.

"I'll just take one of those."

"You got it." He winks and sets down a plate in front of me before rummaging in the fridge. The crab cakes look divine and smell even better. My mouth is watering and I realize now that I haven't had anything to eat all day other than coffee this morning. It takes all of my will power to be polite and wait until he returns to dig in. My eyes widen at the first taste and I actually moan. He laughs before taking a bite himself.

"Oh man, these are *good*. Where did you order from? The Charleston?"

"Handmade by yours truly, actually."

"No fucking way." He grins as he takes a swig from his bottle.

"Yes fucking way." I snort and motion for him to explain. "So, my grandpa owned a restaurant in New Orleans, and I spent every summer there from the time I was ten until I turned nineteen and decided to run off to Hollywood and try my hand at acting. I learned a thing or two over the years." He shrugs but I can tell he's proud, both of his grandfather's legacy and the fact that he can cook. And dear lord he should be because these crab cakes are like heaven.

"Well, props to gramps because these might just be the best crab cakes I've ever eaten."

He inclines his head and extends his bottles across the small table. I do the same.

"To Grandpa Ashmore, good food, and even better company."

"Cheers to that," I say, tapping my bottle against his. He holds my eyes as he takes a sip and I can feel that tension building between us again, that pull that I can't understand and can barely resist. I swallow hard and take a few long pulls on my own bottle to settle myself because with the way he's staring, I have half a mind to lunge across the table and do all manner of depraved things with him. He licks his lower lip before I see that muscle in his jaw ticking again and I'm fairly sure he's having similar thoughts. I clear my throat and tear my gaze away before things get out of hand.

"So, I'm sure you hate talking about your work because you have to constantly, but I just want to say one thing and then I'm done, I promise."

"I don't mind talking about it with you," he says, sounding sincere. "Go ahead."

"I just wanted to say that while I was a total *Shadowlands* junkie—and may or may not have binge watched season one last night actually—and obviously I love Captain Ultra and the *League of Heroes*, I think the best thing you've done was *The Ones We Leave Behind*." His brows arch at that.

"Really? Most people don't even know that one exists."

"Yes, really. It's totally underrated and you did an amazing job. Honestly. It makes me ugly cry, like *ugly* ugly cry. You were just so...raw and real in it. The scene where you're fighting to get your little brother back..." I shake my head. "Gah, it's just *really* good."

"Wow. Thank you." I roll my eyes, but he stops me. "No, seriously. Thank you. It's nice to hear when someone enjoys something I do, that they actually connect with it on an emotional level. Not that people don't connect with Captain Ultra, but it just isn't quite the same. So, thank you."

"You're welcome." I take another sip of beer and then to lighten the mood a bit I add, "Those shirtless scenes in *Shadowlands* are pretty awesome too, though."

He throws his head back and laughs, sounding carefree and relaxed, and I join in. I fiddle with the band at my neck and he nods towards it, the smile still on his lips.

"What's the story with that?"

"That is...a little too heavy for first dinner conversation," I say with a small smile, ignoring the familiar stab of pain.

"Fair enough," he says. I love that he doesn't push me, though I can tell he's dying to know. Finished with dinner, I wander over to the pool and sit on the edge, sticking my feet in the water. It's heated, of course, and feels good on my legs. I lean back on my hands and close my eyes, listening to the sound of the waves in the distance, inhaling the smell of the beach mixed with his cologne as he sits beside me. He's close. So close that our arms touch. I'm about to do something stupid, so I distract myself by asking him more questions.

"So, if you weren't an actor, what would you want to do? Run a restaurant like Grandpa Ashmore?"

He leans back on his hands too, kicking his feet softly in the water in time with mine.

"Hell, I'm not sure honestly. Something...quiet. Slow. Maybe be a fly fishing guide. I used to go all the time with my dad, but haven't been in a while. I always feel so relaxed when I'm out there though, just the sound of the water leisurely bubbling by, the splash of the fish every now and then, the birds chirping. It's so peaceful, so calm. I don't know, it's just something else." He hikes a shoulder but I can tell how much he loves it.

"I've never been, but it sounds nice." He holds my gaze and I swear he wants to say that he'll take me, but stops himself.

"So, I can't believe I haven't asked this yet, but are you from here?"

"Nope, from Texas originally actually. I came to South Carolina for college on a soccer scholarship. I lost both of my parents my freshman year—one to cancer and one to a heart attack not long after."

"Oh, Savvy, I'm so sorry."

I shrug and give him a smile. "Thanks." I still miss them every day, but I made my peace with their passings long ago. "So after that, my roommate, Tiff, and her family kind of adopted me. She's from here and would drag me with her on long weekends and holiday breaks. She refused to let me be alone and I just fell in love with the town." I smile sadly. It wasn't just the town I fell in love with. *God, I miss you, Matt.* I shake away the sadness and choose to remember the happiness instead, the joy and the love. I can't always manage it, but tonight, I can. Tonight, it's as if he's pushing me to be happy, whispering that life can't just stop forever, that this town gave me love and joy once...and maybe it can again.

Easy, killer, I tell him in my head. This is literally only the third time we've hung out and I have the world's largest amount of emotional baggage that I don't even know if *I* can handle carting to a new relationship, let alone if Link would want to try to carry it. Not to mention, I don't even know what he's wanting. A fling while he's shooting his movie? A one night stand? A fuck buddy or booty call?

*And he hasn't even seen the scars...*I shake myself, my head starting to hurt with all the overthinking.

"So, yeah, I'm just a tourist who never left," I say with a laugh.

"I can see the appeal, that's for sure." We sit in companionable silence for a bit, listening to the waves and John Mayer crooning in the background. I shiver when the breeze rustles over the deck and Link stands, holding out his hands for me. "Come on, you."

He leads me to the fire pit and I sit on one of the couches while he runs in to grab a blanket for me even though I insist I'm fine. He really is sweet.

"Here you go." He hands me a plaid throw, and settles beside me as I toss the blanket over my lap and part of his. We watch the fire and chat a bit more, and he does that guy thing where he lays his arm on the back of the couch behind me. I don't know why it's sexy, but it is. I tell myself to hold my distance but every few minutes I catch myself sliding a bit closer to him, my thigh now pressed heavily against his, my shoulder almost against his chest. He takes a deep breath and I wonder again if it's possible that he's as affected by me as I am by him.

"Let's play a game," he says, voice a tiny bit huskier than usual. He clears his throat. "Two Truths and a Lie."

I arch a brow but smile. "Oh, I know this one. Alright."

"You go first."

I shift so I'm facing him on the couch, tucking my left leg up onto the couch and my right leg brushing against his. *Ignore it, ignore it, ignore it.* "Hmm, ok. One: I dyed our dog pink once when I was twelve. Two: I hate thunderstorms. And Three..." I gaze into his eyes for an endless moment, the green so deep it pulls me in and I don't think I'll ever come back out again, the golden flecks catching in the firelight and shining like stars. My eyes dip to his lips, and I swallow hard as I imagine what it might be like to kiss him. I somehow force them back upwards again, meeting his gaze once more. *Just do it. Dive in. Live in the moment and embrace the crazy.*

Carpe. Fucking. Diem.

I take a deep breath before continuing, saying softly, "Three: the past two days with you have been the best I've had in a long time."

He inhales softly. "Number two is the lie—though I'm definitely going to need to hear the story behind number one."

I grin. "I saw a cartoon dog that was pink and thought: I want one of those. A few packets of strawberry Kool Aid later and our husky was very un-husky colored. My dad thought it was hilarious. My mom, slightly less so. I was grounded for a month." He chuckles. "And you're right: I love thunderstorms actually. Sitting out on the porch while a storm rolls through is one of my favorite things." He studies me like every new bit of information he learns is something profound, like he's amazed by me or something. "Ok, your turn."

"One: the past two days with you have been the best I've had in a long time, too." His eyes dip to my lips and my pulse races. "Two: I think you're beautiful." My breath hitches as he reaches out to brush my hair away from my face, hand lingering on my cheek. He leans in, pausing when we're still a few inches apart. "And three: I would really *hate* to kiss you right now."

Lincoln

I told myself I was going to take it slow, that I wasn't even going to try to kiss her yet, but the pull between us is just too damn strong. Every minute I spend with her, the stronger it gets, like magnets trying desperately to reach each other. I've felt more myself with her in the last two days than I have in the last two *years* with anyone else. She's beautiful and smart and funny, and she treats me like a person, talks to me like a normal guy. She even gives me shit for fuck's sake. I'd honestly all but sworn off love and relationships for the foreseeable future after Audrey, but apparently the universe had other plans. I can't explain it, and know it sounds ridiculous and cliché, but I don't care. I know if we do this, it will get complicated because of who I am and the life I lead, and she may not be interested in complicated, but I'm determined to try—if she wants me to, that is.

I hold my breath and wait with a few inches still separating us, letting her make the decision.

"God, I hope number three is the lie," she whispers as she leans forward. *Thank God.* A heartbeat later, her lips press softly against mine. My heart beats wildly against my chest, my pulse racing and my body suddenly on fire. God, kissing her feels *right*.

I gently cup her cheek as I kiss her again, a bit more firmly but still keeping things slow and easy. My head is swimming when I pull back far enough to look her in the eyes. Her lips curl upwards and her eyes seem to be burning. I smile back, feeling like a fucking teenager again, that feeling of excitement and fear and desire all mixed up together.

"I—"

Before I can finish, she grabs the front of my shirt and pulls me to her again. My eyes flash wide before sliding closed in ecstasy. She presses her lips to mine again, this time with more urgency. She sucks gently on my bottom lip and I groan, opening my mouth to her. She doesn't hesitate, thrusting her tongue against mine. God, the feel of her, the taste of her. I keep telling myself to be gentle, to go slow, but when she runs her hands up my chest and to the back of my neck, holding me to her as if I'd try to stop, I tunnel my hand in her hair, holding her to me just as desperately. Kissing Savannah is like coming up for air after being underwater for almost too long. It's sweet relief that I didn't even realize I needed, a balm to a burn I didn't realize had ravaged my body and soul.

"Savvy," I breathe against her lips and she shivers against me. I rest my hand on her thigh, rubbing slow circles with my thumb against her soft skin. She shifts forward, pressing her leg further into my hand, the hem of her dress inching upwards, my fingers along with it. She moans as I continue to gently knead her skin, again forcing myself not to move too fast, too far, though I've never wanted anything more than to explore her body, to kiss and lick every perfect inch, to sink so deep inside her that she screams my name...

She gently digs her nails into the back of my head and it makes me impossibly harder. I shift my hips upward, unable to stop them, desperate, and her thigh rubs against my cock. I hiss in a breath and groan as she moves her leg against me again, knowing exactly what she's doing—*wicked little thing*—and I kiss down her throat. Her head lolls backwards and she whispers my name. I want to hear her whisper it forever, want to hear her rasp it, pant it, scream it. *Take it slow. Take your time. Don't rush this. Don't ruin it.*

I somehow manage to slow things back down again, slowly licking and nipping back up her throat and kissing her again, softer. I gently thrust my tongue against hers and she grazes her hand over my cheek, making a sound of delight when my stubble tickles her palm. My thumb hitches a bit higher on her thigh and I graze the long scar there. She tenses and I worry that I've hurt her. I pull back, searching her face.

"Are you alright?" God, when was the last time I was this out of breath and aroused from making out? Maybe never.

She's breathless too, chest rising and falling in quick, shallow bursts that admittedly draw my eye to her breasts. Again. I hadn't been able to stop myself from staring when she'd first gotten out of the car and I hoped like hell she hadn't noticed. Her dress has shifted slightly now and I can see the edge of a black, lacy bra. I groan, imagining ripping it off of her, wanting to see her breasts so badly I ache for it, want to knead the giving flesh, kiss, and lick...*Focus, damnit.* I force myself to meet her gaze.

"I didn't hurt you, did I?"

"No, no. I'm ok. I just..." She trails off, seeming...embarrassed? Is she worried I'll care about the scar? She closes her eyes and shakes her head. "Sorry, I'm fine. It's just...uh, been a while, since I've done this," she says quietly.

I brush her hair away from her face, and kiss her gently. Her eyes flutter open when I pull back.

"We can take this as slow as you want, alright?" She searches my eyes, as if trying to figure out if I'm serious. Eventually, she nods.

"Alright. Slow is probably...good," she says, though she licks her lips and stares intently at mine again. Fuck, when she looks at me like that, slow is the absolute last thing on my mind, but I'll do whatever she wants, whatever she needs. It's probably smart to go slow for my benefit as well. My last relationship didn't exactly end well and though I try to pretend it didn't, it royally fucked with my head. I've been working on it, but trust is still a fragile thing for me. Despite the intense connection I feel with Savannah, any new relationship gives me pause. *Yes, slow is good.*

"Agreed. Slow." Neither of us seems capable of moving away from the other yet though, so we sit there tangled up in each other for a few more minutes as our heart rates slow and our breaths become normal again.

Eventually she says she needs to head home and though I want to ask her to stay, I force myself not to, instead walking her to her car and offering to drive her home if she'd rather. She smiles, as if my offer is endearing, but declines. She kisses me again before getting in her car and I stand in the driveway staring long after her tail lights disappear.

"Holy shit," I whisper, running my hands through my hair. Tonight was amazing and terrifying and confusing and crazy and I know without a doubt that it's the start of something, at least for me. All I can do is pray that she wants it to be the start of something too. I clean up the dishes from dinner, smiling at how she'd offered to do just that at least four times before she left, and change into some lounge pants for bed.

While I wait for her to let me know she made it home alright, I pull up Instagram. I've been pretty quiet on it lately, on all social media really, though Colin still keeps up with it to an extent on my behalf. I just needed to take a step back from it after the Audrey situation for my own mental health, but part of me feels bad for that. I really do have some phenomenal fans and I know how much it means when I interact with them. Hell, I know how much it means to me when people *I'm* fans of give me a like or a comment on something. It's a razor's edge walk sometimes, social media and being a "celebrity," but usually the good outweighs the bad.

I start to scroll through my feed, liking things here and there, commenting on some friends' posts, and decide to make a post of my own for the first time in months. I pull up a picture I took on the plane ride here and add a simple caption: *on to new adventures.* Within a few seconds, I'm already getting notifications of likes and comments and it makes me laugh.

New adventure indeed, I think as my mind floats back to how beautiful Savvy looked tonight, how she'd thrown her head back and laughed in such a carefree way it made me feel lighter just being around her. I can tell she has some things in her past that she's had to work through, but she's still so...bright. I can't explain it.

Since I'm already on the app, I decide to search for her. I know she said she wasn't too active on social media, but I'm still curious. Apparently, Savannah Riley is a popular name because tons of users come up and I'm not sure which one is hers, but I do find her photography page easily enough. It hasn't been updated in years, other than a post saying that she was taking time off and she would let everyone know if and when she came back. I scroll through the posts anyway and my brows fly up: she's incredible. It's mostly weddings and families, like she said, and those are fantastic, but there are also a bunch of nature shots that are truly stunning. Beach sunsets, the great oaks downtown, flowers on the headstones of one of the old cemeteries. She's extremely talented and I hope that she gets back to it at some point.

As I continue to be a creeper and scroll through her feed, a text message comes through.

Savvy: Made it home. Thank you for tonight. I had a really good time.

I smile and respond:

Link: Me too. Coffee in the morning?

Savvy: Griffey and I will meet you at our spot. Good night.

Link: Good night.

I put my phone down and stare at the ceiling, my thoughts immediately floating back to that kiss. How soft her lips were, how responsive she was to each lap of my tongue, each tiny nibble. I'm hard again just thinking about her, my hips rocking back and forth, and I try to remember when the last time I had sex was. Fuck, nearly a year, not since Audrey. Savvy said it had been a while for her too and again I wonder how someone like her could possibly be single, or at least not hooking up with anyone. Not that I'm complaining of course, but still, I wonder. The cynical part of my mind that is still a bit tangled up from my own issues whispers that maybe she isn't as perfect as she seems, that maybe it's all just an act. I force that thought away, and instead focus back on the kiss, on her hands tangled in my hair, how she'd rubbed her thigh against me to drive me crazy.

I groan as my hand slips beneath the sheet, wishing it was her hand instead of my own. I know taking things slow is a good idea, but damn it if I can stop myself from imagining anything but slow right now. I think about feeding my cock into her mouth, her sucking me hard before I toss her beneath me, slamming inside her hard and fast, her screaming my name, *begging* for me. I want to feel her, hot and tight and wet around me, want to feel her squeeze my cock as she comes apart beneath me, want to fuck her with abandon before I slow things down and make love to her until she can't take anymore. Dear God, are these thoughts all because it's been a while or just because I want Savvy that much? I think the latter. I don't try to stop the thoughts. Instead, letting them grow more detailed as I stroke.

I'm not ashamed that I come harder than I have in recent memory with her name on my lips and her face flashing behind my eyes, cum lashing my stomach and chest.

"Fuck," I groan in astonishment, panting.

This girl is going be the death of me...and I think I'm ok with that.

CHAPTER 6

Savannah

Last night was the best night I've had in years. I can't believe how easy things are with Link, how strong the pull is to him, how much I freaking like him. And don't even get me started on the kiss. *Dear. God.* I'd tossed and turned for half the night, replaying it over and over again in my mind, remembering his touch, his taste, wishing he was there doing it again—and more. The more I thought, the more I wanted, the more I *needed.* It wasn't long before my hand was tunneling into my panties, surprised to find them soaked, and as I stroked, I imagined it was Link's hand, his fingers delving in and out. I careened over the edge harder and faster than I had in a long, long time, shocked and panting afterwards. If that's any indication of what might be to come if we keep at this thing...I shiver at the mere thought.

"I kissed a boy," I blurt to Tiff as I walk Griffey to meet Link for coffee. She'd texted me first thing this morning to forgive me for not calling her the night before, assuming that I'd gotten...*distracted.* I assured her that wasn't the case, I'd just been tired, but damn if I didn't want it to be. Though I know it's the right call because my emotions are all over the place right now, swinging violently from high to low in a way that's making me seasick, going slow is also going to be damn near impossible.

"Ahhhhh!!!" she squeals. "Ok. Details. Now. Full disclosure. Leave nothing out."

"Ok, ok, calm down. He made me dinner, and—"

"Made you dinner? As in he can *cook*??"

"Best crab cakes I've ever had and you know how I feel about crab cakes."

"Damn. Marry him. Marry him right freaking now."

I snort and continue. "So, he made me dinner and had a super romantic spot set up out on the deck beside the pool. Twinkle lights and a fire and the ocean in the distance. It was like something out of a chick flick, dude, like I can't even describe it. He nailed it. Anyway, after dinner and some talking, he kissed me. Or I think I actually kissed him technically."

"Swoooon. That's a pretty impressive first date, I'm not gonna lie. You have no idea how lucky you are. You don't even want to know what the last message I got from a guy I matched with on Tinder was. Seriously, it's slim pickings out here these days, my friend. Sounds like you caught a good one."

"He seems like it," I agreed. "But it's...complicated." Beyond complicated.

"Don't do that. I know this is hard and I'm sure you're having *all* the emotions right now, but don't overthink and talk yourself out of something that might be really great. I can tell you like him, Sav. I know you better than anyone, remember?"

"You're right that I'm in the middle of all the damn emotions, but...it's not just that." I bite my lip, debating on how to drop the bomb on her. In the end, I decide it should be a face-to-face conversation. "Can you do lunch today?"

"I shall have to check my schedule, darling. I'm in very high demand you know." I laugh and roll my eyes. That's her way of saying yes.

"Ok, well pick the place and just text me. I'm grabbing coffee now, but then I'm free until my appointment at Memorial at 3:30."

"Which doctor this time?"

"Cardio. Dr. Fields."

"Ohhh maybe I'll go with you! I hear he's single again and he is *extremely* good looking."

"He's like sixty, Tiff."

"Listen, I don't judge all your stuff, ma'am. Don't judge my daddy kink, ok? He is the epitome of silver fox..."

"Ok, ok, just text me where you want to eat," I say, quickly cutting her off. The last thing I need to picture during my appointment is Dr. Fields with Tiff.

I hang up just as Griffey starts barking and wagging his tail like crazy when he spots Link waiting for us outside the courtyard, two cups of coffee in his hand.

He hands one to me and then bends to rub Griffey's ears.

"Hey buddy, how are you today? You're such a good boy, yes you are." His doggy-voice is adorable and I take a sip of coffee to hide my grin. I arch my brows at him when he straightens, clearing his throat.

"How did you know my order? To my knowledge, I don't have fans on the internet with every intimate detail of my life laid out for the world to see."

"No, but you *do* have a very sweet old lady who runs the coffee shop that you go to almost every day who was more than happy to give 'such a handsome young man' your coffee order so that I could surprise you." He grins and walks backwards through the entry to the courtyard.

"She's nearly blind, don't let it go to your head," I quip, sitting down at my customary table in the corner.

"Ouch, Savannah. Words hurt, you know."

I chuckle as he sits down and we enjoy our coffee.

***

"Ok, I need you to not freak out, alright?" Tiff gives me a look, one perfect brow arching upward. "I mean it. Promise or I'm not telling you jack shit."

"Ok, ok. I promise not to freak out." She rolls her eyes and picks at the nachos in the middle of the table.

"Ok so...the guy...the one I went on the date with...well, it's, um...Lincoln Ashmore."

She freezes with a chip an inch from her mouth, the toppings spilling off the edge and splattering on the table.

"Excuse me, what?" she asks calmly, putting her chip down and staring at me like I might just be losing my mind.

"Seriously. I'm not crazy or hallucinating. He's here to film a movie at the Mandrake."

"Lincoln Ashmore. *The* Lincoln Ashmore? Like...Captain Ultra and Thaddeus McClain and the no shit movie star who was engaged to Audrey Shepheard?!"

"Um, yep, that would be the one." I bite my lip and I show her the pictures from the beach and the few we snapped during our date to prove I'm not nuts. She scrolls through them, mouth wide open.

"I don't...I can't...how?" She closes her eyes and composes herself. Opening them again, she says evenly, "I need you to start at the beginning and leave nothing out. I mean it, not one single detail, Riley." So, I tell her everything, recounting how I met him, how I took him to the Fort, all of it.

"Dolphins?" she says on a soft exhale.

"Dolphins, Tiff. At the Fort. Have you ever seen them there?"

"No, never. Talk about a freaking sign." She yanks my phone back and looks through the pictures again. "Holy shit. This is...holy shit, Sav!"

"Ok, so now you get what I mean when I say it's complicated. He's a *movie star*, Tiff. He lives in Hollywood and dates models and hangs out on yachts and whatever else it is that celebrities do. Our lives couldn't be more different."

She waves that away as if it's nothing. "All of that can be navigated, and from what I've always seen in the media about him, he isn't really the typical Hollywood A-Lister, is he? Or at least, not anymore." She's right, but still. "Have you told him about...?"

I shake my head. "Not yet. It's not like I'm hiding it, exactly, but it's pretty heavy. I didn't think it was something to dump on him right off the bat, you know? 'Hi, nice to meet you. I have a metric fuck ton of emotional and physical trauma I'm dealing with every day, care to hear about it?' Not exactly a great intro."

"I get that, but you're going to have to tell him soon if you're actually serious about whatever this is." She shakes her head in disbelief and pops another nacho in her mouth. "Man, this is nuts. But crazy awesome. You *like* him, Sav, that's huge! And it seems like he really likes you too."

"But he's an actor," I point out. "He could just be putting on a show."

"Why would he lie about it?"

"I don't know. To have a fling while he's here? Hook up with the small town girl while films his movie?"

She shakes her head, unconvinced. "He could do that with anyone. You've seen the man. He could crook his finger and a hundred women would throw themselves at him with no strings attached. He would have no reason to put in the work that he's obviously putting in with you if it wasn't for something more."

She has a point, but my brain refuses to accept it that easily. She holds up a hand. "I can see your wheels turning and burning rubber in there. So, knock it off." I flip her off but smile. She knows me too damn well. "Let's just jump on the carpe fucking diem train for a second, and look at all the checks in plus column, ok? He's handsome. He's sweet. He's hot. Yes, I know I already said handsome, but the man is delicious, so I'm adding it in twice—and we can agree that being handsome and being hot are two entirely different things. He, however, is both. He makes you laugh. You light up when you talk about him, with this adorable little secretive smile that makes me want to puke and go *awwww* at the same time. Forget the fact that he's a movie star or whatever. That doesn't matter, not really. He's a guy. You're a girl. It seems like there's some kind of crazy connection between the two of you."

"I think there...is. It's hard to explain, but it's intense and like I instantly felt comfortable with him, like we'd been friends for years. It felt like..." I trail off, shocked by where I was going.

"Like it did with Matt?" she finishes for me. "Well, at least after you hated him." We both chuckle at that. It was true. I despised him at first, but then it felt like I'd known him forever, like we'd been made for each other.

She gives me a sad smile. "He'd want you to be happy, you know. He was one of my oldest friends and I know without a doubt he'd want you to be happy again, Sav, not to stay stuck in the past forever."

"I know he would," I say quietly, trying to force the tears away. "I really do. I can practically hear him in my head sometimes when I start to slip, telling me how stupid I'm being."

"He definitely would be calling you an idiot—in the most loving way, of course." We both laugh, seeing him so clearly in our minds, remembering how it used to be.

She gives me one of her signature *cut to the quick of things* looks that brokers no argument or bullshit, and asks, "Ok. How are you feeling? *Really* feeling? No sugar coating or bullshit."

"It's...a lot. I'm feeling excited and happy but then also terrified and guilty. So fucking guilty." That had been one of my biggest issues all these years. I feel a deep, unyielding guilt over so much, feel it just for being alive sometimes. I know it isn't logical, but things like this rarely are. I've gotten better with it over the years, with a lot of help from Dr. Forrester, but it's still there.

"You'll get there, Sav. I know you will. You deserve to be happy, more than anyone else in the world. And...fuck, to be happy with Lincoln Ashmore??" She wiggles her eye brows at me and I throw a chip at her.

I feel better after talking it through with Tiff. The guilty feeling is already subsiding, fading to the background a bit and the excitement is taking top billing. I'm excited to see where this might go, despite the fear and all the what-ifs. And if he does just want a fling while he's here? I'll deal with that when the time comes, but I have a gut feeling that this is worth experiencing with him, even for a short time.

And like Tiff reminded me, I've decided to look for the good things—and Lincoln Ashmore is a very, *very* good thing.

CHAPTER 7

Lincoln

The next two weeks fly by in a whirlwind of pure joy. I can't even explain how good it feels being with Savvy. I feel lighter than I have in years, finding that I can confide in her in ways I haven't been able to in a long time. I talk through my fears about the new project, stresses of life in L.A., things I regret, things I want to do. It feels like we've been friends for years, like I can talk to her about anything.

The cynical part of me that's been burned too many times tries to whisper that maybe she's acting so into me simply because of who I am, that she's only so enamored because I'm a celebrity or whatever. I don't *really* believe it, I mean, wouldn't she be pushing things to go *faster* if that were the case, desperate to officially bag the big fish? But the doubts try to worm their way in sometimes regardless of what I actually believe.

Even so, I don't think I've ever felt this way in any relationship before now, and I think...well, I think that I might be falling for her already.

"God, I sound fucking crazy. This is crazy," I tell myself over and over. I don't even know that much about her really if I think about it. Everything is still very new and we haven't dipped into very deep waters yet when it comes to opening up and sharing our darkest secrets, but even so, I'm lost for her. Her laughter makes my heart race, her smile can bring me to my knees. Don't even get me started on how she drives me wild with the slightest touch, the tiniest heated look. I think back to a week ago and shudder.

We'd been watching a movie and had seen almost none of it. As soon as I turned the lights down and the opening credits rolled, the air became thick and heated around us. She started lightly running her hand up and down my thigh and that was all it took. Suddenly, my lips were slamming onto hers and she was in my lap, grinding her luscious hips over my aching shaft. She'd shoved her hand between us, rubbing me through my jeans and my hips had bucked up to her hand uncontrollably. She'd grinned as she bit my lip, giving me a look of pure mischievous sexuality that made it hard to breathe, made my cock throb harder than it ever had. She might want to go slow, but there was also a burning desire in her that was dying to come out. I couldn't imagine what it might be like when she unleashed it completely, but damn if I wasn't looking forward to it.

She kissed down my neck, yanking my shirt open and making buttons fly in all directions. I couldn't have cared less, urging her to keep going, to rip the damned shirt to pieces if she wanted. She planted soft kisses down my chest, running her tongue over the lines of my tattoo and making me groan in pleasure. When she flicked her tongue over my nipple, I let out a strangled cry, so damned surprised and aroused I could barely stand it. She chuckled and continued kissing down, down, down, slipping to her knees on the floor, kneeling before me.

"Savvy, you don't...you don't have to..." My words died in my throat as she kissed just above the edge of my jeans, dipping her tongue just below the waistband. She slowly unbuckled my belt, still planting those soft kisses and gentle laps of her tongue over my stomach, making my muscles flex in response. She glanced up at me through her lashes, the most lust-fueled, sexy look I've ever seen, before she pulled my cock free. Her eyes widened slightly as she got her first look, and she wrapped her fingers around me. She watched raptly as she stroked, up and down, up and down, and I fought to keep my body still. Finally, she leaned forward and ran her tongue over the head before taking me between her lips. Her mouth was so hot, so wet, my eyes nearly rolled back in my head.

I let my head fall back, resting against the back of the couch as she sucked and licked, making me see stars. She released me and my head shot forward in time to watch her run her tongue from the base to the crown, like she was licking a fucking popsicle, moaning, eyes sliding closed like it was the best thing she'd ever tasted.

"Fuck, Savvy," I groaned, voice hoarse. She opened her eyes and gave me a sultry little smirk, holding my gaze as she dipped her head once more. She was a seductress, a God damn temptress, and I was a goner. I tangled my hands in her hair, holding it away from her face because God help me, I had to see this, had to watch her. She started sucking me harder, pumping her hand along the base of my cock in time with the bob of her mouth, and I couldn't stop my hips from bucking upward. Her eyes widened for a moment and I bit out an apology, but she sucked me harder, deeper, as if...inviting me to do it again.

I slowly arched them forward again and she moaned, digging her nails into my stomach. *Fuck. Me. She likes it.* This woman was sin incarnate and she was all mine. At least for now. For as long as she'd have me.

I started to thrust in time with her movements, gently fucking her mouth and it was the sexiest thing I'd ever seen in my life. There was no way in hell I was going to last as long as I would have liked.

"Sav, fuck, I'm going to come. God...Stop...y-you need to stop," I panted but instead of stopping, she met my gaze again and arched a brow, somehow being her sarcastic, snarky self even with my cock down her throat. I bit out the briefest bark of a laugh before the sound died in my throat. She rolled her tongue over the head, dipping it in the slit, before sucking hard and long. I thrust my hips a few more times, bucking to her mouth, knowing I was nearing my end. I felt the tingle in my spine, felt the cum rising and my toes curling.

"Savvy, I'm...fuckkkkkkk!" I came in a rush, hips and back arching upwards, pumping into her hot little mouth over and over and she swallowed every drop. When I couldn't possibly go any more, she finally released me, kissing my lower stomach before resting her head on it. We both sat there, panting, for several long moments before she gave me a cheeky grin.

"And here I was nervous I'd be out of practice."

I threw my head back and laughed before pulling her up into my lap. I kissed her hard. She seemed surprised at first, but she quickly got over it, losing herself in the kiss and slowly grinding her hips in my lap.

"Do I get to reciprocate?" I whispered, nearly begging. I'd wanted to touch her, *taste* her, so fucking badly. I respected that she wanted to take things slowly and would never push, but my God it was getting hard to not show her just how badly I wanted her, getting hard not to pleasure her in the ways I wanted to so badly I felt like I might die. I've always been a highly sexual person, but dear God, I don't think I've had so many urges—or urges this strong at least—with anyone else before.

"Not yet," she'd said, but I could hear the reluctance in her voice. I didn't know why she was holding back, but I wouldn't push. When the time came, I knew it would be worth the wait. Until then, I was happy to kiss her as often as she'd let me, and I'd be lying if I said I wasn't enjoying all the other times she'd found ways to get me off in the last week. I was keeping a mental tally of all the times I owed her for and smirked inwardly imagining paying my debts.

She's shown me all over the town and we've explored several of the nearby islands, spending almost every waking moment together when we aren't both busy. By some miracle, we haven't been bombarded by photographers or fans, and I've managed to go without being recognized most of the time. I'm not sure how much longer that'll keep up since filming starts soon, but I just pray that it won't be too much for her.

I can tell she's still holding a big part of herself back, keeping something big from me, but I don't push. I know she'll tell me if and when she's ready and until then, I'm happy to just be with her, soaking in every single possible second.

"So, are you ever gonna tell me her name?" Colin asks as I wipe sweat off my face.

"And if I say I don't have any idea what you're talking about?"

"I'll say you're full of shit and must have forgotten that I've known you for almost fifteen years." I laugh and toss the towel into the hamper. I did a pretty punishing workout this morning and now I'm in desperate need of a shower.

"She's amazing, that's all you need to know for now."

"Listen, as your manager and friend, I probably need to do some checking into this girl to make sure we don't have another Carolyn Crawford situation on our hands."

I wince remembering that situation all too clearly. Carolyn Crawford was a very disturbed woman who had become obsessed with me a few years back. Though intense when we'd met at cons and other events, she'd been relatively harmless—at first. But she started to cross more lines as time went on, finding her way backstage and into dressing rooms, leaving gifts for me and threatening messages for co-stars and friends. When she broke into my house and Colin found her waiting for me, *naked in my bed*, the police had gotten involved. She was convinced that we were soul mates, meant to be together or something. I'd agreed not to press charges so she could get the help she needed, and she'd entered into a deal: no jail time but she would be remanded to a mental health facility for treatment.

"She isn't like Carolyn, I promise."

"But you said you haven't even been to her house?" He gives me a pointed look.

"I've been there...outside anyway." I'd picked her up a few times, but she'd never invited me in and never wanted to hang out there. I've told myself over and over that I will not push her to share whatever it is she's holding back, but...well, I wish she would. I'm starting to worry that she's hiding something huge.

As if reading my thoughts, Colin says, "But what if she doesn't want you to come inside because she's hiding something crazy? Like a secret husband or lamps covered in human skin??"

"You need to stop watching so much *Criminal Minds*," I say, rolling my eyes, but the doubts do start to nag at me.

"Whatever you say, buddy. I'll let you keep your secrets for another couple weeks, but I'm sure I'll get it out of you down at Gatorcon." *Oh shit.* I'd almost forgotten all about that. It's Florida's largest comic-con event and I'm scheduled to do some *Shadowlands* and *League of Heroes* panels and meet and greets, and then Drew planned to rent a boat so we could all hang for a few days. I'm looking forward to it actually, but I'd be lying if I said I wasn't going to miss Savvy, even for just a few days. *I'm like a lovesick fucking puppy.* An idea springs to mind and before I stop myself, I tell Colin to put a guest down for me for the con, full access, and rattle off a few more requests.

"You've got it bad, dude," he laughs, shaking his head, but promises to take care of it for me, like always. I was extremely lucky to meet Colin early in my career and we hit it off from the get go. Eventually he was in a place where he decided to start his own management company, and I was in a place where I needed a new manager. It just worked out perfectly and we've been together ever since. He's helped me through some of the hardest times of my life and I honestly don't know where I'd be without him. I owe not only my career him to him, but my life really.

I realize that Savvy may not want to run off to Florida with me for a week, but it can't hurt to ask, right? Colin and I go over a few more things, and he heads out to catch his flight. I head to shower because, as Colin so kindly reminds me as he's heading out the door, I'm disgusting.

I start the water and toss my sweat-drenched clothes in a pile by the door just as Savannah calls.

"Well, good morning, beautiful," I say, leaning back against the counter. She blushes ever so slightly but smiles.

"Morning..." She trails off as her eyes shift, taking in my bare chest. They widen slightly and she wets her lips. I *might* shift the phone a bit so she gets a better view and she straightens, sitting farther up against the headboard, the thin strap of her shirt slipping down her shoulder. "Are you *naked*, Lincoln Ashmore?" she asks, somewhere between bemused and breathless.

"Perhaps..." I rub a hand through my hair and she mutters something that I can't quite hear other than *"fuck."*

"I just got done working out, so I was about to take a shower." I keep catching her eyes flickering downward. "Hey, my eyes are up here, Savannah," I scold with a grin.

"Listen, I can't be held responsible for what my eyes do when you're standing there looking like *that*, ok?"

I chuckle and ask her about her plans for the day, and after a bit of chatting, we decide on dinner at my place tonight. I figure I'll ask her about Gatorcon when I've buttered her up with shrimp étouffée. After we hang up, I head to the shower but pause. On a whim, I take a picture of the stall and send it to her with the caption *wish you were here.*

To my delight, she responds almost immediately.

Savvy: don't tempt me...

I groan, my imagination running off the rails in an instant. Savvy underneath the streaming water, hands digging into the blue tile, me behind her...her in my lap on the wide bench...*her* on the bench and me on my knees in front of it...

"Fuck," I grate as I step under the hot stream, immediately throwing the dial all the way cold.

***

"So, I have a kind of crazy question...and it's completely fine if you say no..."

She gives me a suspicious look, arching one golden brow as she reaches for a cucumber, and I playfully swat at her hand. She's sitting on the counter of the island while I work on dinner, looking sinfully gorgeous in a yellow sundress, the color beautiful against her sun-tanned skin. She glares at me and steals another one, making an exaggerated chomp before gesturing for me to go on.

"Do you want to go to Florida with me?"

"What?" she laughs. "Wait, seriously?"

"Yes, seriously," I say with a roll of my eyes. I swat at her thigh with a dishtowel before tossing it over my shoulder and leaning in to give her a quick kiss. I move back to the stove, stirring the shrimp before turning to meet her gaze again. "Hear me out before you say no, ok? I have to go down for this big comic-con in a couple of weeks and I thought you might want to come with me. You'd have a full access pass, so you'd be free to check out anything you wanted, all the panels, meet and greets, the whole nine yards. You were just saying the other day how you've always wanted to go to one and Gatorcon is one of my favorites. I told Colin to get a suite with two bedrooms, so you don't even have to share with me, unless you want to." I give her a smile and she thankfully returns it, not looking like she wants to run for the hills yet. It gives me hope so I push on.

"And I know you're worried about paparazzi and all that crap, but you don't have to be seen with me if you aren't ready for that. Like, you can hang out with Colin and we can tell people you're part of the management team or whatever you want. I promise I won't grope you in public—unless you want me to." I grin and she laughs. "We'll fly out on the twentieth and be gone for six days, but if you need to come back sooner that's totally fine. And it's completely my treat," I add, realizing that jet-setting out of town for a week on a whim might give people pause from the financial aspect. Of course we haven't talked about that kind of stuff, and I'm not *assuming* she can't afford it or anything, but I don't want to put any kind of burden or pressure on her in that department either. She snorts, as if me offering to pay is some kind of joke, but I'm not sure why. "I know it's kind of short notice, but...well, what do you think?"

"I...I would love to go with you, actually," she says, but before I can get excited, she adds, "But, um...well, I don't fly."

"At all?"

"At all," she confirms, a strange tremor in her voice. Fear of flying? Not uncommon. My mom hates it and has to basically be sedated to get on a plane, so I get it. She chews her lip, clearly conflicted and it makes me happy to know that she truly does want to come with me and experience this together. "But maybe...I could drive down and meet you there?"

Lightbulb.

"What if we drove together? We'll just road trip it."

"What?"

"Yeah, we'll just drive down together. It'll be fun. We can have Boy Band Karaoke, buy way too many road snacks, stop and see the world's largest ball of twine or biggest cast-iron skillet or whatever the hell might be on the way. Get frisky in a rest stop parking lot," I add with a wink and she bites her lip, smiling. "Come on. A road trip with Captain Ultra would be *very* CFD. Just sayin'." I give her my most imploring smile. "Please?"

"You don't have to do that for me," she says quietly, staring at me like I'm something special, like...well, I don't want to name what it looks like for fear of being let down.

"Of course I do. I want to make the trip with you. I want you to come to Florida. I want you to experience this with me. I want...I just want..." I trail off as the conversation takes a turn. Suddenly, we aren't talking about Gatorcon anymore. We're talking about much, much more. I take a deep breath and that thick tension settles over us again, like a powder keg just waiting for a match. I turn off the stove and slide the skillet off of the burner before turning back to face her.

"Wh-what do you want?" she asks, breaths becoming quick and shallow, pulse beating wildly at the base of her throat.

"Savvy," I whisper as I move closer. When I reach her, she widens her knees and I wedge my hips between them, placing my hands on either side of her thighs on the counter.

"What, Link? What do you want?" she asks again.

"I want *you*. I want you more than I've ever wanted anyone in my life, Savannah. I don't understand it, but I'm drawn to you in a way that I can't explain, in a way that I've never felt before. I know it's still new, and I know we still have so much to learn, but I want to. I want to do this with you. I want...*everything*."

She swallows hard. "I want that too," she whispers.

That's all the answer I need. I press my lips to hers, kissing her hard and deep. She arches her hips forward and hitches one of her legs over my hip, pulling me closer and holding me tight. She dips her hands beneath my shirt, running them upwards across my bare stomach, and my muscles jump in response. Her touch is burning and desperate, and I want her hands everywhere, want her touch on every inch of me. I tunnel my hands in her hair, trying to tell myself to be gentle as I thrust my tongue against hers.

"Savvy," I breathe against her lips.

"Link, no more going slow," she pants.

I pull back and arch my brow, asking if I heard her right. Her pupils are blown wide, her lips red and swollen from our kisses, and I've never seen anyone look so hungry; so desperate; so sexy. She whispers *please* seconds before she pulls me back in for another scorching kiss. Her soft plea breaks the last bit of my self-control. I grip her ass and lift. She wraps her legs around my waist and I walk us back into the living room, settling on the oversized couch with her on top of me. She spreads her knees on either side of my hips, straddling me, and we both make sounds somewhere between groans and moans when she settles down against my cock, already hard and aching.

"Fuck," I hiss as she shifts her hips forward and back, grinding slowly against me. She digs her fingers into my shoulders and kisses me again, sucking and biting my bottom lip in the way that drives me absolutely wild. I'm not going to last for shit at this rate. I grip her hips, grinding her just a bit harder as I thrust upward.

"Oh God," she moans. She moves her hands down my chest and yanks at the hem of my shirt, jerking it upward and I help her get it over my head. She sits back for a second to stare, running her tongue over her bottom lip as she runs her hands over my bare chest, tracing my tattoo. "I'll never get tired of seeing you like this," she whispers before leaning in to kiss me again, threading her fingers through my hair, tugging gently.

I slide my right hand in between her thighs, rubbing lightly over her silk panties, and nearly groan.

"Fuck me, your panties are soaked, Sav," I grit out.

"I blame you," she pants, a hint of a smile in her voice as she kisses me again, rocking her hips again hard against my hand. "God, I want you, Link. So much."

"Let's get this off then," I say, moving both hands to her thighs, just above her knees. I slowly move them upward to grip the bottom of her dress, and when my fingers graze the scar on her upper thigh, she freezes. I want to tell her that I don't care about a scar, that it doesn't matter to me one bit, but she speaks before I can say anything.

"Hold on," she says, pulling away enough to look at me. "Just...give me one second."

My chest is heaving and I want her so badly I think I might die, but if she isn't ready, if she's changed her mind again, then I'll wait. I'll wait forever for her.

"It's ok, Sav. We don't have to—"

"No," she interrupts quickly. "No, I want to. God, I want to. I just...need to warn you." My brows draw down and she takes a deep breath. "I've got some pretty gnarly scars."

"Like this one?" I ask as I lightly skim my fingers over the scar on her thigh. Her eyes slide closed and she bites her lip, rocking over my lap again. "And this one?" I whisper, tracing the very top of the scar that I can see between her breasts. She shivers, thrusting her chest forward, all but begging me to touch her more, but nods. "And you think I'd care? That they'll bother me?"

"No, it's just...I didn't want you to be surprised is all." She chews her lip, clearly nervous.

I lean in and kiss her, gently this time, savoring the taste of her, the feel of her lips and tongue. She relaxes and I grip the bottom of her dress again, slowly tugging it upward. I graze her skin with my fingertips on the way and she gasps quietly. Finally,

I pull the material over her head and toss it to the floor. I don't say anything at first, just take in the sight of her. She's still in her bra and panties, and I don't think any woman has ever looked so sexy in lingerie before. Her bra is black lace, with tiny strings arching from the center over the swells over her breasts and connecting to the straps. Such a simple design and yet, it's so erotic, so fucking arousing. Her panties are matching black silk with a strip of lace along the top.

It takes a long moment before I really notice the full scar between her breasts and my eyes widen slightly, surprised by what I'm seeing despite her warning. A long scar runs along her center, thick and jagged. I've seen scars like this before. My blood chills a bit as I realize why: my dad has one from his bypass a few years ago, calls it his zipper. *God...had they cracked her chest open?*

Another large scar sits on one side of her stomach and looks like it wraps around to her back. The one from her thigh extends up the side of her hip. Another smaller one rests over her ribs. I swallow thickly, suddenly overcome with emotions I can't completely understand. I'm sickened, not by the scars, but by what possibly could have caused them. *My God, what did she survive? How* did she survive it? I want to take away the pain she must have felt from all of these injuries. My mind runs wild, scenarios of someone hurting her making me see red.

She's staring at my chest and I don't think she's breathing.

"They're...a lot, I know. It's ok if you...I mean if they're...too much."

CHAPTER 8

Savannah

My heart is about to beat right through my chest. *My stupid, scar-ridden chest.* I hate that he's seen them now, that he knows how broken I am. He's just staring, not saying a word. He must be so disgusted. I feel my cheeks heat, embarrassment and...shame rising up, and I hate myself for that. It's not like I asked for the scars, not like I want them, but they *are* a part of me, a big part. They're my penance, my punishment, my reminders, and I hate that I'm feeling this way about them.

Link puts one finger under my chin and raises my face to meet his. He doesn't say anything, just stares, and I don't see revulsion in his eyes. I don't see pity or disgust. I see...*desire.* Holy fuck, do I see desire. I swallow at the intensity of that look, heat rushing through every inch of my body, turning my blood into fire. He leans in and kisses me, deep and forceful, pouring emotion into the kiss that I can't quite wrap my head around at the moment. He pulls back just enough to speak, but I can still feel his lips moving against mine.

"Does it bother you for them to be touched?" he asks softly.

"N-no," I breathe. He kisses along my jaw, slowly driving me mad. He licks just below my ear before planting a soft kiss there, and I shiver violently, dizzy with lust.

"Good, because I plan to touch and kiss and lick every last inch of you, Savvy." He plants another kiss before adding in a sexy whisper, "*Every. Last. Inch.*" I gasp as he drags my ear lobe through his teeth. *Dear God.* My nipples pucker even more, begging for him to do as he promised, and I can't stop shaking. I've never wanted this badly before, never been so wet, never needed someone so much. As if he can read my mind, he reaches behind me and quickly unclasps my bra, tugging the straps down my arms. I'm not shy of my body despite being hesitant about my scars, so I toss the garment aside and he makes a low rumbling noise in appreciation.

He takes a moment to stare before reaching out and covering both breasts with his large hands, kneading gently, and my head falls back with a guttural moan. Something so simple as his hands on my breasts has me writhing in his lap, has me desperate to come. It's been too long, every touch is ten times more intense than it should be and I can't get enough. He rubs the pads of his thumbs over my throbbing nipples and I buck my hips forward in response.

He chuckles and whispers, "Oh, noted. You like that."

He suddenly moves, shifting us to the side and lying me down on the long couch, his body hovering above mine. He kisses slowly down my neck and then places soft kisses down the scar on my chest before finally locking his lips firmly around one aching nipple. I cry out, my entire body jerking in response, arching upward towards his touch. The sensation is so strong, it's like an electric shock. He sucks gently before releasing it and twirling his tongue around and around.

"Oh God, Link...Fuckkkkk that feels good."

He continues to lick and suck while he rolls my other nipple between his thumb and forefinger, pinching with just enough pressure. God, I feel like I could come just from this. *Hell, maybe I will.* He moves to put his mouth on my other breast and slowly traces his hand downward, slipping his fingers beneath the silk of panties and quickly thrusting one inside me. I make an obscene noise and my hips rock upward like a shot.

"Christ," he grits out, leaving my breast to kiss me once more. "You're so fucking wet, Sav."

"Need more," I pant. "Don't stop."

He kisses me hard and adds another finger, thrusting them gently in time with the laps of his tongue against mine. I can feel his cock, hard against my thigh as he rocks his hips subtly against me, and memories of it in my mouth float to the forefront of my mind. How big he is. How hard. How good he tastes. I dig my nails into his shoulder, barely able to think. He suddenly moves, going up on his knees and yanking my panties down my thighs. Though it's been years since anyone has seen me this way, I don't hesitate to kick the silk away. He catches my eyes for a moment and his are wild and sexy. I bite my lip and let my knees fall open.

He pulls his gaze from mine and stares, rubbing his hand across his mouth before settling between my thighs. His head dips and my world tilts. The first lick is ecstasy. The second? My soul leaves my body. He groans and continues to lick and it feels so fucking good I can't see straight. The pleasure is too much but not nearly enough. He thrusts his tongue inside over and over before languidly tracing it upward, flicking it over my clit, making my hips buck wildly.

"Don't stop, don't stop, don't stop. Oh *GOD*," I moan, gripping his head. He doesn't stop, instead presses my inner thighs down with his big hands, spreading my legs wider and pinning them there, spreading me wide open. *Oh. My. God.* It somehow makes it even more intense, making me feel so open, so exposed, so vulnerable, but it's pure pleasure, pure bliss. He pulls back and stares for a long moment.

"God, I could do this forever, Sav. I could lick your pussy for hours. You're so fucking sexy, taste so good."

His words make me whimper. I've always liked when guys talk during sex, especially a bit of dirty talk and apparently we're in accord on this front too, just like on so many other things. We just...fit each other. He continues to stare as he uses his thumbs to spread my lips before leaning back in and lapping his tongue slowly from the bottom of my opening all the way to my clit and back again. He does it, over and over, keeping the pace slow and sinful and agonizing. It's so good. It's too good. I need to come so badly but I don't want it to end. It's the most delicious torture.

He slowly starts to increase his speed, and I feel myself climbing, climbing, climbing.

"Oh God, Link. Don't stop. Please don't stop. I'm going to come. *Please...*"

"Come for me, Sav. Want to taste it."

Fuck. Me. He sucks on my clit and I chance a peek downward. The sight of his head between my thighs, his face buried in me, his mouth covering my pussy as he licks and licks—I'm done for. It's too erotic, too sexy, too fucking hot. My back bows as I come in a rush. I cry out and he moans against me, setting back in to thrust his tongue inside me, as if he really does want to taste my orgasm. I ride it out and my thigh muscles quiver by the time the tremors subside. He kisses the inside of my thigh and then up my stomach, brushing his lips over the scar on my side and the one on my ribs, before planting soft kisses up the long one between my breasts again. I have a feeling he plans to kiss them as often as possible.

He hovers above me finally, and his eyes are wide and wild.

"Are you alright?" he asks, panting. I can't even form words, so I just nod before shooting upwards, slamming my mouth to his. He freezes for half a second, but then kisses me back, his tongue dominating mine as if kissing me after that is arousing to him. Hell, maybe it is. It kind of is to me, honestly. I yank at the fly of his jeans, nearly breaking the button off, and shove the zipper down. I don't hesitate before thrusting my hand inside, finding him so hard and ready that I nearly combust. I've waited long enough, can't possibly wait any longer.

"*Fuck*," he groans as I glide my fist over his cock, using my thumb to spread the bead of moisture all around the tip. He surprises me, quickly shifting so that we're standing, my ass in his hands and my legs around his waist once more. He manages to get us to the bedroom without tripping and quickly tosses me onto the bed. He follows me down, somehow kicking out of his jeans on the way, and settles his body over mine.

"Mmmm," I moan as he grinds against me. I arch my hips up against his, desperate to feel him, even as my mind starts to spiral. I'm about to have sex with him. I'm about to have sex with *Lincoln Ashmore*. I'm about to have sex for the first time in almost a decade. What if I'm out of practice? What if I cry? What if he doesn't like it?

He seems to feel the shift inside of me as my mind goes into overdrive. I don't want it to, though. I *want* this. I truly want this so badly, want Link so badly, but my mind is just spinning and spinning like one of those tops I had when I was a kid, and I don't know if I can stop it.

He pulls back, resting on his elbows. "Savvy? What's wrong? Do you want to stop?"

"No! No, no, no, I really don't. God, I don't. I just...I can't...my mind is too loud...I need..." I can't even get the words out. I run my hands over my face and through my hair, out of my mind with desperation and frustration.

"Tell me," he says, sounding desperate. "Tell me what you need."

"I need to stop thinking," I say, anguished. Desperate. He stares at me and I can see the calculation in his green eyes.

After a long moment, he asks, "Do you trust me?"

"Yes," I say automatically and the absolute truth of the statement staggers me.

"Then, stop," he commands, his voice shifting subtly. The timber is slightly different, a bit deeper, a bit more...authoritative? *A bit more drop dead fucking sexy.* My body and mind both jerk to attention, my thoughts blanking for a minute. *Ohhhh, interesting.* "Stop thinking about anything except what I tell you to," he says and I swallow hard, unsure what exactly is happening but knowing damn well that I'm here for it. "Put your hands over your head and grip the headboard." My mind stays blissfully blank except for concentrating on his words, on watching the intense way his eyes burn as I follow his instructions.

"Good girl," he whispers and fuck me, it's the sexiest thing anyone has ever said in the history of the world. "Stay just like that. Don't you dare move an inch." He shifts on the bed to take off his boxer briefs, and grabs a condom from a drawer. I keep my mind blank, concentrating on his words, on his commands, and I can't believe it's actually working. I'm panting by the time he returns, writhing my hips in anticipation, watching every movement he makes, the way each beautifully hardened muscle flexes and moves. He climbs on the bed, kneeling in front of me.

His voice is gruff when he says, "Spread your legs," eyes riveted to my thighs.

I immediately let my knees fall wide and he makes an appreciative "mmm" sound as he runs a finger down my pussy before pushing two of them inside, thrusting once, twice. He strokes his cock with the other hand and I've never seen anything so sexy in my life. He's big and part of me wonders how he's going to fit, but I'm aching for him to try. Literally *aching* in a way I didn't even realize was possible. I can't keep my hips still until he commands that I do. God, this is...amazing. Powerful. Sexy. Sinful. Erotic. Too much and not enough and I'm eager to explore even more of it. I want him to command me, want him to dominate me. Visions flash through my mind: him pinning me down, binding my hands, demanding things of me...*Fuck me.* I need it. I want it. I never knew it until this moment, but now that knowledge is seared into my soul like a brand.

He moves forward, forcing my thighs wider to accommodate his hips. He runs the head of his cock up and down my pussy and my entire body trembles in anticipation.

"Look at me," he demands, and I drag my eyes upward. "What do you want?" he asks, voice pitched low. I swallow, not sure how to answer, not sure I even *can* answer. "Tell me what you want, Savannah," he says in that voice that's too sexy to be legal. "Do you want me to go slow? Or do you want me to fuck you hard?" I shudder. "Tell me..."

I want it all, but right now, I'm on the razor's edge, and I need him too much. My mind is blissfully blank thanks to his dominance, but I know that my emotions could tip at any moment. This is a big deal, but it's something I want so damn badly. I need to just rip off the band aid, so to speak.

"Hard," I manage to get out between shaky breaths. He inhales sharply and I can tell the answer floors him. He keeps running the head up and down, up and down and I arch my hips, trying desperately to get it inside. I need to feel him, need to be filled by him. I lift my head and hold his gaze. His eyes seem to burn with a desire I don't think I've ever seen before. "Fuck me, Link. Fuck me hard," I say, a command of my own. His eyes blaze hotter.

"Keep your hands on the headboard until I tell you to move them." Somehow, his commands are keeping my mind blank, keeping the thoughts from running wild despite the enormity of what's happening. He's a genius. An absolute perfect, sexy, genius who is about to fuck me within an inch of my life if I have my way. I'm sure most people would want slow and sweet for their first time, especially after so long and after everything I've been through, but I need the opposite. I need desperation and passion, I need to feel exactly how badly he wants me, need it to match exactly how badly I want him. I can't explain, but it's what my mind and body and soul need, at least in this moment. The idea of making love, of him kissing me softly as he slowly glides in and out of me, of me riding him in a slow grind while he whispers in my ear, is tempting and I need that part of him too, but not right now, not yet.

He feeds the head of his cock inside and I gasp at the same time he groans. He shifts so that he's above me, holding himself up on straightened arms.

"Alright?"

"Yes," I pant, desperate for him to start moving, desperate for more of him inside.

"Hold on tight," he whispers.

CHAPTER 9

Lincoln

Fuck. Me.

I hadn't exactly planned to bust out the semi-dominant side of myself this early, but when I could sense her pulling away, getting lost in her thoughts and overthinking everything, it just happened. It's tricky, learning to share these parts of yourself with others. Some people would be out the door in a heartbeat if you told them to grip the headboard or...other things that I haven't demanded yet but that are sitting just at the edge of my tongue. Audrey was absolutely not into it at all. And that's totally fine. Everyone is entitled to do and say and think and feel whatever they want in the bedroom. But Savvy seems to enjoy it, at least this little bit so far.

She immediately lit up when I started tossing commands at her, both sagging with relief that her mind could just blank, could just listen and obey, and seeming to spark with excitement, those hazel eyes seeming to burn with desire. It's just yet another way that we fit together. I don't always need to command and demand, but there *is* a part of me that enjoys it from time to time, and it seems like Savvy is into playing the commanded too. God, I can't wait to explore more of this with her, learn what else she likes, what else she needs. Her most secret desires, her deepest fantasies. I want to fulfill them all for her, want to be anything and everything she needs me to be.

When she told me she wanted me to fuck her hard. *Dear. God.* I almost came right then and there. Hell, I almost came going down on her on the couch. I wasn't lying when I said I could do it for hours. She tasted so good, was so God damned wet and responsive. I don't think I've ever seen anything as sexy as Savannah Riley, spread and open before me.

Now, she stares at me wide-eyed, body trembling with need, as I rise above her, the head of my cock just inside her.

"Hold on tight," I say and I see her muscles in her wrists flex as she grips the rails of the headboard tighter. With that, I thrust forward, slamming my cock inside her as far as I can.

Fuck.

She cries out and arches her back upward. I give her a second to adjust and she shifts her legs slightly, wiggling her ass a bit to get me settled inside her even more.

"Fuckkkkkk," she half hisses, half groans.

"Alright?" I ask again, somehow managing to hold myself still and steady.

"Yes," she rasps.

"Good."

I pull back and then slam inside her again, over and over, building into a torturous rhythm. She gasps and cries and moans and it's like music to my ears. She begins rocking her hips upward in time with my thrusts and it feels so God damn good. She's so tight around my cock, so slick and warm. I slant my mouth over hers, thrusting my tongue in time with my hips, punishing hers just as I'm punishing her body. She meets me though, lapping her tongue against mine and biting my lip, which drives me mad. I like to dominate, but I also need her to push back, to give as good as she gets. It's too good. *She's* too good, too perfect.

"Want your hands on me," I bite out through harsh breaths.

She releases the headboard and tunnels one hand into my hair at the back of my neck and digs her nails into my back with the other. *Fuck yes.* Just want I wanted, what I needed.

"Harder," she demands. "Harder, Link."

I smile, kissing her again before rising to my knees. I hook my right elbow under one knee, opening her more and letting me get even deeper. She moans, long and deep, and my cock swells even harder. I pin her hip with my other hand and pound into her, over and over. Her tits bounce with each thrust and I decide to push my luck.

"Grab your breasts. Massage them for me, baby," I pant. To my extreme delight, she obeys automatically. Cupping them in her hands, rubbing and squeezing, moaning. I shift her leg so it rests on my chest, her ankle near my shoulder, shoving further inside her again. She pinches her nipple with one hand, reaching out to rake her nails down my stomach with the other. "God damn you're so fucking sexy, Savvy."

"God, Link, keep going. Don't stop." I reach down and rub her clit with my thumb and she bucks up wildly, head thrashing against the pillow, golden hair fanning around her like a halo. "Oh Goddddd, don't stop. Right there. Rightthererightthererightthere." I force myself to think of other things as best I can because I'm not ready to come yet, I'm not ready to be done. She screams out as her back bows upward, and I can feel her orgasm ripping through her, her pussy clamping and pulsing around my cock. Her eyes slide closed and her beautiful lips part as she pants through her climax. Beads of sweat glide down her forehead and neck, across her chest. She's gorgeous. Absolutely fucking gorgeous.

Her eyes fly wide again and she meets my gaze.

"Kiss me," she demands and I'm helpless to deny her. I shift again, pulling her upwards against my chest as I maneuver beneath her. She wraps her legs around my waist and our sweat-slicked bodies writhe against each other as I kiss her, tangling one hand her in hair, gripping her ass with the other. Her necklace is cool against my heated skin. I knead her flesh, trying to be as easy as I can, but I'm nearly lost in the sensations of her, in the primal need that's riding both of us. She starts to move on me, sliding up and then back down on my cock, impaling herself over and over. I can get even deeper at this angle and she moan-screams into my mouth as I begin to thrust upward at the same time she slams downward.

"Oh God, Link," she says, breathless, as she meets my gaze. She holds my stare and I've never felt more connected to another person in my life. She's mine. I love her. I know it so strongly in this moment that it staggers me. Of course, I don't even think about saying that yet because then she really would bolt, but I know it to the core of my being. I will do anything and everything in my power to be with her forever. *Please don't hurt me, Savannah. Please...*

She throws her head back as she comes again and I kiss her neck, biting gently as I follow her over the edge, thrusting a few more frantic times before I'm completely spent. She wraps her arms around my neck and collapses against me, resting her head on my shoulder. We're both out of breath and it's a long while before either of us can speak.

"Bravo, Captain," she finally says and I can't stop the boom of laughter that erupts from my chest. I feel her giggle against me and I don't think a moment has ever been so perfect.

We disentangle ourselves and I get rid of the condom before lying back on the bed, pulling her into my side. She rests her head on my chest and we just lie there for a bit, catching our breaths and processing the mind-blowing sex we just had. At least, that's what I'm doing. I have no idea what's going on in her head and after a while, her quiet starts to worry me.

"You alright?"

She nods against my chest.

"Link." I tense when I hear the slight tremor in her voice. She lets out a long breath, as if she's trying to settle herself, to keep control over her emotions. "Link, I know that this is new and there's still a lot that you don't know about me, that we don't know about each other, but..." She cuts off on a sob and I shoot upwards, fear and concern spearing through my chest.

"Savannah?" Tears spill down her cheeks and my heart splinters. "Savannah, oh God. Did I hurt you? I'm sorry, I'm so sorry."

"No, no, it isn't that. I promise. I...damnit, *I'm* sorry," she chokes out through her sobs. She slaps a hand over her mouth and squeezes her eyes shut.

"Tell me what's wrong, tell me what I did." I know I got a bit carried away but I didn't think I'd lost control, didn't think I hurt her. I thought she was enjoying it as much as I was. How did I get this so wrong, how did I mess this up so badly? "God, Savvy, I'm sorry. I don't know...I don't..."

She goes up on her knees and cups my face, confusing me. She holds my gaze and each tear that slips free is like a knife to my heart.

"Link, I need you to listen to me, ok? Ignore this breakdown as best you can, alright? This has *nothing* to do with you or what just happened. That was amazing and I plan to have so many encore performances, you're going to get sick of me. This is about me and my stuff and the fact that my emotions have a mind of their own sometimes, especially right now."

"I...I don't understand," I say honestly, rubbing her arms, trying desperately to figure out what's happening.

She takes a shuddering breath. "Link...the last man I had sex with was my husband. He...he died, almost eight years ago." *Oh God. The band on the chain.* I had an inkling that maybe that was her secret, that she'd been widowed, but to hear her say it cuts me to my core. I'm angry at the world on her behalf. Someone like Savvy shouldn't ever have to go through something like that. The scar on her chest catches my eye and something cold creeps into my chest. Had they been in some kind of accident together? Is that what she's been holding back?

"Savvy, I...I'm sorry. I'm so sorry." I brush hair and tears from her face. She gives me a watery smile through her tears.

"I'm sorry I didn't tell you before and I'm not...I'm not ready to tell you everything yet, I'm sorry, but—"

"Hey, shhh, don't worry about any of that, Sav, please."

She nods and leans in to kiss me. "I'm sorry. I'm ruining this."

"You couldn't possibly." I keep stroking her cheeks, her hair. I don't know how to take her pain away and it's killing me.

Her tears finally slow and she lets out a long, slow breath.

"Phew. That was…" She shakes her head and rolls her eyes. "That was ridiculous." She laughs a little and I give her a small smile, though I'm still worried. "Link, I have so much baggage and more issues than Sports Illustrated, but if…if you want to try to deal with it all, I would like that very much."

I let out a shaky laugh. "Sweetheart, we all have issues. This is all new. We both have histories and secrets and we'll take our time learning them, ok? You don't have to apologize for anything, do you hear me?"

She nods before leaning in to press her lips to mine. I cradle her face and kiss her softly, trying to somehow take all her pain away, even though I know I can't. I can't even begin to imagine what she's been through, what losing a spouse could possibly be like, but I know that I would do anything in my power to keep her from ever feeling pain like that again.

CHAPTER 10

Savannah

I cannot believe the earth-shattering sex I just had with Link...or the breakdown I had afterwards. I mean, I can, but it's still embarrassing. I've told him a piece of my dark secret and I feel better for it, but I'm not ready to go all in yet. The look in his eyes when I told him I'd lost Matt...well, I'm not ready to see what will be there when I tell him everything.

He's such a *good* guy, I can't really believe it. How many guys would react the way he had tonight? Beyond concerned and afraid that he'd hurt me at first, and then completely understanding when I broke down, only worried about me and nothing else? Basically none. I don't deserve him, but I'm going to keep him anyway, for as long as he'll have me.

I lean in to kiss him, soft and slow as I trail my hands over his shoulders and arms, back up again and over his chest. He's so damn gorgeous and I can't seem to stop touching him. His skin is flushed and hot beneath my palms, but so smooth. He has a few scars of his own here and there: one near his right collar bone, another just below his left peck. I make a point to kiss them as he had mine and he takes a shuddering breath.

I trace my fingers downward, grazing his stomach and his abs clench in response. I don't know that I've ever known anyone in person who has a legit six pack, but Link sure as hell does—and those damn indentions beside his hips that make me think nothing but X-rated thoughts. I know he works hard to maintain his body and I plan to remind him repeatedly just how much all that work is appreciated.

I continue to let my fingers drift lower and his breath catches. "Savvy, we don't—"

I cut him off with another kiss, still languid, but something ferocious building beneath the surface. I grip his cock, delighted to find him hardening again already, and slowly begin to stroke. I kiss down his neck and he lets his head fall back, giving me better access to his throat. I lick and nip my way across to the other side and back up, making him groan when I bite his ear lobe. As if he can't stand it anymore, he reaches out and cups my breasts again. I moan quietly against his lips and just like that, the kindling goes up in flames, fire spreading through every inch of me again.

I lean back, pulling him down with me. He levers himself above me on his elbows.

"Are you sure?" he asks, studying me in that way he has.

"Please, Link. I want this. I want you." I kiss him again and pull back. "I'm ok," I add softly, holding his gaze. I need him to understand that I am actually alright, despite what that breakdown may have looked like. I want this, I want *him*, more than just about anything in the world.

He nods and leans in to kiss me again, biting gently on my bottom lip. The flames fan higher and my breaths are coming quick and shallow, my breasts rubbing against his chest with each inhalation. This burn is so unlike the desperate fire from before, but just as consuming, just as dangerous. Maybe even more so. I reach down and grip him again, positioning him in the right spot, and he hisses in a breath. I grin and he kisses me again as he starts to shift forward. I'm already moving my hips, desperate for him again, but he freezes.

"Wait. Fuck, hold on." He starts to pull away but I cling to him, hand tight on the back of his neck. I realize what he's going to get and decide to say fuck it.

"I...I can't get pregnant," I say, biting my lip. "And I'm definitely clean..." He stares for a second before his eyes widen, realizing what I'm saying.

"I am too," he assures me quickly. "I got tested after I found out about Audrey cheating, just to be safe, and I haven't been with anyone since."

"So, um...you don't have to wear anything, if you don't want to..."

He doesn't seem to be able to speak, but gives me an eager, jerky nod in response. I chuckle a bit as I pull him close again, reaching downward.

"Then..." I grip him again and get him in the right spot, pressing the head inside without hesitation.

"Fuuccckkk," he moans. He slides inside, slowly this time, and the pleasure is so intense my entire body shudders. When he's in as far as he can go, he pulls back, almost completely out, only to move back in again. Slow, measured thrusts while he kisses my lips, my jaw, my neck. I rub his back, digging my fingers in, but not in a desperate, mad clawing this time. No, this time I'm silently begging him to stay with me, desperately trying to keep him this close to me forever. He gently strokes my cheek and then grabs my wrists, one at a time, prying them from his back. I wonder for a moment if I hurt him, but then he pins my hands on either side of my head, slowly raising them upward and interlock his fingers with mine. I squeeze his hands as I move my hips in time with his slow thrusts, hooking my leg around his hip to fuse his body to mine.

The pressure builds slowly this time, a low burn within the coals of a fire, stoking hotter and hotter with each languid slide of his body against mine. This is so different than before, so different than anything I've ever felt. The embers begin to catch, the flames rising, higher and higher, and after what feels like a blissful eternity, they reach a fever pitch. I cry out his name as I come, arching my back.

"Can feel you," he rasps at my ear, before kissing my neck. "God, Savannah..." He thrusts a few more times before following me over the edge, groaning into the crook of my neck as he comes.

We lie tangled together for an eternity after that, my head on his chest as he strokes my hair. No tears come this time, only a sense of pure satisfaction and contentment that I haven't felt in far too long.

CHAPTER 11

Lincoln

Savvy and I are like horny teenagers, barely able to keep our hands off of each other. Since that first night—and the following morning—it's been insane. Not that I'm complaining, not in the slightest, but I don't think it's ever been like this for me with anyone else. We're figuring each other out and learning all of our likes and dislikes is exceptionally fun. I love how open and free she is with herself. If she wants something, she tells me. If she needs something, she demands it. She's inquisitive and eager and it's honestly been the best sex of my fucking life. Not just because it's good—and it is *damn* good—but because everything with Savvy just feels different. Bigger. More important.

Everything is perfect. *Maybe too perfect?* We've just come in from lounging at the pool most of the day. Swimming, playing, napping...waking to play some more. I grin at the memories of sliding her bikini bottoms to the side while she sat on the edge of the pool, hooking her knees over my shoulder as I leaned in...

Another perfect day...yet something dark and ugly is creeping into my mind and I'm powerless to stop it. The trust issues I've tried hard to move past, to pretend don't exist anymore, are worming their way into my thoughts, and I can feel myself starting to go on the defensive.

"Pizza?" she asks, pulling her hair out of her messy bun and running her fingers through the wavy strands. I lean against the counter and watch her, wondering how something as simple as fluffing out her hair can be so sexy. She notices me noticing her, notices the heated look in my eyes despite my wayward thoughts, and comes to stand in front of me. My hands automatically settle on her waist and she smiles as she turns my hat backwards. I've noticed she particularly likes it that way for whatever reason and something about that makes me fall even harder. She likes me for *me*, in jeans and an old t-shirt with my dirty old ballcap backwards. She doesn't care if I'm dressed to the nines, doesn't care where the hell my clothes came from one way or another. It's nice not to have that weird added pressure that I often find in L.A. to have designer everything, to always be worried about what I have on or how I look.

She goes up on her toes to kiss me, long and soft, but making my blood boil all the same. She pulls back and slides one hand to my chest, giving me a look that makes me feel so at ease. Everything is easy with her. *Too easy,* that stupid pessimistic voice in the back of my head pipes up. My conversation with Colin comes back to the forefront, nagging at me again. *Damn it.* This isn't going to let up, so I decide to go at it head on. Maybe I'm just being paranoid or overly sensitive, maybe I'm reading too much into it. Maybe she'll give me the answers I need to hear and all of this will just be chocked up to too much sun and too little food.

"Hey, why don't we stay at your place tonight?"

She tenses and pulls away to grab a bottle of water out of the fridge. My stomach knots, knowing that this isn't going to turn out the way I want it to, the way I *need* it to. I've already got it so bad for her, but that doesn't mean I can just ignore the unease, to stop the nagging feeling that she's hiding things and lying. Doubts start to bubble up and I can't seem to stop them.

She turns back and gives me a smile, bumping the door closed with her hip. I'm momentarily distracted by the movement, by the way she looks in those damn cutoffs, unbuttoned over her bikini bottoms. *Mercy.* I rub a hand over my mouth, but force myself to yank my gaze back upwards.

"Why would you wanna slum it at my place when you have this?" she teases, gesturing to the grand space around us, but I can still hear the tension beneath her easy tone. Something is up. *Maybe she really does have a terrible secret that she's hiding from me.* "Plus, Griffey has grown accustomed to a certain lifestyle..." She cuts her eyes to where the Golden lounges on one of the plush, oversized chairs beside the window. Ignoring her attempt to brush it off, I push on.

"Come on, please? I want to see your place—the inside of it," I add when I can tell she's about to point out that I have seen her place. It's a gorgeous farm-house style home nestled among thick woods and overlooking a lake at the edge of town, but the farthest I've ever gotten is the front steps. Why? What kind of secrets could she be hiding there that she doesn't want me to see? Is she embarrassed for some reason? Does she think I'll care that it isn't a mansion? I don't understand and I *want* to understand.

She crosses her arms over her chest. "Why are you pushing this tonight?" She sounds defensive and I don't know why, which makes *me* even more defensive. I think I've been pretty patient with this whole thing, especially for someone in my position. I don't mean to sound haughty or whatever, but I *am* an extremely well-known celebrity. I should be way more wary about all the unknowns in this situation than I have been. It hasn't really bothered me before, but now Colin has gotten in my head and her defensiveness isn't helping matters. Maybe I'm just hangry. Who the fuck knows.

"I'm not pushing, but I do want to know why you're so hellbent on keeping me away from your house, from your life."

"I'm not keeping you from my life," she fires back, but she averts her gaze slightly, which she does anytime she isn't being completely honest. I'm not saying she should share every detail of her life with me. This is all new and we're still figuring this thing out between us, so we're both allowed to have our secrets, but I feel like I'm giving a whole lot more than I'm getting. I'd felt that way through my entire relationship with Audrey and I never want to feel it again. My haunches go up and my defensive walls start fortifying themselves. I'm not quick to anger, but once I start towards it, it's like a runaway train: a crash is inevitable.

"You are, Savvy. I'm not saying you have to share everything with me right now, but hell, you can't even invite me to your house? What's that about? What could you possibly be hiding?"

"What do *you* think I could possibly be hiding?" she snaps.

I throw my hands up in frustration. "Hell, I don't know! You could be...you could be a serial killer for all I know at the rate you're sharing with me!" I know how ridiculous that is, but—runaway train.

Her mouth pops open and she barks out a humorless laugh.

"A serial killer? Seriously??"

I take off my hat to run a hand through my hair, and then shove it back on again. I know that was a stupid thing to say, but I'm not about to apologize. I don't think I'm in the wrong here.

She already told me about losing her husband. Is that the problem? She doesn't want me in the space she shared with him? That...hurts. I don't exactly know why, but it does.

"It's fucking weird, Savannah!" I thunder, the train reaching the point of no return. *Crash imminent.* "Why won't you tell me anything real about your life for the past decade? Why won't you tell me where your scars came from? Why won't you let me come to your house? This is a two-way street, Sav, but I'm the only one fucking driving! Why won't you let me in?"

"Because!" she yells back. Her eyes are wild and her mouth opens as if to say something, then snaps shut. She presses her lips into a thin line and shakes her head. "You know what, screw this." She grabs her keys off the counter and storms through the living room towards the front door. I grit my teeth and go after her. I'm pissed but I don't want her to leave.

"Savvy, come on—"

She whirls on me, casting me a killing look and stopping me in my tracks.

"No, you don't get to follow me. I've got bodies to go dismember according to you," she sneers, the sarcasm so thick it could choke a cat. "Griffey, let's go!" The dog lifts his head for a second, but then lays back down with a huff. She grits her teeth. "Fine. You stay here, you Benedict Arnold. Wouldn't want you to be witness to all my heinous deeds anyway!"

I roll my eyes, annoyed with how much she's harping on the stupid serial killer comment.

"Fine. Go. Have a good fucking night." I turn my back on her and stomp back into the kitchen. I hear her mutter *fuck you* before leaving, slamming the door behind her for good measure. Pictures rattle on the walls and Griffey lifts his head again barking out a low huff of annoyance. He looks from the door to me, tilting his head. *Your guess is as good as mine, buddy.*

I yank my hat off again, slamming it down on the counter with a curse. I scrub my hands over my face, wondering what the hell had just happened. I'm an idiot. I know I'm an idiot. I'm still pissed and annoyed, but I know it wasn't exactly fair to go after her that way.

"Fuck," I mutter as I sprint towards the door. I yank it open, determined to chase her down, but freeze. She's standing on the porch, hands opening and closing at her sides. My chest constricts and I exhale roughly.

She didn't leave.

She couldn't leave any more than I could let her go.

Our gazes collide and just like that, the tiny spark lights an inferno. She closes the distance between us and jumps into my arms. I lift her easily, gripping her ass with both hands as she wraps her legs around my waist. Her lips slam into mine as I walk us back into the house.

"You drive me fucking crazy sometimes," I whisper against her mouth as I kick the door closed behind us and lurch towards the entry way table. Decorations and keys and other odds and ends go flying as I sweep them aside with too much force, setting Savvy down and wedging my hips between her thighs.

"I know," she breathes as I kiss her throat, fingers tunneling into my hair. I yank the triangles of her bikini top aside and dip my head to her breasts. She moans as I take one nipple into my mouth, sucking hard and biting gently. She bucks her hips forward against me as she tears at my shorts. In a heartbeat my cock is in her hand, and I hiss out a breath. I latch on to her other breast as she strokes, licking and sucking and biting until she's writhing. I straighten and lean my forehead against hers.

"I'm still annoyed," I pant as she continues to stroke, driving me wild.

"I know."

I step back and pull her with me, tugging her shorts and bikini bottoms down. I plunge a finger inside, biting back a groan to find her wet as hell. I walk her backwards until she's against the wall beside the table, fingering her harder as passion and anger and lust all collide. She spreads her legs wider, welcoming it. I yank her forward and spin her around, pinning her front against the wall again, my chest to her back. She glances back at me, panting and writhing as I grind my cock against her ass. I lean in and kiss her neck, and she wiggles against me, desperate. My cock pulses with need, so hard it's painful. I step back enough to pull her hips out and bend her over *just* enough so I can fuck her hard against the wall. I kick her ankles apart and position the head before slamming forward.

She cries out but I know it's in pleasure, and I pull back only to slam forward again. I press my chest against her back, covering her body with mine, surrounding her. I bite her shoulder and she moans, reaching behind her to wrap one hand around the back of my head, nails digging in. She draws me to her lips for a searing kiss. She claws into the wall with her other hand as I pound into her, over and over in a punishing rhythm.

"Drive me. Fucking. Crazy," I say again at her ear before running the lobe through my teeth.

"Fuckkkkk, Link. *Oh God.*" As much as this is an outlet for the anger from before, it's also something more. I cover her hand on the wall with mine, intertwining our fingers.

She couldn't leave. And I couldn't let her go.

The sounds of my flesh slapping against hers, pictures rattling on the walls, and cries of bliss fill the room, echoing all around us. I don't let up, fucking her hard as she begs for more, urging me to go harder, not to stop, to make her come. I slip my hand around and rub her throbbing clit, and she thrashes against me. Finally, she screams as she comes hard and I don't hesitate to follow her over the edge. Her legs give out and I ease us both down to the floor, wrapping my arms around her and pulling her tight against my chest. I kiss her sweaty forehead and my heart drums wildly. I wonder if she can feel it against her back.

"I know you aren't a serial killer," I whisper.

She huffs out a hoarse chuckle. "I know." She sighs. "I'm sorry I'm so...weird."

I wince. "I shouldn't have said—"

"No, you're right. It *is* weird. It's really fucking weird. If I were you, I'd be annoyed too, or at the very least confused. I just...I have a lot of stuff I'm dealing with and working through and I'll share it all with you at some point, I promise. If you can just give me more time and be patient with all of my *stuff*..."

I exhale roughly and decide to give her as much time as she needs. Already my irritation from earlier seems stupid and I don't really know where it came from. Sure, I want to know what's going on inside her head, what she's not ready to share with me yet, but as someone who has zero privacy from prying eyes ninety-nine percent of time, I refuse to take hers away from her. *I really think I'm just hangry.*

I shift her so I can see her face. I stroke her cheek before leaning down to kiss her softly.

"Ok. I won't push again," I promise. "Now: shower and pizza."

She grins and I lean in to nip her bottom lip again, planning to apologize properly on the bench in the oversized shower.

"Maybe we should fight more often," she says with that sexy mischief in her eyes. "I think making up might be my new favorite thing."

I chuckle softly, nuzzling her hair.

Mine too.

CHAPTER 12

Savannah

The road trip turns out to be fantastic. I'd been nervous that it would be a disaster, that he'd be annoyed at having to drive instead of fly first class or in his private jet or whatever, but he seems to be having a blast. We laugh and sing and I ask him endless questions about Gatorcon and what I might expect. I can't even pretend not to be excited, bouncing in my seat as I scroll through the website, nearly shrieking several times as I go through the attendee list.

"Oh cool! There's a Cosplay contest."

"We'll have to get you a costume for the next one."

"Oh I'm so in. I'm thinking Slave Leia?"

He groans and says, "Only if you model it for me in the bedroom first..." I giggle and go back to reading about the event. We make a few pit stops along the way, posing for pictures in front of each new state's welcome sign, buying dumb souvenirs, and honestly having a blast.

I've tried to mentally prepare myself for the possibility of our relationship coming out to the public at this thing, tried to prepare for what that might mean. But, I'm trying not to think about that too hard—no use worrying about things that might not happen and freaking out for no reason. We'll deal with it if and when it happens.

So, instead of thinking of all the what-ifs, I keep my mind occupied with...other things. I glance sidelong at Link, looking too good for words with his Aviators on, backwards ball cap, and a sexy grin on his face as he sings along with the radio.

We've only got about forty-five minutes left and I decide I can't wait that long. He's driving with his left hand on the wheel and his right on my thigh, rubbing slow circles with his thumb that drive me wild. Ever since that first night, we've been damn near insatiable. I don't know what's come over me. It's like I'm making up for all of those years without and I just can't get enough. I feel so free and safe with Link, have loved exploring this new side of our relationship and learning all kinds of new and sexy tricks. Lincoln Ashmore is an undercover sex *god*. The things he can do, the way he can touch, the desires he brings out in me that I never even knew I had...I shiver just thinking about it. Even our anger bang against the wall had been hot as all hell and I'd be lying if I said I wasn't tempted to pick a fight with him again just to bring that fiery passion out once more.

My eyes rove over him again, my blood starting to heat. He's been working out even harder lately and it's showing: his shirt is stretched tight across his chest and the sleeves strain over his biceps. He's got an even thicker five o'clock shadow right now and I long to feel the scruff against my inner thighs as he kisses...

I can't take it anymore. I reach over and stroke him through his jeans, feeling him harden beneath my hand. He shifts in his seat and grips the wheel harder, coughing in surprise. I undo his pants and quickly yank his erection free, making him groan. I grin, loving all the noises he makes, all of the ways I can drive him crazy. I continue to stroke, gliding my hand up and down, up and down.

"That's just mean, Savvy..." He trails of when I make the reckless and totally unsafe decision to unbuckle my seat belt and maneuver so that my head is in his lap. He makes a choking sound when I suck him deep. "Fuck!" he bites out.

I giggle around a mouthful of cock and pull back long enough to tell him, "Keep your eyes on the road, Captain." He gives a hoarse chuckle that tappers off into a moan as I lick and suck. He keeps one hand on the wheel and the other rests on the back of my head. He pushes down gently and my toes curl. I don't know why it's sexy, it just is, alright? When he's free to move his hips and he literally fucks my mouth? Forget about it, I'm a goner. Don't ask me to explain.

All too soon, I'm swallowing him down, loving the taste of him. That's probably weird, but it's the truth. I love taking him with my mouth, love feeling him come on my tongue, love tasting him. Almost as much as he likes doing the same to me. I shiver at the thought, wanting his tongue on me so badly right now I have to clench my thighs together. I twirl my tongue around him once more before I pull back and grin. He licks his bottom lip before biting it in the extremely sexy way of his, and I know I'm in trouble as soon as we get to the hotel. My heart races with anticipation and my imagination runs wild with all the possibilities of what he'll do.

"Just you wait," he whispers with a wicked grin, grasping my thigh again and starting up his torturous rubbing again.

We thankfully aren't met by hysterical fans or hordes of paparazzi, only Colin and a few security types in the private parking garage.

"Nice to meet you officially," Colin says, shaking my hand. He's a bit younger than Link I think, maybe my age but definitely not older than mid-thirties at any rate, with deep brown eyes, black hair, thick-rimmed glasses, and a warm smile. I like him immediately, possibly because he's wearing a t-shirt with *Goonies Never Say Die* sprawled across the front, or possibly because I can tell how much he really cares about Link. Anyone who makes Link smile like that, lighting up with genuine joy, is alright in my book.

He escorts us up to our room and though Link tries to, I don't hold his hand through the hallways, just in case. He arches a brow but doesn't say anything, letting it slide. I'm not thrilled about "hiding" our relationship because I...well, fuck me, I think I love him and part of me would like nothing more than to flaunt it to the universe, to say "ha! Suck it! You serve me shit sandwich after shit sandwich, but here I am—winning!" but the longer I can avoid being part of the media circus, the better.

"Alright, Savvy, I've got you all squared away for tomorrow. You've got full run of the whole shebang. You're welcome to explore or stick with me whenever Link is busy, totally up to you." Colin hands me a pass on a lanyard that I guess acts as my Golden Ticket to the chocolate factory. He rattles off a few more things about the next day, times and events and whatnot, and asks if either of us need anything.

"I think we're good, Col, thanks," Link says with a smile, but I can tell that he's desperate to get back at me for the car. I'm desperate to let him.

Colin looks between us and gives us a knowing look, but attempts to hide his smile.

"Alright then, I'll see you two in the morning."

The door has barely shut behind Colin when Link's hands are in my hair, pulling my mouth to his. He moves us to the dining table, unbuttoning my shorts and shoving them and my panties down as we walk. I kick out of them and he quickly lifts me atop the table, the cool wood making me gasp.

"I believe I owe you..." he rasps as he sinks to his knees before me. I bite my lip, ready to receive my due.

***

"Lincoln Joseph Ashmore!" a British-accented voice calls accusingly from the doorway. "How *dare* you!" We're already awake but still lounging in bed, and Link shoots upward, throwing an arm across me protectively.

"Drew, get the fuck outta here!" he yells. Drew? As in...

I shoot up, holding the sheet over myself and gape. Andrew Faraday is standing at the end of the bed, looking at us in mock outrage. He's almost as tall as Link, and attractive—if you're into blondes with piercing blue eyes who look like they just stepped off of a Viking warship. Which I think everyone on the planet is, so, yeah, Drew is sigh-worthy.

He'd had a hugely successful career after *Shadowlands*, was arguably an even bigger star than Link. He'd even won an Oscar for crying out loud and had been nominated for tons of other awards, winning a few here and there. He's slowed down a bit in recent years, and I remember seeing an interview where he talked about getting burned out and being more selective about projects these days. Hell, I don't blame him. His IMDB page is a mile long with all of his roles.

He's a bona fide mega star, one of my favorite actors...and he's standing five feet away from me while I'm stark naked in bed with his best friend. *What in the fuck is my life even!?* For the thousandth time since meeting Link, I wonder if this is all just some kind of hallucination.

Completely ignoring Link, he says, "Snuggling during cons is *our* thing, and here I find you in bed with some..." His eyes shift to me and the mock indignation fades, a salacious grin taking its place. "Some absolute *angel*," he finishes smoothly. "How do you do, love? I'm Drew. Please tell me you're available and maybe just threw Link here a pity fuck because he's Captain Ultra and got his heart broken and all that?" I bust out laughing and Link pinches the bridge of his nose, though he's clearly trying to hide his amusement.

"God damn it, Drew, *get out*."

Instead, he leaps into the bed and I squeal as I try to remain covered.

"I've missed you too, sweetheart," he croons, blowing Link an air kiss.

"Fuck me," Link grates, exhaling in defeat. "Savvy, this is Drew. Drew, Savvy. This isn't exactly the scenario I had in mind for introducing the two of you, you know."

"Really? It's pretty much exactly what I figured would happen," I quip and Drew tosses his head back, laughing.

"Oh, I like you. And so does Link. He talks my ear off about you constantly, you know. If I didn't know any better, I'd say he's in lo—" A pillow hits Drew square in the face. "Oy!" he yells, though it's a bit muffled. He yanks it off and shoves it behind his head, making himself comfortable and I can't tell if Link wants to laugh or murder him.

"Really nice to meet you, love."

"It's nice to meet you too." I sound relatively calm, at least in my own ears. Maybe I'm just a pro at meeting celebrities and acting normal? It's like my super power.

"Now, I'm sure you want a photo, but it's probably in bad taste to do it while you're naked—unless I am likewise so." He wiggles his blonde brows and Link mutters curses under his breath. I can't help but laugh. He's a lot like Link in that I feel instantly comfortable with him, like we're already old friends.

"What if we'd been...uh, busy?" I ask, brushing hair out of my face.

"Filmed it, of course, and sold it to the highest bidder online. Oh don't worry, love, I'd blur your face out first. I am nothing if not a gentleman."

"Alright, get the hell out, asshole. We'll be there in a second."

Drew acts exasperated, but agrees to wait for us in the living room of the suite.

"I'm so sorry. He's...well, he's Drew," Link says as if that explains the situation entirely. I laugh and tell him it's alright. And surprisingly, it is. Talk about a crazy story to laugh about later. We get dressed and head out into the insanity.

***

Comic-cons may be my new favorite thing ever. It's a full on, never-ending nerdgasm and I can't get enough. Everywhere I look, there are cosplayers and merchandise and actors from shows and movies that I've loved for decades. I'm trying hard not to geek out, but it's difficult. My idea that I was just a pro at meeting celebrities and remaining cool? Yeah, I was wrong. Link and Drew are special cases. I lose my mind several times over the course of the morning as I meet some huge stars, gushing and even tearing up a few times. I'm literally speechless when I meet

Nathan Fillion, but he graciously gives me a minute to collect myself and I assure him too many times that I'm not usually so spazzy. He and Link have apparently been friends for a few years and chat about plans to go fishing soon while I stand there unable to speak or breathe or hold a normal conversation like I have half a brain.

"I feel like I should be offended that he's the one that you go completely starstruck over. I mean, I *get it*, but...well, I thought *I* would be your favorite Captain," Link pouts, barely holding back his smile.

"Captain Malcom Reynolds will forever hold that honor, I'm very sorry to break it to you," I retort, sticking out my tongue, but then I remember the encounter and my cheeks heat. "I'm so embarrassed," I groan.

Link chuckles. "You'll do better next time." *Next time. Because there will be a next time. This seriously cannot be my life.* At my dumbstruck expression he grins and starts singing the *Firefly* theme song.

I get to sit in the front row with Colin for the *Shadowlands* panel and it's absolutely amazing. The entire cast is fantastic and they're so kind to all of the fans asking questions. Link catches my eye more often than he should, grinning like an idiot, and Drew makes a point to do it as well, putting his arm around Link's shoulders and holding my gaze as he answers pointed questions about love lives and filling it with plenty of innuendo. I blush and just hope no one else is putting two and two together.

Now I stand off to the side with Colin as the *Shadowlands* cast do meet and greets and sign autographs. Without looking at me, he says, "So, not to sound like the overprotective brother or whatever, but I'm going to say it anyway: if you hurt him, we're going to have a problem."

"I don't plan on it," I tell him honestly. "Scouts honor."

He turns to study me, as if searching my face for any hint of a lie but finally nods. "Good because I like you and he obviously does too." He shifts to lean against the wall, nodding towards the table and what seems like a never-ending line of fans. "This part can get a little boring for us on the sidelines, so if you want to go explore, that's totally fine. I'm sure Nathan is still around," he teases.

"Listen, I was having *a moment,* alright?" I say and he laughs, pushing his glasses up on his nose. I stick around for a while, watching Link with his fans. The way he is with them is really special. He lights up and seems interested in each and every one, never seeming bored or annoyed or like he's pretending to be happy to see them. It makes me grin like an idiot, and I quickly force myself to rein it in and act normal.

After a while, I decide I'm going to go explore on my own for a bit after all, remembering all of the things from the website that I wanted to check out.

"I think I am going to..." I trail off as a kid comes up to the table in front of Link and catches my eye. He's maybe seventeen or eighteen, and he's grinning from ear to ear, wearing a *Shadowlands* shirt and a Captain Ultra hat. He's *definitely* a fan. Link greets him warmly, but the boy shakes his head, pointing at his ear. Link frowns slightly, not quite understanding, and the boy holds out a tablet where he's written something on the screen. I'm moving forward before I can stop myself—or before Colin can haul me back.

The boy notices me approaching and his eyes widen as he takes me in, blushing a bit. He's super cute, with sandy blonde hair, baby blues, the faintest smattering of freckles across his nose, and a lip ring. I peek at the screen and my suspicions are confirmed.

I sign to him, asking if he speaks ASL.

A grin splits his face. He nods enthusiastically and tells me that he does, beginning to explain what's going on. I quickly introduce myself, and, with his permission, begin to interpret for him.

"He's deaf, but knows ASL," I say to Link, keeping my eyes on Michael. His smile is contagious and I can't stop grinning back. "His name is Michael and he's a huge fan. Like huge, mega huge, oh God this is embarrassing. I'm sorry." We all laugh and he shakes his head, blushing a bit, before continuing. "His older brother usually comes with him to act as an interpreter, but he was sick today. No way was he going to miss this though, so he came alone."

Link is looking at me like I have five heads.

"You know sign language?"

"I'm a woman of mystery, Lincoln Ashmore," I say with a sly grin and a wink.

"That's for damn sure," he mutters before turning to speak to Michael directly.

He tells Michael, through me, that he's happy to meet him and the two have a nice conversation with me interpreting. I catch Drew watching me with something close to astonishment on his face, but I just shrug. It isn't a big deal. Michael gets a few pictures, and Link autographs a few things for him and his brother before it's time to move down the line to the rest of the cast. I happily go along, helping him meet the stars he so obviously loves and have real interactions that he wouldn't be able to have with his tablet. The rest of the cast are all equally kind to Michael and give me looks of encouragement, excitement, surprise, and thanks. Now *I* start to blush, feeling weird with all the attention directed my way. I don't get why everyone is making such a fuss.

When we reach the end, Michael thanks me profusely and asks for a photo with *me*. I laugh but can't say no to him, so we snap a few selfies, one of which has Link and Drew being ridiculous in the background. Before Michael leaves, I have an idea.

"Hey, would it be ok if I tagged along with you for the rest of the afternoon?" I ask.

"Oh, it's ok you don't have to do that."

He looks like he's already on cloud nine, but if I could help keep his entire day going this way? I want in.

"I'd really like to, if you don't mind. It's kind of boring just standing there watching everyone sign autographs, so I want to explore, but this is my first con ever and I don't know anyone else here and it's all a little intimidating, honestly. Think you could show me the ropes?" I put my hands to my chest, pleading. He laughs and rolls his eyes, but eventually nods. I can tell that he's secretly excited and very grateful for my help. I smile and hold up a finger, asking him to give me a second.

I jog over to Colin. "Hey, do you have another one of these pass thingys?" I ask, yanking on my lanyard. "Can he get the same access as me or can he be like my plus one to everything or something?"

"I'm way ahead of you," he says, smiling and handing another pass over. "This is so cool, Savvy. Buzz is already spreading through the whole place about it. You just made a few hundred thousand new friends." I gulp a bit at that, making Colin laugh. He's got to be messing with me, right? I eye him and he merely grins and shrugs. I shrug it off, deciding that even if it's true, it's worth it for how stoked Michael is about to be.

I jog back towards him and hold up the pass, wiggling it with a grin. I loop the lanyard around my wrist so I can sign, **"Are you ready for the best day of your freaking life?"**

He stares at the pass, dumfounded for a long moment, eyes getting glassy. I put the pass around his neck and pat his shoulder.

"Man, even if I could talk, I couldn't right now. You have no idea what this means. I've been saving for a whole year just to get enough for my ticket and the meet and greet pass for Shadowlands. I must have mowed at least a thousand lawns. I'd never be able to go to all of these other panels and stuff, not in a million years." He swallows hard. **"Thank you. Seriously. Thank you."**

My nose burns a bit from the tears starting to blur my vision, but I force them away and give him a smile.

"Well, let's go kick the shit outta this con, then." We fist bump and I'm actually thrumming with just as much excitement as Michael. This is going to be awesome.

I head back to Link, who's staring at me like I just walked on water or something, to tell him bye.

"Savvy, you're...you're amazing."

"I know," I smirk. "I'll meet back up with you for the *League of Heroes* panel tonight?" He nods and without thinking, I lean across the table and give him a kiss goodbye. I pull away and we both freeze. It had been instinct, habit. I hadn't even thought about it but now I realize what I've done. I slowly turn, eyes wide as cameras flash around us and a collective gasp sounds down the line of fans. *Fuck.*

I don't know what to say or do, so I mouth *sorry* to Link, give the crowd an awkward wave, and quickly turn back to Michael. He's staring like everyone else, but his lips curl into a shit-eating grin.

"Shut up," I sign before grabbing his arm and tugging him away as fast as humanly possible.

CHAPTER 13

Lincoln

Savannah Riley may just be the most amazing woman I've ever met. No, the most amazing *person*. What she did for that boy yesterday was simply...amazing. I can't stop using that word but it's the one that fits best: She. Is. Amazing.

The look on Michael's face when he realized he would be able to have conversations with the cast after all was like a kid on Christmas. The look on his face when she'd given him the all-access pass and decided to hang with him all day? Like he just saw the sun for the first time. I'm fairly certain he fell in love with her before the day was done. *Join the club, kid.*

The only downside to the day was that now the media was in a frenzy about the mystery woman who was kissing Lincoln Ashmore at Gatorcon. Fans waiting in line hadn't missed the swift goodbye kiss and had snapped plenty of photos, as had the con photographers, and everyone had been quick to start posting them all over social media. She's taking it surprisingly well and so far, actually seeming more worried that *I'd* be upset that she'd outed us. Of course, it doesn't bother me at all other than me worrying that it's going to be too much for her. I'm not sure she can really be prepared for what the media might say and do.

People say some pretty cruel things online without the slightest care for the person on the other side. Thankfully, it doesn't appear that anyone has been able to dig up any real information about her, so that's a plus. For now, she's just my unnamed blonde lady friend.

On the upside, the media had *also* gotten wind of her day with Michael and the heartwarming story was spreading like wildfire, taking at least part of the attention away from my relationship status.

We're all hanging out in Drew's suite when her phone rings. She grins before answering.

"Hey Tiff."

"So apparently you're the universe's hottest good Samaritan *and* Lincoln Ashmore's mystery kissing bandit. Can I get your autograph?" Savvy rolls her eyes and flips the camera off. "Seriously, you're all over my feed today. Do you know how many of our friends have texted me asking if that's *you* in the picture or not? Of course I tell them they're nuts, playing the whole wouldn't I know if my best friend were dating Lincoln Ashmore card—which is really going to hurt the street cred of our friendship when it comes out that you are, in fact, the one sucking face with him in those pictures you know."

Savvy scrunches her nose. "I was not *sucking face*—" She cuts off when a bark sounds in the background. "Aw, how's my boy?"

"Currently floating in the pool on his raft and living a life of luxury, of course." Savvy giggles and I'm assuming Tiff panned the camera to show the golden mutt lounging in the pool. I laugh, picturing it. He has special doggy-proof floats and everything. "So, you're like a legit little mini celebrity right now, it's so crazy."

"Convince her to do an interview!" Colin calls from across the table.

"Who was that?"

"That was Colin, Link's manager. He wants me to do interviews—about the whole thing with Michael, not the kissing—which is ridiculous," she adds pointedly.

Drew pops behind Savvy's head, giving the camera one of his signature panty-melting smiles as he likes to call them. "And I'm Drew," he purrs. "Hello, darling."

Unintelligible sounds come from the other side of the phone and Savvy catches my eye, biting her lip and smiling.

"Oh my fucking God," Tiff finally gets out. Drew quickly yanks the phone out of Savvy's hand and walks away, chatting happily with a stunned Tiff. Savvy lets him and it makes my chest clench at how easily they've hit it off, how comfortable she seems to be among my friends and how much she fits in with all of us perfectly.

"Just got *another* interview request..." Colin says, giving Savvy pleading puppy eyes.

"Just tell them I said it wasn't a big deal, I was just being helpful. Right place, right time kind of thing, that's all," she says with a shrug. Colin and I both give her *seriously?* looks and she rolls her eyes. "Ok, ok." She bits her lip and scrunches her nose again, looking too adorable for words. "Would I have to be on camera...?"

I watch as she and Colin start talking about potential interviews, soaking up seeing her here among my friends, in the thick of the crazy that is my life and not completely freaking out. In fact, she unknowingly just endeared herself to two entire fandoms, plus practically every nerd on the planet. Not to make comparisons, but Audrey wasn't the nicest when it came to fans. She never attended events like this with me, only red carpets and after parties. When fans approached us out in public, she would stand to the side, usually looking annoyed and would typically be irritated with me once we walked away, demanding to know why I *always* had to stop and talk and disrupt our day. Yes, I know hindsight is 20/20, but man, I wish I'd had glasses back then. She really wasn't right for me and I don't know how I didn't see it, or at least how I convinced myself that I didn't see it. I was colorblind to the red flags, I guess. It wasn't all bad, and I did love her, at least in a way, but it was most definitely not like how it is with Savannah.

Colin and Drew are already head over heels in love with her and...I know I am too. I know it's batshit crazy, know there is still a fuck ton of stuff I don't know about her—like the fact that until yesterday I had no clue she knew ASL (which she knows because her father had been deaf, so ASL had been her second language growing up)—but I don't care. I'm lost for this girl and I'm not going to try to fight it.

***

"Are you ever coming out?" I call from the bed. She's been in the bathroom of our luxurious cabin on the admittedly ridiculously large yacht that Drew rented for thirty minutes changing into a swimsuit. I hear her curse and then she emerges looking so damn sexy it's criminal. She's in a black bikini, the small triangles covering her breasts making my mouth water. The bottoms were made to perfectly hug her exquisite ass, strings tying at the sides of her hips. I'm seconds away from untying them with my teeth and doing all manner of illicit things with her, but I can see how tense she is and I pause my wayward thoughts. I move to the edge of the bed as she comes closer. I automatically wrap my hands around her waist as she settles in between my knees and rests her hands on my shoulders.

"What's wrong? What are you over-thinking?"

She gives me a half smile before answering. "I'm thinking that maybe I should have worn a one piece? Or a full wetsuit..."

"You're worried about your scars." She nods. I've all but forgotten about them for the most part. I still make a point to kiss them as often as possible, to reassure her, but overall, they're the least most remarkable thing about her. Other than her initial apprehension of me seeing them, she seems completely ok with them. She wears two pieces all the time back in Sandlapper Cove and must have thrown them in the suitcase without thinking.

"Babe, don't," I say softly. "Every inch of you is gorgeous, scars or not. You do know that right?" She bites her lip and I lean in to kiss the one on her side, then run my tongue upward until I reach her ribs, and she shivers, gripping my shoulders tighter. "Do I need to remind you how beautiful I think you are? How delectable your body is?" I ask in a low voice practically dripping with lust.

Her voice is breathy when she answers. "Yes, please..." I grin and plant another kiss against her skin. She shudders, and I start making my way south, deciding that everyone can wait on us just a bit longer, but she forces herself backwards. I give her a pouty face and she giggles.

"Behave. We're supposed to be hanging out with your friends, remember?" She runs a hand through her hair. "I guess I just...I don't want them to think that you could do better or something? That you deserve the perfect model instead of...this," she says, gesturing to herself.

"Trust me, they're all wondering how I got so lucky and why you're slumming it with me." She rolls her eyes. "No, seriously. Those were Kira's exact words." That makes her laugh and seem to relax a bit. "Them seeing that you have scars isn't going to change that opinion, trust me." I know it's naïve to think that no one will ever say anything about them, especially negative things. I know that the superficial haze that's settled over so much of Hollywood and the media these days will touch her at some point, it's just a matter of when. But I also know that the people I choose to surround myself with fall outside of that haze and won't react the way she's dreading, and, for now, that's all that matters.

She lets out a long breath and nods. "Alright, let's go then. I've never partied on a yacht with a bunch of celebrities. Let's see what the fuss is all about." She reaches for my hand and I take it, my lips curling upward. She surprises me at every turn and I agree with everyone else: I don't know how I got so lucky.

***

Drew, in true Drew fashion, immediately makes a comment about the scars, but it actually seems to make Savannah feel better. I think she'd rather have the elephant in the room in the spotlight than everyone trying to avoid it and keep it in the shadows.

"My guess is cage fighting Bengal Tigers," he says, squinting at her and turning his head this way and that. "Hey, that one kind of looks like a cat if you close one eye!" She smiles and squeezes my hand, letting me know she's alright.

"Check mine out!" He grins, turning his back to her. "I've got four screws in my spine right there. Bloody brutal recovery that was. The pills weren't so bad though." Savvy laughs and that's that. No one asks about them or mentions them again. It doesn't even seem like anyone notices them after that initial "shock" of seeing them.

We have one of the best days in my life probably, full of laughing, swimming, drinking, and dancing. I feel utterly *content* and my lips curl. *It's a good fucking feeling.* It seems like Savvy is feeling the same way, looking weightless and perfect as she smiles and laughs and spins to the music.

We party well into the evening, anchored not too far off shore. After way too many drinks, Drew stands on a table out on the deck. Savvy and Kira stop their conversation to watch the show, Kira whispering something to Savvy that makes her snort with laughter, clamping a hand over her mouth to stop from spitting out her drink. She meets my eyes across the way where I'm chatting with Ethan and Zach, and smiles. It's innocent enough, but quickly transforms into something much more. We've been stealing heated looks at each other all day, and I've been stealing kisses every opportunity I get, but seeing her in that damn bikini all day and not being able to have her has been torture. Worth it for the blast we've been having, of course, but torture none the less. She bites her lip, as if reading my mind, and I slowly shake my head, letting her know she's killing me. Drew clears his throat loudly and we both pull our gazes back to the idiot on the table.

"I need everyone's attention please. Link, you're my best friend, so I'm truly sorry to do this to you, mate, but I simply *must* steal your woman. Savannah, I love you. You are far too good for Lincoln here. Also too good for me, that's obvious, but I'm better looking, and I do believe it is common knowledge that I have the bigger...sword." He winks and everyone laughs. He holds one hand to his chest and reaches towards her with the other, like he's about to recite a sonnet or some shit. Hell, he really might. He'd been part of the Royal Shakespeare Company for a few years for crying out loud. Drew is twice the actor I'll ever be, that's for sure.

Savvy meets my gaze again and gets a mischievous look in her eyes that is so damned sexy I can't even explain it. Whatever she's planning is going to be fun...

She pretends to debate, tapping the tip of her finger against her chin. "Well, I *was* team Elias back in the day, you know...Plus, what girl doesn't want a man with a *big sword*..." I narrow my eyes at her, giving her a challenging look. She bites her lip again and arches her brow in response. *Oh yes. This is going to be fun.*

Drew whoops in triumph and I stride across the deck. Savvy squeals with laughter when I pick her up and toss her over my shoulder.

"She has clearly had too much to drink and needs to go to bed."

"Oy! I was winning!" Drew calls as I head towards the stairs leading below deck.

"And for the record, your *sword* is not bigger than mine," I yell over my shoulder.

"Alright, let's do this then." Everyone roars with laughter and I turn enough to see Drew starting to unlace his swim trunks to prove me wrong.

"Oooo contest time!" Savvy says, and I hear her smack her palms together, rubbing them eagerly. I chuckle and turn away, back towards the stairs "Hey! Wait! I wanna be the judge!" she pouts as we head down the stairs. "Take me bacckkkk," she giggles, waving to everyone as we disappear out of sight.

Back in our room, I slide her slowly down my chest and press her back into the door. She licks her lips as her gaze collides with mine. The gold in her eyes is bright tonight, and she's just tipsy enough that they're filled with a reckless and wild abandon.

"Team Elias, huh?" I ask as I shove the two triangles of her top aside, freeing her breasts and quickly palming them. She arches her back, pressing them into my hands harder, moaning.

She somehow manages a shrug. "I had a thing for bad boys," she pants as I knead her flesh, rubbing her jutting nipples, wanting my mouth on them so badly it waters.

"Hmm," I murmur as I lean in to kiss her neck. She digs her fingers into my back as she pulls me closer. At her ear I whisper, "You liked bad boys? Well, I like *good girls.*" I bite her ear lobe and she cries out, bucking her hips forward as she yanks mine against her.

"Fuckkkk," she moans. I chuckle, knowing how much she likes when we play these little games, how much it turns her on when I say those two little words. *Good girl.* I'm hard as stone already at the thought of dominating her tonight, of using that sassy little mouth of hers for another purpose. I pinch her chin and tilt her head back so she can meet my gaze.

"On your knees, beautiful," I command. Her eyes blaze with desire and my cock pulses. She eagerly obeys, sliding down to her knees before me. She glances up at me as she unties the laces of my swim trunks, quickly freeing my aching cock. She strokes it, her palm so soft and warm, and I grit my teeth. "Between those pretty lips, baby." Again, she obeys, taking my shaft into her mouth.

"Fuck," I groan as she twirls her tongue around the head and sucks me deep. Over and over, nice and slow, driving me mad. "Eyes up," I demand. She releases me from her mouth and strokes my wet shaft as she meets my gaze. "Do you want me to fuck your mouth, Savannah?"

Her eyes widen and she nods, licking her bottom lip in that way that makes me crazy. I don't know why she loves it so much when I do it, but she does. She actually fucking *adores* it, encourages me to do it even. *This woman...*I barely stifle a groan.

"Eyes on me," I tell her again as I feed my cock back in between her lips. She holds my gaze as I start to move my hips, cock gliding in and out of her hot little mouth. She moans in delight as I fuck her mouth over and over, letting me get so deep in her throat.

"Good girl," I rasp and her eyes slide closed with a soft moan. I never thought two little words could elicit such pleasure out of both of us, but *my God.* One of her hands grips my thigh and the other...trails downward between her thighs. *Fuck me.* She starts to play as I continue to move between her lips and it's the sexiest thing I've ever seen. I can feel her moans against my cock and it's almost too much. I pull away, not wanting to come yet.

I scoop her up and yank her hand to my mouth as I move her to the bed. I suck on her fingers, eyes sliding closed for a moment before I release them.

"Bed over," I growl. Eyes wide and burning with lust, she complies instantly and I yank my shorts all the way off, stroking my cock as I stare at her ass. I can't stop myself from reaching out to grip it, fingers digging into the giving flesh. Reminded of her sass from earlier, I give one cheek a light smack before kneading the spot again. She gasps and I freeze for a second. *Hadn't really planned on doing that. Not sure what she's thinking.*

"Ok?" I ask, holding my breath.

"A-again," she says, voice gruff and breathy. *Ooo, this is new.* I rub my palm over the other cheek before giving it a swift spank.

She moans and grips the sheets in her fingers, arching her hips higher into the air, as if asking me for more.

"Fuck me," I rasp. *New kink unlocked? Who knew??*

I kick her feet out, spreading her wider and the sight is heaven. Ass up. Legs spread. Clear view of her wet pussy. *Dear. God.* I want to do too many things right now: Just stare. Lick. Fuck. My brain is short circuiting. I continue to run my hands over her ass, squeezing. Her legs tremble from want and anticipation. She wiggles her ass, as if begging for me to make a move, and I spank her once more.

"Goddddd," she moans, writhing on the sheets. "Need you, Link. Fuck me. Hard. *Please.*" She sounds mindless. Desperate. Sexy.

I move forward and run the head of my cock up and down her pussy and she quivers. On a whim, nearly out of my mind with lust, I run the head up her ass as I spread her cheeks. I don't plan to fuck her there—yet—but by the way she groans and grips the sheets, I think she might want me to. God, learning all of her desires, fulfilling them, it's my greatest pleasure.

"One day," I whisper, as I glide the head of my cock up and down her ass again, stopping for the briefest moment in the right spot.

"YES," she cries, sounding enthusiastic, and bucks her hips backwards, making me chuckle.

"Not tonight, greedy girl." We'll have to work up to that. We've only dipped our toes in the shallowest of pools when it comes to that stuff. *But if she's game to dive in...*I nearly shudder.

I slap her ass once more and move my dick back to her pussy. I shove my hips forward, slamming inside her without warning and she cries out, tumbling forward a bit, chest sliding across the sheets. So slick. So hot. So tight. I grip her hips and pound inside her as she digs her fingers into the bed, moaning and screaming in pleasure.

"Right there. Just like that! Fuck, Link," she grits through clenched teeth. "It feels so fucking good."

I wrap her hair around my fist and pull back slightly as I pound forward, making her back arch. Over and over, I fuck her hard until she comes, pussy squeezing my cock in tight pulses.

"Link!!" she screams into the covers. My spine tightens and I thrust forward a few more times before I'm coming hard inside her. Her legs give out and I collapse on her back, quickly maneuvering us so we're lying on the floor together, panting and blissed out.

"Good girl," I say again as I kiss her sweaty forehead.

"Mmmm," she mumbles, eyes closed and a sleepy smile on her lips. "Maybe next time I won't be so good." She turns her head and kisses my chest.

"Oh I can't wait for that," I mutter, sleep and intoxication already trying to pull me under too. I know we don't need to pass out on the floor, but my muscles all seem to made of jelly at the moment, so I merely tug the blanket off of the bed and wrap it around us. "That would call for a good spanking," I whisper against her hair.

"Mmmm, promise?" I love exploring all of this with her, awakening things in each other. I chuckle and kiss her temple. Her breaths start to slow and I can tell she's almost asleep. I'm not far behind, but my heart thuds against my chest like a jackhammer when she whispers, "I think I might be falling in love with you, Lincoln Ashmore."

"Ditto," I whisper, but she's already passed out.

CHAPTER 14

Savannah

"Well, I seriously question their journalistic prowess when they can't even get the reference right," I say holding up my very first tabloid cover. Never thought that would be a thing, but here we are. Some paparazzi had managed to get shots of us on our last day on the yacht after Gatorcon and now photos of me and Link cozied up on the deck are plastered across the front of some crappy magazine, and all over the internet of course. I can't say I'm completely shocked or completely unprepared. I'd started working on handling this potential reality when things became so serious with Link so quickly. I talked about it at length with Dr. Forrester, told myself over and over again that it didn't matter, that this was just part of Link's life and if I wanted to be a part of that life, then this came with the territory.

And I'm actually more ok with it than I thought I would be. I just wish our first paparazzi shots had been of something other than me in a damn string bikini where the entire world gets to ogle my scars and start digging into the story behind them. Link still hasn't asked me to explain and it makes me fall even more in love with him, but I feel guilty for continuing to keep him in the dark.

Neither of us has brought it up, but I *know* I dropped the L Word bomb in my tipsy, orgasm-riddled state of bliss on the yacht. I don't know if he hasn't mentioned it because he isn't there yet and doesn't want to hurt my feelings, or if he's worried that I only said it because I was drunk, or what. Or maybe he didn't actually hear me. There's a fifty-percent chance that he was already passed out, or maybe just drunk enough not to remember.

I've personally avoided the topic because I can't believe it came out like that. Not because it isn't true—it is. As crazy as it sounds, I'm already completely in love with Link—but I just can't believe I actually *told* him that already. Guys aren't usually known for being thrilled with girls confessing their love after only a few weeks of dating. No, that usually ends with manly-shaped holes in walls where they bolted like a cartoon character, little puffs of smoke curling in their wake.

Plus, it isn't fair of me to tell him that I love him when there's still so much other stuff that I *haven't* told him. Important stuff. Heavy stuff. Stuff that may make him decide that my baggage is way too much to carry around for the rest of his life.

I can tell Link's upset and worried that this tabloid thing will hurt me or, worse, make me rethink this relationship. I give him a smile and point at the headline. *Monster Mash: The Vampire and Frankenstein.* Of course, they're alluding to this vampire character from *Shadowlands*, trying to be clever.

"I should be Frankenstein's *Monster* in this case, not Frankenstein. He was the doctor. Everyone knows that." He huffs out a laugh, rolling his eyes and pulling me in close between his knees on the kitchen stool. He wraps his arms around me and kisses the top of my head.

"You know not to pay any attention to this garbage, right?"

"I know," I sigh, running the band against the chain on my neck out of habit. "It comes with the territory I guess." I'm comfortable with my body, and Link's is really the only opinion that matters on the subject. If he's ok with how I look, then the rest of the world can suck it. I give him a slow, languid kiss before patting his chest. "I should get going."

"Alright. Tell Tiff I said hi."

He and Tiff officially met when we got back from Florida and had immediately hit it off (after her initial freak out over meeting *the* Lincoln Ashmore, of course). I'd watched them from the corner of my eye across the pool while I chatted with Colin and his fiancé, James, suspecting that she was giving him the "hurt her and I'll kill you" talk. Whatever his response was, it had absolutely been the correct one in Tiff's eyes. She'd smiled, nodded, and then shoved him in the pool like he was any other guy friend in the world.

As soon as I pull out of the driveway, I miss him. How ridiculous is that?

"I've got it so fucking bad," I mutter before I turn the radio up and start singing along with Tim McGraw about Barbeque stains on white t-shirts.

Tiff and I go down to South Shores and get lunch at The Salty Pirate and she gives me non-stop shit about my not-so-gentle thrust into the spotlight.

"I never would have thought I'd see you on the front of The Gossiper," she says, shaking her head. "I'm officially besties with a celebrity! Well, a mini one as of right now. I guess it isn't too much longer before all hell breaks loose on this though, huh?"

I sigh. So far I was still mostly just the mystery blonde and Gatorcon queen, but I know that soon enough, one of the vultures will break the story, dig into my past and unleash all of my secrets to the world. Plus, they were set to start filming Link's new movie in just a few days now. The town is already starting to crawl with fans and photographers, so it's only a matter of time before Link and I are seen and captured on film together regularly. I'm not going to maintain my mystery blonde status for long once that happens.

So, yeah, it was only a matter of time before the shit hit the fan.

"Yeah, I guess."

"And you're ready for that? To be in the media crosshairs?"

"I think I have to be. If I want to be with Link, then this is just part of the deal." I snort. "He's really getting the short end of the stick if you think about it. I get media attention and he gets so much emotional baggage it could fill the Grand Canyon."

"Shush. He's getting the absolute best part of the stick being with you." She frowns. "You know what I mean. Anyway, yeah, sure, you've got a past that would rival most superhero—or supervillain," she adds thoughtfully, "—origin stories, but so what." She shrugs, as if all of my epic skeletons aren't a big deal. I wish it were that simple. "That being said, you know you have to tell him everything. And soon. You owe him honesty, Sav. Plus, you don't want him to read it on Instagram or on the cover of some gossip rag, do you?"

I groan and bury my face in my hands. She's right, as usual. I know I need to tell him everything I've been holding back, but truth be told, I'm terrified to. What if it *is* too much for him? What if he decides I'm too broken? Sure, I'm doing so much better than I have in the past, but that doesn't mean that I won't slip, that I won't have dark days and flashbacks that are sometimes so real and visceral that I can't breathe, can't think, can barely make it through. That's a lot to put on someone, even someone as great as Link. His life is already complicated and he has a million responsibilities. What if he doesn't want another one?

As if reading my roiling thoughts, Tiff leans over and grasps my wrist. I meet her gaze, knowing mine is weary.

"You know I have a sixth sense for reading people, and he's one of the good ones, Sav. I know it. So, whatever you're worried about, don't be. But you *need* to tell him."

"You're right," I sigh. "I'm going to tell him everything. He's wrapped up the next couple of days, but then we'll have the talk." I blow out a long breath, wondering how in the hell to even start that conversation. *Hey honey, let's play a game: name the worst trauma you've ever experienced. I'll go first—loser buys dinner!*

"Until then, I think we need more hush puppies."

CHAPTER 15

Lincoln

I've just finished up with a podcast interview when the doorbell rings. I arch a brow. Only Colin and Savvy have the code to the gate. Colin usually calls first when he's in town, and Savvy was doing her own thing since I was busy on and off all day.

I open the door and bark out a stunned laugh.

"You fucker," I say, shaking my head. "Who gave you the code?"

"Colin, of course," Drew says as he pulls me into a hug, slapping me on the back before we head inside.

"What the hell are you doing here?"

"I had some time off and you were talking this place up so damn much, I figured I'd check it out myself. Plus, I missed my girl," he adds with a wink. I shove him playfully in the shoulder.

"Well, there's a great breakfast joint around the corner. You hungry?"

"I'm fucking ravenous."

We eat way too much, chat about a few roles he's been offered and whether or not he wants to take them, and indulge a few fans with pictures and autographs. Word is getting out about filming and my presence, so more and more people are showing up. I knew the peace could only last for so long, but I hate that it's already come to an end. I pray that it isn't too much for Savvy. If she can just stick with me through the initial crazy, I know that we can make this work together *without* having to be in the spotlight non-stop. Plenty of celebrities do it, I know we can figure it out...but even as I think the words, doubts seep in. I know exactly how insane the next year or more of my life is going to be. There will be chaos nonstop between filming, promoting, awards season...How in the hell am I supposed to live out of the spotlight during all of *that*? I push the thoughts away, not wanting to worry about them right now.

"So, how is the lovely Savannah? Missing me like a lost limb, no doubt." I toss a piece of bacon at Drew who catches it easily and pops it in his mouth.

"She's good. Great. Beyond great." He gives me a knowing smirk and I flip him off, signaling to the waitress that we need our check.

I know it's still early on in our relationship, but I know already that I'm completely in love with her...but I don't know how *she* feels. I know that she cares about me, and I know that I make her happy. I know that she said she was falling for me on the boat, but was that just the alcohol talking? Did she mean it? Neither of us have brought it up again—is it because she didn't actually mean it? Or because she doesn't remember saying it? Or because she's worried that I won't feel the same? *Ugh.* I know one of us just needs to bite the bullet and say how we actually feel and see what happens. *Not it.*

Despite agreeing to let her have her secrets until she's ready to share them with me, I think the fact that there's so much about her I don't know about her is holding me back from telling her that I love her. What if the things she's hiding are things that would keep us apart for some reason? I shake the thoughts away, deciding to enjoy my time with Drew and think about all this later.

Drew and I head back to the house and he gets settled into one of the many guest rooms and showers while I hop on my next conference call. I rub my eyes and stretch when I'm done, already tired of talking for the day, though I'm scheduled to do a podcast interview in a couple of hours. To kill time and take my mind off things, Drew and I play some pool.

"Eight ball, corner pocket," he smirks, sinking the shot and beating me for the third time in a row. I roll my eyes and flip him off. "So, how are you feeling about things with Savvy, for real? In light of your recent exposure as a couple and everything?"

"I feel good. I think we can navigate all of the crazy, and I want to because...Fuck me, man, I...I'm in love with her." I rub the back of my neck and he looks at me like I'm a moron. "What? I know it's quick, but she's—"

He holds up his hand to stop me. "I know, idiot. You really think you could hide that fact from anyone, me especially?" I sigh in relief and grin.

"That obvious, huh?"

"Might as well have it tattooed across your fucking forehead, mate." He chuckles and leans back against the pool table while I grab us a couple of beers. "How did she take her first taste of tabloid life?"

"Surprisingly well, actually."

He nods, as if he isn't surprised at all, and looks contemplative. "She's a tough one, that girl. I can tell."

Drew had an extremely rough childhood and his teenage years didn't bring brighter times. He came out the other side stronger and knowing exactly what kind of man he did and didn't want to be, what kind of life he would and wouldn't have. It would have been so easy for him to just fall into a cycle and become resigned to a life of sorrow and pain. Instead, he made something of himself and he's one of the best men I know.

But because of everything he's been through, he has a sense about pain and suffering and survival, and can see it in others. *And he sees it in Savvy?* A cold feeling skitters down my spine as I think about her scars, about the strength it took for her to survive whatever had caused them.

His phone dings, some kind of alert. He mutters, "this oughta be good," and swipes his finger over the screen to open whatever it is.

He chuckles and holds the screen out to me. One of our former cast mates from *Shadowlands* posted some "Throwback Thursday" pictures from our days on set, and there are some real gems: Kira asleep in the makeup chair, the rest of us crowding behind her for the picture; me and Drew covered in fake blood after filming a fight scene; Zach and Lily having a donut eating contest.

We laugh and he quickly types out a comment. He continues to scroll through his feed and I start racking the pool balls again.

"Oh fuck," he says.

"What? Another marriage rumor about you?" I muse. By my count, he'd been engaged or married at least a half dozen times according to the media. He had been married *once* for real, but for whatever reason he always seemed to land in the wedding rumor mill.

"No, mate...I...Christ," he mutters, running a hand through his hair and staring at the screen intently, eyes flying across it as he reads something. He pushes away from the table, his body gone rigid and face pale. I tense in response, reading him like a book after all these years. Something is up. Something bad.

"What happened? What is it?" I demand. He keeps staring at the screen and covers his mouth with one hand. A ball of ice forms in the pit of my stomach, slowly spreading cold throughout my body.

"Oh God..." he whispers.

"I need you to start talking right fucking now, Drew." Had someone died? One of our friends? Had there been an accident? What the fuck was going on??

"Link, there's a story out about Savannah." Right on cue, a rumble of ominous thunder echoes in the distance, a foreboding feeling settling over me like a heavy blanket. I knew the media would dig until they found out who Savannah was, but I'd hoped it would take them a bit longer, that I could prepare her a bit more. But...what had they found that has Drew so freaked out? Looking so...devastated?

"What kind of story?" I ask slowly, not knowing if I want to hear the answer or not, though I find myself reaching for his phone. He yanks it away and shakes his head at me.

"You need to go see her. Right now. This is her story to tell, not the fucking media's." He looks torn between being enraged that they'd posted whatever they had, and that look of devastation that was making my chest clench. "You need to hear it from her and...and if she's seen this already, she's...fuck, she's probably not going to be having a good time of it, alright, mate?" My blood feels like ice in my veins, my legs and chest feeling heavy. What the hell is going on? When had I last gotten a text from Savvy? A few hours? Had she seen whatever Drew had already? Was she alright?

I'm grabbing my keys before I can even think, sprinting into the downpour that started a few minutes ago and jumping in the car. I vaguely hear Drew assuring me that he'd handle the podcast for me and get with Colin. I think I nod as I peel out, but I'm not sure. My thoughts are running wild and I try to focus on the road, trying to figure out what had been posted, wondering if Savvy is ok. I've never felt worry or dread like this, like it's a living thing crawling and clawing inside my chest. I text her, nearly running off the road.

"Fuck!"

I know I need to focus. It won't do either of us any good if I end up in a ditch right now. I keep the phone in my lap, but she doesn't respond. Is she mad at me? Blaming me for whatever is out in the world now? The rain is coming down so hard I can barely see and the fact that I have to drive twenty-five is a special kind of torture. Thunder rumbles again, louder this time, the dark clouds rolling towards me in thick waves.

"Come on, come on..." I bite out through gritted teeth. I finally make it to the turn off, the long private road that leads to her house feeling like it's fifty miles long instead of five. I turn down the driveway, heart pounding. I barely let the car stop completely before I throw it in park and leap out. I sprint up the wide stairs and across the porch, and ring the bell before I can stop myself. I have an *oh shit* moment then: what if she doesn't actually *want* to see me?

I wait, feeling so uneasy that my stomach is in knots. The storm grows louder, the wind starting to make the branches sway violently, the Spanish Moss flying sideways. I gaze out, and the clouds in the distance are nearly black.

A big one is barreling towards us, in more ways than one.

After what feels like a lifetime, she opens the door. Her hair is up in those messy buns I love and she looks gorgeous as always, but her eyes are red and puffy. *She's been crying.* I speak before she can.

"If you want me to go, I'll go, but I just...I needed to make sure you were ok."

To my utter relief, she steps out onto the porch and leans her head into my chest, wrapping her arms around me and squeezing so hard, like...like she's holding on for dear life. While I'm relieved she didn't throw a punch or kick me off her property, not knowing what's going on is killing me. I stroke her hair and let her squeeze as hard as she wants.

"I'm here, Sav. I'm right here." Lighnting spears through the sky, thunder cracking not long after so loudly we both flinch. She pulls away and wipes her nose.

"Did you see...?"

I shake my head. "No, Drew saw something and just said that...that I needed to come, that whatever is out there now is your story to tell me yourself. And that you might not be ok," I add quietly, trying hard to keep the worry and desperation out of my voice though I'm not sure I succeed.

She swallows hard and takes a deep, shaking breath. I brace myself, somehow knowing that whatever she's about to say is going to hit me like a physical blow.

"Almost eight years ago, I was in a plane crash." I inhale sharply. *A fucking plane crash?* That's where she'd gotten her scars? My God. She continues, and I somehow sense that this story gets worse, that there is a hammer about to fall. "A plane crash that killed every other person but me. A crash that killed my husband..."

A tear streaks down her cheek.

"And my daughter."

CHAPTER 16

Savannah

He's staring at me like he couldn't have heard me right. Shock. Sorrow. Pain. Pity. Anger. His emotions seem to be running wild. When I'd seen the post a few hours ago, I'd been shocked and then gutted. It hit me so hard and out of nowhere, like someone jumped in front of me and tossed a vat of acid in my face then sucker punched me in the gut. I thought I'd been prepared to be the focus of the media because of my association with Link, but I'd somehow never dreamed that I'd see the biggest tragedy of my life splashed across the internet like it was nothing, like it was just gossip.

I'd only managed to skim the first post, eyes burning with tears and shock keeping me from really seeing much, but they'd managed to find photos from the crash, a few of me in the hospital right after, and...photos of my family. I'd lost it then, feeling like I should have somehow sheltered them from this, that I'd failed them all over again.

"Savannah," he whispers. I lead him inside and we curl up on the couch. Griffey immediately jumps up on my other side and puts his head in my lap. I stroke his ears with one hand and hold Link's with the other. "Savvy...I don't know what to say."

"It's ok. No one ever does," I say, trying to give him a half-hearted smile. I take a deep breath, ready to tell him everything. He squeezes my hand and I start talking, wondering if I can make it through without breaking down completely. I've told the story a million times it seems, a million different ways to a million different people, but this time is so different. This time I'm not just telling my story, I'm sharing *my life* with Link, showing him the deepest, darkest parts and exposing the wounds to him, letting him see exactly how bruised and broken I am.

"I was shooting a destination wedding down in Costa Rica for a man named Lionel Drake's daughter. He owns all of the Chicken King restaurants in the southeast and had been a friend of my husband's family for decades. He'd begged me to shoot Kinley's wedding, and I'd agreed, of course. He flew us all down on a private jet so that we could make a family vacation out of it." My heart starts beating too fast and my throat feels tight, but I push through, trying to remember to breathe and focusing on Link's hand in mine. "The plane went down in Georgia, not far from the Florida line. I...I remember bits and pieces of the before and the after." I squeeze my eyes closed.

"Savvy, you don't have to."

I open my eyes again and run my thumb over his hand, concentrating on the slow circles, the feel of his skin.

"I do. I need to. I want to." Drew was right, this is *my* story to tell Link. *Deep breath in...long breath out.* "I remember knowing something was wrong, even before they told us. I remember the attendants looking terrified and just having a bad feeling that crept up my spine, like someone running an ice cube along my back. I remember the alarms going off and oxygen masks dropping down from the ceiling, just like in a movie." My ribs feel like they're shrinking, pulling in too tightly around my lungs. *Breathe, breathe, breathe.* "I remember feeling fear but also this strange numbness, like it wasn't real, like it was a dream. Or a nightmare, I guess." I meet his gaze and the hurt there, the worry, makes me fall even more in love with him.

"The biggest thing I remember was Mia being scared, not understanding what was happening." I choke on a sob, my heart splintering and my throat closing. I release Link's hand and clutch at my chest, nails digging into my flesh. "God, Link, she was so scared. And I couldn't protect her from it. That was my *job* as her mother and I failed her. She died terrified and I couldn't stop it. I *failed.*"

My ribs close in completely, crushing my lungs to dust, and I can't breathe as I completely break apart. Link tugs me into his lap and holds me while I cry, shaking violently in his arms, gasping for air. He holds me so tightly, like he thinks if he can just hold tight enough, it'll keep me together or somehow put the pieces back together again when it's done. Hell, maybe he can. *If anyone could, it would be him.*

I've told this story too many times over the years, or versions of it anyway, but I've only ever said those words to Dr. Forrester and Tiff. They are the only ones I've ever confessed my greatest sin to, my greatest regret, my most monumental failure. I failed my daughter. *I failed her. I failed her. I failed her.* I'm spiraling, crying so hard my chest hurts, but I somehow force myself to focus on the feel of Link's heart against my cheek, the smell of his cologne, the deep rumble of his voice. It brings me back from the brink, and though it feels like it takes hours, the pressure in my chest fades and I can suck in ragged breaths again.

"Savvy," he finally says, sounding anguished, his own voice breaking quietly. I pull back and find his eyes glassy and it somehow breaks my heart all over again and makes it stronger at the same time. My pain is his pain. *I'm not in this alone.* I sniffle and grab a handful of tissues from the coffee table, scratching a whimpering Griffey on the way. After a few more minutes, I can speak again.

"I don't remember much of the crash itself," I continue. "Bits and pieces sometimes surface, but I mostly remember meeting Matt's gaze, silently saying all the things we'd never be able to, and then the two of us holding Mia as tight as we could, trying to shield her from it all, though we knew we couldn't." I run my fingers over Matt's wedding band around my neck. My own had been cut off during the initial chaos at the hospital, but they'd brought Matt's back to me...after. I swallow thickly and take a few more deep breaths. My brows furrow as I try to recall the details.

"The next thing I remember is waking up on the ground. I could smell fire and gasoline, and I could hear sirens and people shouting, but it was all muffled, like I was underwater. I learned later that I had a ruptured ear drum among about a million other injuries. I remember excruciating pain. They say that adrenaline kicks in and you don't feel pain during something like that, but either that's bullshit or my adrenaline factory was on the fritz." He tenses, as if hearing of me in pain is painful to him. "I remember trying to move and scream, but I couldn't. Or maybe I did, but just couldn't register it, I'm not sure. It's all fuzzy. I *do* remember seeing a giant piece of metal sticking up through my stomach, right here." I tap the large scar on my side. "I was skewered, lying there in a bloody, broken daze."

I hesitate for a heartbeat before saying, "I...I couldn't see them, but I was told later that they died on impact, that they didn't suffer." I let out a long breath before I can continue, ears ringing loudly and my chest aching like someone just took a sledgehammer to it. Finally, I manage to push through. "And that's about it. The rest is just kind of a hazy mess of images that don't usually make sense or connect in any kind of order. The next thing I really remember clearly is waking up in the hospital a few weeks later."

"Savannah, I can't...God, baby, I'm so sorry."

I give him a small smile, feeling better for finally having shared it with him, like the extra weight that had been pulling me down and away from him is finally gone and now, I'm free to just be with him, completely and totally. *If he still wants me...*

"After that, it was lots of time in the hospital, tons of surgeries—I think I'm up to twenty-seven now—tons of rehab, tons of pain. It took me almost two years before I could walk again on my own, another full one before I could walk *normally*. Mr. Drake was beyond himself with grief and guilt. He felt responsible, though of course it wasn't his fault. Once I was stable enough, he had me moved to the best hospitals, made sure I had the best doctors, and paid for all of my medical bills. Every last one of them. He still sends me flowers every month without fail, calls me every holiday, and I eat for free in any Chicken King in the universe, so that's something," I say with a half smile.

Link doesn't laugh, just stares at me with an unreadable look on his face.

"And in the background of all the medical stuff was the legal side of things. Turns out, they *knew* a piece of equipment in the plane was faulty, but the owner of the company was afraid to lose

Mr. Drake as a client by causing the photographer to miss his daughter's wedding. If they'd really known the man, they would have known how utterly fucking stupid that was," I spit, the anger rising right along with the pain. They were never far apart. "They have recordings of the pilot confirming it as the plane was going down and another employee came forward afterwards too with irrefutable evidence."

"Oh my God," Link whispers, going rigid all over again. The muscle in his jaw ticks and I know that he's trying his best to keep his anger in check.

My mouth goes a bit dry and I tangle my fingers together, remembering those early days. I promised myself I would tell him everything, every last bit.

"I was...I was in a really bad place at the beginning, barely surviving and not just because of all of the injuries. I think the only reason I made it through at first was the need to make somebody answer for what had happened, to hold someone responsible, ya know?" *Make them pay.* And they did. Big time. Both literally, with me ending up with millions upon *millions*, and figuratively, their lives utterly destroyed and the head of the company serving sixty years in prison for ten counts of involuntary manslaughter. They'd given him the max sentence, and though it wasn't nearly enough, could *never* be enough to right the devastation he'd caused, I'd forced myself to make peace with it—eventually. It had taken years.

Link keeps touching me, rubbing my arm or squeezing my leg, brushing my hair back or a tear from my face. I don't know if he's trying to make sure I know he's still here, or if he's trying to convince himself that *I'm* still here.

"After I got justice so to speak, I wasn't sure why I was still around. I...I thought about trying to remedy that, on more than one occasion." I feel him tense but I push through. I need to tell him all of it, even the dark and scary parts. I need him to know everything. I *want* him to know everything, to know me unlike anyone has in nearly eight years, maybe even better than anyone *ever* has.

"I was in the darkest place imaginable inside my own head for a long time. I was alive, but not really living. I called it being on autopilot. I went through the motions and there were good days in the mix, but mostly, I was just...there." Another deep breath.

"On what would have been Mia's tenth birthday, I had a very, very dark day. Tiff stayed up with me all night, watching me and talking me off the metaphorical ledge...while I held a loaded pistol in my hands, turning it over and over, just thinking to myself 'why not?'" Link takes an uneasy breath and squeezes my hand. "I wasn't allowed to have weapons here, of course, so I'd stolen one from Tiff's house. That was probably my lowest point, stealing from my best friend, ready to do something really terrible just to make the pain stop, make the guilt go away. And to make her be there to witness it?" I shake my head and press my lips into a hard line, hating to remember, hating what I put her through.

"But she saw me through it, kept me talking all night, let me cry, let me scream, and, eventually, I let her take the gun from me. Really, she should have reported it to the police and I probably should have been locked away in a mental institution somewhere, but she didn't. You are the only other person on the planet who knows about it."

He squeezes my hand, but remains quiet.

"So, yeah, I could never quite bring myself to go through with it, despite having the thoughts—often. Even when I got a grip on those thoughts and no longer wanted to join my family, I still went through bouts where it was so bad, I stayed in bed for weeks, could barely even move. Tiff was with me, every step of the way, making me eat, helping me bathe, taking care of me like I was a child. I owe her more than I can ever repay. My therapist, Dr. Forrester, too. Tiff is the reason I'm still here, and Dr. Forrester is the reason I'm here and somewhat healed."

"Then I owe them both more than I could ever possibly repay," Link says softly. I give him a small smile, and keep talking. Opening up to him fully is actually really cathartic. He asks about my injuries, so I tell him the mile-long list of them, about the ups and downs, the surgeries and the recovery, how I never wanted to hear the word "miracle" again after being called one so many times.

"It was a miracle I survived the crash, a miracle that the piece of metal hadn't been a fraction of an inch this way or that, a miracle that they'd been able to repair my heart at all, let alone bring me back when it stopped beating on the operating table— twice. Miracle that my spine hadn't been shattered, miracle that I'd been able to walk again, miracle, miracle, miracle," I say, shaking my head and trying to keep the anger out of my voice. "I know nobody understood that every time they said I was a miracle, it was like a knife to my heart. I don't blame them, but to me, when they said 'miracle' it sounded like an accusation in my ears. Me being a miracle meant that I failed them by surviving when they didn't, that I somehow stole life from them. It shouldn't have been *me*. The miracle should have been *her*." I shake my head again and angrily wipe tears away.

"Tell me about them?" he asks quietly, stroking my hair. I find that I want to. It hurts to remember them, but God, it also feels so good. I loved them so fucking much, it makes my heart want to burst to remember them as they were, to think on the good times and all the love we shared.

"Mia was six and a half, going on sixteen, and a total goofball. She had the best laugh, this contagious giggle that could make even the coldest hearts melt. I don't think she ever just *walked* anywhere, it was always some kind of crazy dance or skip, everywhere she went." He huffs out a laugh and I smile, remembering my girl. I glance up at her portrait above the couch and he follows my gaze. This was the reason I'd never wanted him to come inside the house before. How could I have explained the reminders of her and Matt everywhere? I could have taken them all down, hidden them away, but that didn't feel right either. So, I'd shut him out of this place. Now, I'm happy to have him here.

"She was beautiful." His eyes roam over Matt's face and then back to Mia's. "She looked a lot like you, but she had his eyes." I smile and nod.

"She was so smart, too. I know every parent says that, but she really was. She was a fish, constantly in the water, whether it was the ocean, lake, or pool. I swear she was a mermaid in a former life. And she was obsessed with dolphins. Like *ob-sessed*. They're all over her room, if she saw any article of clothing with a dolphin on it, she had to have it. We did dolphin watching tours at least once a month—one of the captains actually re-named his boat after her as a tribute. It was very sweet." His eyes alight in recognition, remembering my reaction to the dolphins that first day. *You don't even know the half of it, babe.*

I go on and on before I realize I might be boring him, but he seems nothing but interested.

"I would have loved to meet her," he says. "I love kids. My niece is nine now and she's like my little bestie." I grin, remembering seeing pictures of them together at Disneyland on Instagram not too long ago. "And what about him?" He nods towards the thick wedding band at my throat. To his credit, he doesn't sound the slightest bit jealous or threatened, the way some guys would, no matter how ridiculous that would be.

"I hated him when I first met him," I say with a scrunch of my nose.

He barks out a surprised chuckle. "What?"

"Yep, absolutely loathed Matt at first. The first night I met him, he was completely drunk off his ass at a party and knocked me into the pool—fully clothed with my brand new phone in my pocket, totally ruining the blowout I'd gotten earlier that day too. He then attempted to "save" me, but only managed to leap into the water directly *on top of me*. Gave me a bloody nose and a concussion and nearly drowned me."

"Oh my God," Link laughs.

"That wasn't even the worst part! I hated him because the next time I saw him, he had no recollection of the entire night! *Zero.* Literally introduced himself and tried to shake my hand like he didn't nearly drown me in the pool, ruin my phone, and almost put me in the hospital a few weeks prior. He was such a turd." I shake my head and smile. "But he was one of Tiff's oldest friends, so we inevitably kept getting thrown together every time I came home with her on breaks or long weekends from school, which was pretty much non-stop after my parents died freshman year. Eventually, I forgave him and not long after that, fell head over freaking heels. He'd always tease that he grew on me and I'd always respond *like a fungus.*" We both chuckle a bit.

"He was an architect—designed and built this house himself," I say gesturing around us. "The land had been in his family for generations and when his parents died, he inherited it all. The house he grew up in is on the other side of the lake—Tiff actually lives there now. He was a really good guy. Funny. Ridiculous. Loved to sing but sounded like a cat in a blender. He used to volunteer with the local rec league every year, coaching or running concession stands, his firm always sponsored a team. And he was an amazing father." I sigh, remembering them together. "Mia was the happy accident that came along just after I graduated. I still felt like a kid myself, but we were so stoked, knowing it was going to be the best adventure. We eloped to New Orleans a week after we found out, came home, and he started on our dream house."

"He sounds great."

"He was. I think you would have liked him. Things weren't perfect, of course, no relationship is, but man, we really did have it good. I loved him hard, in that young, stupid, first love kind of way, ya know?" He nods and brushes hair from my brow.

"I know it doesn't help and I know you've heard it too many times to count, but I'm so sorry, Savvy. God, I just can't imagine what you've been through, what you've lost. I can't imagine how you've survived and are so...God, you're amazing, you know that? I wish I could bring them back or take the pain from you somehow. I just..." He exhales roughly, voice hoarse and sounding thick with emotion.

"It's ok, Link. It took a long time, but I'm in a good place now. I think about them every day, but now it's..." I frown. How to explain it right? "It's kind of like a show you put on in the background for noise while you're cleaning or folding laundry, you know? It's there, and you can hear it, and every now and then you'll stop what you're doing to watch a few scenes, getting drawn in for a bit, but then you go back to your chores and the show fades to the background again. I understand now that it doesn't mean I love them any less and it doesn't make me a terrible person. It's just part of surviving, of moving forward. It took *a lot* of hours with Dr. Forrester to finally accept and understand that. That's when I adopted my mantra."

He rubs his fingers over my wrist, gently brushing the tattoo.

"CFD," he says softly, and I smile.

"CFD," I confirm. "I was starting to feel better mentally, making real progress with Dr. Forrester, finally feeling good, like maybe I could do this after all, like maybe I could be ok. I went out to the beach and...and it sounds crazy, but I swear I *heard* Mia beside me telling me to be happy again. And hand on the Bible, the second after I heard her voice, three dolphins swam by, right in front of me."

"Dolphins..." he breathes on a soft exhalation, brows flying upward, comprehension really dawning this time. Now he understood how significant seeing them that first day with him was to me, why I'd teared up. It was like it had been another sign from Mia, telling me that Link was special, that this was the start of something. *To be happy.*

"Yep," I say, giving him a meaningful smile. I take a deep breath, knowing it was time. *Nut up or shut up, Riley.*

"Grief is weird, Link. It isn't a linear path, at least not for me. Parts of it are curvy and terrifying and sometimes it doubles back on itself, seeming to go in circles and drop me right back at the beginning again. It's full of peaks and valleys and sometimes it's like trying to drive through quicksand in some places. I'm still very broken, on so many levels. I'm still figuring out this strange grief road trip and sometimes I still have really bad days. Sometimes, I still get turned around and have to pull over and just scream in my car for a while. And...and I understand if that's too much for you, if all of this is too much for you, but I needed to tell you all of it because...because, well, it wouldn't be fair for me to tell you that I've fallen completely in love with you, without you knowing exactly what you're getting yourself into."

His green eyes widen in surprise and he inhales a soft, sharp breath, but then his lips curl upward into the most devastating smile.

"Say that last bit again," he says, leaning toward me and gently sliding his hand around to grip my nape.

"I love you, Lincoln Ashmore. I know it's fast and that things are only going to get crazier as we navigate this, but I'm in. A thousand percent. I'm throwing all my chips in the ring."

He chuckles softly, his eyes dancing. "That's definitely not the saying."

Before I can argue that I'm fairly sure it *is* the saying, his lips meet mine in a searing kiss. Slow. Deep. He's speaking to me through this kiss, telling me so much, telling me things that words couldn't possibly convey. He finally pulls back and stares into my eyes. His are so gorgeous, it makes me want to cry.

"I love you too, Savvy. I think I've loved you since the moment I heard you tell that runner to go fuck himself in that sweet, southern drawl of yours." I narrow my eyes at him and he grins. "I wish I was joking, because I know how ridiculous it sounds, probably borderline creepy, but it's true. I couldn't take my eyes off of you that morning. I fucking stutter-stepped at the sight of you, hand to God. I thought you were the most gorgeous person I'd ever seen and I was immediately drawn to you, but after spending that day with you, I was already a goner."

My heart beats wildly, my stomach fluttering. I hold my breath as I ask quietly, "And now? After everything I've told you? All of my baggage and broken pieces that I've got stuck together with Elmer's glue…It doesn't scare you?"

"No." I roll my eyes, but he forces me to look at him again. "I mean it, Savvy. Learning all of this doesn't change how I feel. If anything, it makes me love you even more. You are strong and resilient and you amaze me every single day. You could have taken all of this tragedy and turned against the world, shutting everyone out, but you haven't. You're still so *good.* Genuine and sweet and kind."

He kisses me again and something gives way in my chest, like the tourniquet I've had on my heart for the last eight years finally gives way. I've always been terrified that if I loosened it or, God forbid, took it off, that I would bleed out, that I wouldn't survive. But now it's like the love I have for Link, and the love he has for me in return, is stemming the blood without strangling my heart in the process, like my past and present are coming together to heal me in a way I never thought possible.

Be careful with my heart, Lincoln Ashmore. It won't survive another break.

CHAPTER 17
Lincoln

"Come onnnn," I beg Savannah. "What about CFD?"

She narrows her eyes at me, but I can see the hint of a smile on those gorgeous lips and I know she's thinking about it.

"How dare you use my hard-earned psychological breakthrough against me like this?!"

I chuckle and pop a grape in my mouth. When Gabriel, our director, had seen Savannah visiting me on set a few days ago, he'd insisted she have a small role. In his thick French accent he'd said, "How can I not have such a beauty in my film?" He'd looked contemplative before adding, "And there is just something about her, no?" There really is. Something about Savannah just draws every eye to her, and it isn't just her physical beauty, though that is breathtaking. It's something more, something from inside her that radiates outward that's unquantifiable.

She stands in front of my stool and wraps her arms around my neck, leaning in to kiss my lips, flicking her tongue to steal the bit of juice left there from the grape. She gives a low "mmm" of appreciation and I groan, my hands settling on her hips and wrenching her close. I'd thought we'd been insatiable *before* she told me about her past, about her family—and officially told me that she loved me. I can't help but shiver when I think back to that afternoon:

"So...are all your chips in the ring too then?" she asked from the doorway. She'd gone to let Griffey into the bedroom to cuddle with his stuffed monkey as he liked to do during storms. I'd stood at the large backdoors, staring out into the rain, watching the drops bounce off of the lake and replaying everything she'd told me. I glanced to the portraits over the couch, realizing that they were the reason she never wanted me to come here before now. It would have meant trying to explain them before she was ready. I felt like an even bigger ass for our argument about it now and vowed I would spend hours and hours making that up to her later. I turned my gaze back to the rain. I could still scarcely wrap my mind around it all and was sure I'd have a private breakdown over it all later, imagining the pain and loss she'd felt. It gutted me to even think about it.

She pulled my attention from the glass with her question and I turned as she approached. She was biting her lip and her eyes shined. They were red-rimmed from tears, but a blinding hope glimmered there, a hope that made my chest clench. The rain remained steady, beating an oddly soothing rhythm on the metal roof and making it feel like we were in a strange bubble, away from the rest of the world. Just me and her, where nothing else could touch us.

She stood a few feet away, and as our gazes collided, something blazed to life, hotter and deeper than ever before. Her lips parted and her breaths shallowed as I moved towards her. I could only imagine the look on my face, the hunger in my eyes. The depth of what I felt for her hit me like a wrecking ball, nearly taking me to my knees and making it hard to speak.

"Every last fucking one," I said, voice low and husky. Just as I reached her, lightning flashed outside and thunder rumbled on its heels. I tunneled my fingers in her hair, the clip holding it up slipping free, and drew her mouth to mine. My lips crashed into hers with a desperation I didn't quite understand. She gripped my shirt in clenched fists as her tongue met mine again and again. Deep, frenzied thrusts as she held me close and I backed her into the wall. She ran her hands under my shirt, splaying her fingers over my chest. I reached down and placed one of my hands over hers, holding her hand steady over my thundering heart.

"It's yours, Savvy," I whispered brokenly between panting breaths. "It's all yours for as long as you'll have it, until the damn thing stops beating." I'd never felt this many emotions before, all clamoring inside at once. I loved her so much, it hurt. I needed her so much, it felt like I would die without her. I wanted her so much, I couldn't catch my breath.

"Link," she whispered, eyes glassy, but this time, I could tell they were tears of joy. I swooped down again and kissed her, throwing everything I was feeling into the kiss, willing her to understand the depths of my love for her, the depths of the connection I was feeling. She ran her hands across my chest and down my stomach, making my muscles clench. She settled them on my hips and yanked me forward, holding me tight against her. I pulled back just enough to yank my shirt off, then hers. I was dimly aware of the sound of ripping fabric as I tore her bra from her, freeing her breasts. I groaned and gripped her hips, lifting her up, and she immediately wrapped her legs around my waist. I pressed her hard against the wall again, arching my hips against her, making her cry out. Her chest pressed against mine, the friction and heat making me gasp.

She wrapped her arms around my neck and kissed me like she couldn't survive another second without it. Soon, we were breathing for each other, ragged gasps keeping each other going. I turned and dropped to my knees, easing her down on the plush rug in front of the wall of glass. I eased back long enough to pull her shorts and panties down her tanned legs. Her nipples jutted and I could barely wait to run my tongue along them, to suck them hard as she panted and writhed, then to travel lower, kissing every last scar on my way before tasting her, making her scream. I unbuckled my belt and removed my jeans and boxers while she watched raptly. God the way she looked at me made me shudder with pleasure, made my cock shoot harder. Need inside her. *All of my other plans evaporated in an instant, the need to bury myself in her too strong. I'd make it up to her later, would worship her all night long.*

She reached for me and I eased down, wedging my hips between hers. The look in her eyes told me she needed me as much as I needed her.

"Link," she said again, pupils blown and voice both pleading and demanding. I gripped my cock with one hand and positioned the head, hissing when it met wet heat. I wasted no time, immediately sliding inside her in one long thrust. We both groaned and I gave her a second to adjust before I raised up on straightened arms and began to move. She gripped my hips, fingers digging into my lower back and urging me to keep going, to keep up the punishing rhythm. My thrusts were long and deep, and she held my gaze through each one.

This was...different. Something about this time was so much more *than every other. Because we both knew for sure how the other one felt now? Because I was finally letting myself let go of my heart completely? Without realizing it, I'd been holding part of it back, but now it was like the flood gates had been opened wide. No, not opened, but* destroyed—*there was no holding it back now, no way in hell to ever close them again. I'd given Savvy my entire heart and was just hoping like hell she didn't break it.*

I slowed my pace a bit, making each arch of my hips measured, making her feel each one. I felt like I was marking her as mine somehow. She sure as shit was searing me to my core with each soft lap of her tongue, each encouraging buck of her hips. The lightning flashed around us in a frenzy, illuminating her beautiful face, so beautiful I could fucking cry. Thunder and rain hammered in the background.

"I love you, Savvy," I rasped as I started to increase the pace once more.

She craned her head up to kiss me again, driving me wild as she sucked on my bottom lip. After what seemed like an eternity more, she screamed my name as she came apart and I followed her soon after, collapsing on top of her as we both caught our breath. She gently trailed her fingers across my back, whispering "I love you" over and over.

"Isn't this like...nepotism or something?" she asks, drawing me back to the present.

"So what if it is?" I say with a hike of my shoulder. "Come on, it'll be fun. You've been on screen before."

She rolled her eyes. "Ok I was like five and it was a commercial for a local car dealership. That doesn't count! I still can't believe Tiff showed you that." The footage of an adorable little Savannah standing in the bed of a Ford truck, blonde pig tails peeking out from beneath a cowboy hat was pure gold. *Y'all come on down, ya hear?* she'd said to the camera with that adorable southern drawl and a giant missing-tooth grin. It had been about the cutest thing I'd ever seen. Tiff had showed it to both me and Drew, and Savvy had hidden her face in a pillow, groaning and vowing revenge on us all. Drew thought it was the greatest thing on Earth and had immediately leapt up, demanding we go line dancing.

"Do you even know how to line dance?" Tiff had asked him.

"No, pet, but you're going to teach me," he said with a confident grin, chucking her under the chin with one finger. She looked simultaneously amused and...well, I'll call a spade a spade: horny as hell.

"Do *you* know how to line dance?" Savvy had asked me with an arch of her brow as we got ready to head to a local place down by the beach.

With an exaggerated drawl, I'd said, "I grew up on a farm in Oklahoma, honey. What do you think I did every Friday night?"

The night had turned out to be fun as hell. It was fairly dead on a Tuesday night, so we had a blast with the few patrons that were there and all of the staff. Though I was a bit rusty, I'd found my rhythm again pretty quickly. Drew had caught on quickly as well and looked annoyingly *not* stupid in his cowboy hat. He ended up dancing on the bar at one point, and I'm fairly certain someone slipped a fiver in the waistband of his jeans—because of course he'd danced on the bar *shirtless.*

Savvy moved like liquid sin as she wound her way around the floor, blonde hair flying and shaking her ass in those tiny cutoffs. Every eye had been glued to her as she moved and I didn't blame them one bit. At one point, the music had slowed and I'd pulled Savvy close as Chris Stapleton sang about Tennessee Whiskey.

I leaned down and whispered in her ear, "When this song came on in the car that first day, I nearly came across the seat for you." She shivered against me before meeting my gaze.

"I nearly wrecked the car," she admitted. Our eyes locked and that familiar fire flared to life. We may or may not have found ourselves in the backseat of her SUV not five minutes later, her hands bound behind her back with my belt while she rode me hard. I'd be lying if I said it wasn't hot as fuck. Apparently Drew and Tiff had found themselves in a similar state of lust and by the time Savvy and I had made it back inside, they'd left in an Uber. Savvy had looked at her phone and cracked up, shaking her head. She showed me the text from Tiff explaining their disappearance, and I couldn't help but laugh: fourteen eggplant emojis.

I shake myself, again pulling myself back from memories and focusing on getting her to agree to be in the movie.

"Please?" I ask, giving her my best puppy dog eyes. I grin when she sighs and I know I've got her.

"I hate you," she mutters with no conviction, a smile playing on her lips. I know she's excited about it beneath the nerves.

"You love me." I lean in to kiss her neck and whisper in her ear, "I'll remind you how much later..." She shivers and I chuckle before I'm called back to work.

***

Weeks fly by and things have been both amazing and chaotic. Filming is going well, but it's also grueling. Long hours, night shoots, early mornings. I don't even know what time it is most days, thanking God once more for Colin and Savvy keeping me straight. Savvy impressed everyone with her small part, and Colin got that look in his eye, the one that said *I just found a hidden gem.* I have no idea if Savvy would ever want to try her hand in this world, but she honestly has a shot. Though she'd been nervous, she'd hidden it once the camera started rolling. She was confident and just had that *thing*. There was no way to explain it, but she had it in fucking spades. *Of course she does.* My girl is simply amazing.

Though jarring at first, Savvy is slowly getting used to paparazzi flashes every time we step outside. They are ever-present, but thankfully they haven't been suffocating and have been surprisingly polite as far as paparazzi go. They've mostly remained a respectful distance away and haven't invaded our privacy. No one has shown up in my trash can, at least. So far, so good.

Fans have flocked to the area and teem all over town, which is great for local business, so I try not to feel too guilty for the insanity. We can barely go out to dinner anywhere without being spotted now, but Savvy never complains, even urges me to interrupt our meals or walks to go interact with fans when I don't do it on my own. I really don't know how I got so lucky. Funnily enough, a lot of them actually want to meet *her*, having seen the stories about her and Michael from Gatorcon. The first time a girl had said *I actually wanted a picture with her, if that's ok?* nodding towards Savvy with a sheepish smile and blushing slightly, Savannah had actually looked over her shoulder with a confused look on her face, before turning back and pointing at her chest, blurting "me??" It was both adorable and hilarious.

We've settled into life together, despite all the crazy, and I've never been happier. I keep thinking that it's too good to be true, that something is going to go wrong or I'm going to wake up and all of this will have been a dream.

Thankfully, right now I wake to Savvy pointing a camera at me and know it's real. I give her a sleepy smile from my lounge chair by the pool before realization really hits. I jolt up, eyes wide. She'd told me that she hadn't picked a camera up since the crash. Photography was all wrapped up in the guilt she carried for that day—if not for her job, they never would have been on that plane. She'd waived me off when I'd started to protest and gave me her wry smile, tapping her temple.

"Illogical, remember?" She's had to remind me time and time again that the biggest thing she's learned navigating her path of grief was that thoughts and emotions and feelings weren't often logical, but it didn't stop her from thinking them and feeling them. She was so comfortable in her skin, in her journey, but at times I could see the fear behind her eyes. She keeps warning me that bad days will come, and I know she's afraid of what I might think or do when it happens, worried that it will all be too much for me to handle.

I wish I could explain to her in a way to make her understand that nothing—and I mean *nothing*—could keep me from her or ever change the way I feel about her. Good days, bad days, smooth roads and detours—I'm here for it all, want it *all*. It's her road trip of grief, but now I'm right here with her, a passenger that will forever be there holding the map to lead her back to the right path again whenever she needs it.

"I dunno," she says before I can ask, hiking a shoulder and playing with the camera in her hands. "I've been wanting to pick it up again lately, even been carrying it around in my bag for the last week. When you fell asleep, the light was hitting you just perfectly and I had it in my hands before I could even think." Her cheeks flushed slightly. "You're an adequate model, I suppose."

I grin and reach for her, tugging her onto the oversized lounger beside me.

"Adequate my ass," I mutter, kissing her temple. "So, do I get to see?"

"Do you not get to see enough of yourself online?" she teases, but scrolls through the pictures for me. Not to toot my own horn or sound conceited, but they're *really* good shots. That fact that she was starting up again had me floored. I know how much she'd loved it—and how damn good she was at it. It was such a huge part of her and she'd locked it away for almost a decade. I'm happy that she was healing enough to want to let it out once more.

She sets the camera down on the table and lays her head back on my chest, tracing shapes and making my eyes slide closed.

"So, can I ask you something?"

"Yes, that *is* my real butt in the second Captain Ultra. No ass doubles for me."

She chuckles. "As if I wouldn't be able to pick your ass out of a lineup." She raises up and cocks her elbow, resting her head on her upturned hand. "What happened in Memphis all those years ago?" I tense at the mention of my past, but remind myself how much she's shared with me, that I owe her a peek at all my skeletons as well. It isn't like I've been hiding it from her, exactly, but I haven't found a good way to bring it up. She studies me, reading me too well, as always.

"You don't have to talk about it if you don't want to. I've just always wondered and it was mentioned in an article about you and a stunning blonde chick that I read this morning..." She wiggles her eye brows at me and laughs, but then turns a bit more serious. "The details around it were always murky..."

I rub the back of my neck and sigh. Here goes nothing.

"Just after *Shadowlands* really started taking off, it was insane. I went from an Oklahoma farm boy to teen heartthrob in a matter of months it seemed. All of the attention and fame kind of went to my head. I started living life like a "real" celebrity, you know? I started down a bad path, fell in with the wrong type of Hollywood crowd. Drew tried to steer me away from all of that, but I was blinded by all the glam, the high I got from being at those parties, from drinking and drugs and women. I was a walking cliché of young Hollywood." I shake my head, hating to remember how I'd been. It hadn't lasted long, but I'd done plenty that I regretted during that time, and there was plenty that I couldn't even remember.

"Anyway, I was in Memphis for an event and went out with a few people. I got way too drunk and got in a bar fight. I...I almost killed a man." Her eyes go wide and her lips part on a soft gasp. Despite my fear of what I might see there—disgust? Horror?—I make myself meet Savannah's gaze. Thankfully, I only see confusion and concern. *God, I don't deserve this woman.*

"How...how did that not make the news?"

"Colin is a miracle worker is the short answer." I exhale roughly. "There weren't that many people around that night, so it was easier to keep it quiet, but there *were* enough witnesses to prove that I'd acted in self-defense so no official charges were filed. Apparently, the guy had a history of violence and this fight had been his fifth or sixth strike. And I *had* acted in self-defense, that wasn't a lie. He started the fight, broke one of my friend's— and I use that term loosely—jaws and came at me with a broken bottle." I hold up my arm, showing her the scar on the back of my forearm, near my elbow. She gently runs her fingers across it, leaning in to brush her lips over the faint line, as I've done to her scars too many times to count. She gives me a soft smile and I try to return it, but my stomach is in knots. I take a deep breath and let it out slowly. "But...I couldn't *stop*. I was like an animal, like all of the things I was feeling at the time—self-doubt, self-loathing, too much pressure to perform and succeed—just became too much and exploded through my fists. I beat him until he was barely breathing, even after he stopped fighting back." My voice pitches low as I remember that night.

Despite the alcohol in my system, I can vividly remember the crunch of his bones beneath my fist, the cracking of my own knuckles as I struck again and again. I can still smell the blood and see it all over the floor, all over my hands. I will never forget the look in Drew's eyes as he stormed inside and dragged me off of the man: part fear, part pity, part disappointment. He said that he'd just had a feeling that he needed to be there. If he hadn't shown up when he did...I shudder at the thought. I've believed in divine intervention since that moment and will never doubt anything Drew says or feels. Savvy has her dolphins and I have Drew.

"Drew saved my life that night. He and Colin both, but Drew in ways I can't even explain. He dragged me out of that bar and then dragged my ass all the way back to Oklahoma the next day. Thank God *Shadowlands* was in between seasons otherwise I probably would have been fired. He and my parents had a full-on intervention when we got there." My lips curl into a half smile as I remember my dad and Drew standing next to each other, arms crossed, looking so similar despite how drastically different they were physically. Drew, the giant blonde Viking; Dad, the weathered dark-haired farmer.

"Dad put me to work on the farm again like I was a teenager, which was like hell on earth while I was detoxing. Ever try to move hay bales while you're puking and shaking from withdrawal? Not a good time. But he had me out there every day, telling me some good old fashioned manual labor would help clear my mind and get me right again. And it did. Not just being out there and working hard, but...seeing the disappointment in my parents' eyes was enough to put me on my ass. We stayed there for two months, Drew sticking with me every step of the way, canceling everything he'd had planned over break, and I came back to L.A. with a different outlook on life."

I'd started handling everything differently after that and it had made all the difference. A few of the guys I'd been running with around that time had ended up ODing, one had wrapped his car around a telephone pole and killed two other people in the process. That could have easily been me if not for Drew, for my parents.

"I'm sorry you had to go through all that," Savvy says, squeezing my hand.

"I'm not. I think I needed to get knocked down to the bottom. I needed to see that I was heading in the way wrong direction so I could be better." And I'm pretty sure I have been. I honestly try to be a good person, a good friend. I use my fame and fortune to do as much good in the world as I can. I've started several charities, do as many *Make-A-Wish* grants as I can, try to be good to fans. Not that it matters, but the media has often dubbed me one of the "nicest guys in Hollywood." It seems like such a stupid thing, but I take that designation to heart.

I reach out and cup Savannah's cheek. "Plus, I wouldn't have you if not for all of that. You wouldn't have touched the guy I used to be with a ten-foot pole. That guy would never have been good enough for you. Not that I think I am now by any means, but—"

I'm cut off by her lips on mine. My eyes slide closed and I pull her over to straddle my lap, running my hands through her hair and down her back as she deepens the kiss.

"I love the man you've become, Link," she whispers against my lips.

"And he loves you back."

***

Savvy's scream jolts me awake. She's thrashing in the bed beside me, face pinched in pain and fingers clenching the sheets.

"Savvy? Savvy! Wake up, baby. It's just a dream." I shake her gently, but urgently. She's never had a nightmare like this before, and panic makes my heart race. She looks like she's in agony, sweat plastering her hair to her temples, and I grit my teeth at how useless I feel to stop it. "Savannah!" I yell again, urgency and my own fear and pain making my voice rise. I shake her again and her eyes finally flash open. They're wild and unfocused, tears streaming down her cheeks. She's breathless, choked sobs breaking from her chest in great heaves.

I pull her into my arms and rock her gently while she shatters. I hold her tight, praying that I'm enough to put the pieces back together afterward. She cries into my chest and each tear that lands on my skin scalds me, branding me over and over. I hate that I can't take this from her, hate that I can do nothing to help. I feel so useless, though she's told me time and time again that me just being here is enough. It doesn't feel like nearly enough. Each one of her tears guts me, each one of her screams feels like a knife to my chest.

"Shhh, baby, I've got you. I'm here."

She eventually settles and scrubs angrily at her tears. "I'm sorry, Link. God, I'm so sorry." She puts her head in her hands, looking so tired and defeated. "Why do you want to deal with this?" she whispers, almost to herself. "You deserve so much more than this, so much better. You could have someone normal. Someone not so fucking broken and fucked up."

I pry her hands away and grip her chin between my thumb and forefinger, gently pulling her face upward.

My tone is gentle but absolute when I tell her, "Listen closely, Savannah Riley. I do not want anyone else. I want *you*. I want every last bit of you."

"Even the jagged, broken bits?" she whispers brokenly.

"Especially those," I tell her, brushing my thumb over her bottom lip. She holds my gaze and I add, "You are *not* broken, Savvy." I need her to understand that I don't see her that way, never will. She is the strongest person I've ever met and I'm in awe of her every single day. It kills me that she thinks of herself that way, or that she could ever believe that I would think it.

Her eyes water and I can't tell if she believes me or not, but she throws her arms around my neck and pulls me into a searing kiss, quickly moving to straddle my hips and maneuvering our scant clothing out of the way. I choke out a surprised gasp, not at all expecting things to go in this direction, but there is a desperate need burning like a wildfire out of control in her right now, and I would be a fool to try to stop it.

She strokes my cock as she thrusts her tongue and it doesn't take long until I'm hard as a rock. I hiss in a breath when she slides down on me with hardly any warning, and my fingers clench her waist. *So hot. So tight. So slick.*

"Fuck," I grate as she begins to move, twisting her hips in a sinful rhythm that already has me aching to come. I lean forward and lave her breasts, capturing a harden nipple between my lips. She gasps and throws her head back, moaning in pleasure while I continue to suck and lick. She rides me harder, whipping her hips up and down, digging her nails into my shoulders. I let her do whatever she has to do, letting her deal with her nightmare and the aftermath however she needs to. She holds my gaze while she moves on me, over and over. I reach between us and massage her clit, and her eyes slide closed in bliss.

"God, Link. Don't stop..." she breathes.

"Never," I growl. Never going to stop pleasuring her. Never going to stop loving her. Never going to stop bringing her back from the brink and holding all of her broken pieces together as best I can. Never going to be without her.

Soon she whisper-screams my name, her breathy moans like music to my ears as she comes around me, clenching my cock over and over.

"Fuck, Savvy. Can feel you. God..." I wrench her hips up and down, again and again, and feel the tightening in my spine. One more thrust and I climax, arching my hips beneath her as I come hard. I rest my head against her chest as we both come back down from the high of release, trying to catch our breath.

"I love you, I love you, I love you," she whispers.

I'll never tire of hearing it.

CHAPTER 18

Savannah

"I can do this, I can do this, I can do this..." I whisper to myself as we enter the hangar at the private airport not too far from Reid's Island. I've been preparing for this for the last two months, talking about it endlessly with Dr. Forrester and Tiff and Link. Colin is getting married at a luxurious mansion on a vineyard in Napa Valley. The pictures he'd shown us were so gorgeous that my fingers itched to take my own camera out and attempt to capture the beauty of the place myself...but getting there meant getting on a plane.

Colin and his fiancé, James, had both assured me that they understood completely if I couldn't attend, though they both wanted me there, of course. Colin and I had become close since the day we met at Gatorcon, and James was amazing. We were both from Texas and had actually gone to rival high schools if you can believe it, so we sing *it's a small world after alllllll* at the top of our lungs every time we see each other or facetime, much to everyone else's dismay. It kills me to think about missing their big day, but...*plane.*

If the filming schedule wasn't quite so insane right now, I know that Link would have done a cross-country road trip with me to get us there. Which is ridiculous, but I love him all the more for being completely on board with the idea. Unfortunately, he only has two and a half days off, so barely enough time to even get there and celebrate when flying—a road trip is out of the question. His part of shooting here is almost done and we've been avoiding talking about what that might mean for us. Did we do the long-distance thing? Would he even be able to do that with everything else he would have going on with promoting and events and all of that? Did I think about moving to L.A. to be with him? Did we...break up?

That last one feels like a knife to my heart every time I even dared have the thought, but I'm not sure how the other options will work out. Hence, the avoiding of the conversation. We'll have to have it soon though, and we both know it. I'm so in love with him, but I don't know that I'm ready to give up my life here, to leave the house that holds so many memories of my family. But he can't very well leave his life either. *Later*, I tell myself. *Think about it later.*

Right now, I have bigger fish to fry. My heart starts to beat wildly as we enter the space—again. I've already *tried* to walk in three times and had to turn back around again before I even made it through the door. This time, I make it inside at least. *Progress!* But as soon as I see the plane, my throat starts to close and my ribs start pulling in tight until my lungs feel like they're going to burst. I try my best to hide my reactions, embarrassed by them. I don't want anyone to see this, not even Link. *It's ok, it's ok, it's ok. Just breathe.*

I try the visualization exercises Dr. Forrester had suggested: *Ok, I'm going to walk from the doorway to the stairs. Then I'm going to ascend them, gripping the handrail for balance. The metal will probably be cool to the touch. I'm going to step foot onto the plane and turn to the right, walking down the small aisle. I'm going to sit next to Link in one of the large, comfortable chairs and buckle my seatbelt. He's going to hold my hand and I'm going to focus on the feel of his skin against mine. The plane is going to take off and we are going to fly across the country, landing safely in northern California.*

Easy.

Simple.

Impossible.

I freeze, my feet simply refusing to move any farther. Dr. Forrester had suggested something to calm me for the flight, but most medicine doesn't sit right with me and I don't like feeling out of it. Plus, the idea of being out of it on a plane, not being fully aware of my surroundings if anything should happen...Nope. Big nope.

I want to laugh at myself. I'd been *convinced* I could handle this, actually believing that I had this in the bag. Obviously, I was so, so wrong.

Drew studies me and shares a look with Link before saying, "I'm going to go check out the snack situation. See you in a minute, yeah?" I think I nod, but I'm not entirely sure. He walks towards the plane, inclining his head to a few of the people milling about, and heads up the stairs. Just like I should be doing, but my feet won't move.

And it's so hot in here.

And I can't breathe.

And it's so loud. Why is it so loud?

There's a low din echoing in my head, but it's getting louder and louder. *No, no, no.* I squeeze my eyes shut as memories rise.

Then they don't feel like memories, they feel real. Everything is happening, right here, in this moment:

The dull roaring turns into screams and alarms, screeching metal and the sound of flames crackling nearby; my stomach drops as the plane plummets; Mia screams my name; Matt squeezes us both so hard it almost hurts; impact so jarring it rattles my bones; Mia is ripped from my arms; pain flares across my entire body; the smell of blood and gasoline and fire fill my nose.

I fight to claw my way back, to force my mind to accept that it isn't real. Or at least, it isn't happening *now*. I sway as my vision blacks out for a second, and I can only imagine how pale I must be right now. I vaguely register how worried Link looks when my vision clears again. He ushers me towards a metal trunk near the plane, half hidden by a service vehicle of some sort to give us a tiny bit of privacy, and I sit down heavily, leaning over and putting my head between my legs. I try to breath but I can't. I straighten as Link hands me water and I take a sip, not sure how the liquid passes through my closed throat, but it must somehow. He kneels in front of me and gently cradles my neck between his big hands, his thumbs stroking my cheeks.

"Savvy, look at me. Focus on me." I try, but the screams...I squeeze my eyes shut again, battling the memories. "It's ok, baby. I'm here. Everything is ok." I take a few gasping breaths, but manage to fight back against the panic, little by little. I focus on the feeling of his warm skin on mine, the slow strokes of his thumbs, the scent of his cologne. Slowly, the sounds dim, the memories fading away. I open my eyes and meet his gaze. "There's my girl. It's ok, just breathe with me." I nod and he takes a long, deep breath while I mirror the action. We hold them for several seconds, then release them together. Again and again. My heart calms. My head clears.

"I'm sorry, Link," I whisper, hating myself for this. I feel so fucking *weak*. Another reminder that Link should be with someone else, that he deserves so much more than the mess of broken pieces that is masquerading as a person named Savannah Riley.

"Hey, none of that," he says, that slight command in his voice. He always seems to know when I need to hear it. He gives me a tiny smile and I try to return it.

I don't know how much time has passed, but apparently enough that I'm delaying our departure. People are talking around the space, muttering about flight schedules and the like.

"Here, drink some more water. I'm gonna go talk to Drew for a second."

I nod, and take the bottle, tilting it up with one hand and rubbing sweat from the back of my neck with the other. Link stands but before he can step out from behind the car, we hear a couple of the crew members talking a few feet away. They must not realize we're here.

"Blondie probably thinks she's hot shit because she's fucking Ashmore," a guy with a nasally voice says, then snorts with a derisive laugh, "Hell, she's probably fucking *both* of them. Small town star chaser going knees to the sky for a bit of *Shadowlands* on her resume." *What a dick.*

"See, this is why no one likes you, Jay," a second guy says, sounding like he's tired of dealing with Jay, but doesn't really have anywhere to escape to at the moment. "You're such a dick." *Glad I'm not the only one who thinks so.*

Jay continues, unfazed. "Whatever. Where did Ashmore and the headcase go anyway? Did you *see* her? I mean, Jesus Christ, it's just a plane. Get a grip, right?" He sounds like he's smirking. I wince, feeling way more hurt by his words than I should.

I glance up to see Link shot through with tension, the muscle in his jaw ticking and looking...dangerous. I've never seen him look so angry before and I get a flash of what he might have looked like during that fight in Memphis, when he'd lost his mind and gone animalistic on that guy. My eyes widen but before I can get the words out to beg him not to do anything stupid, that the guy is just a jerk and it doesn't matter, we hear Drew.

"Oy!"

Link and I jump up and race around the corner of the car, both of us gasping in shock. Drew has a skinny ginger guy up against the side of the plane, clutching the front of his shirt in clenched fists. I've never seen Drew so much as in a bad mood, but now? He looks *scary*. He'd played a lethal vampire warrior on *Shadowlands* but right now, he looks even more formidable than that character had ever been. Jay looks terrified.

"I—"

"No, you're done talking now." Drew bares his teeth in the most menacing expression I've ever seen. The pilots rush over and so does Link. I stand there, dumbfounded. Others gather, all looking shocked. Some don't seem concerned for Jay, sharing *serves him right* looks with each other. Apparently, he really is just a dick. Part of me wishes Drew would deck him, and I'm not even ashamed of it.

Drew seems to struggle for calm and leans in close to Jay's face. "That woman is the bravest person I've ever met. The last plane she was on *crashed*, you stupid fuck. The fact that she's even here *trying* to get on this plane again is God damned astounding." Jay's eyes go wide as they cut to me.

"I...I'm sorry. I..." Drew pulls him off of the plane only to slam him back again. Jay whimpers and I honestly wouldn't be surprised if he pissed himself.

"What did I say about you talking? Hmm? Pay better attention, mate." He releases Jay and steps away. Looking at the pilots and the other personnel that arrived to witness the altercation, Drew adds "He's done. *Now,*" he adds in a tone that brokers no argument. "I don't typically throw this card around, but here it is: I'm Andrew Fucking Faraday and that is Lincoln Fucking Ashmore. Do with that what you will." The threat is clear in his voice. *Fix this or you'll have a PR nightmare of epic Hollywood proportions.* A chorus of *yes sirs* ring out as the other crew members and a manager for the small private airline joins the fray to try to smooth things over. Someone ushers Jay out of the hangar into a back office on unsteady legs, his freckled face beet red.

Drew turns to me. "Savvy, you alright, love?"

I nod numbly, still trying to figure out what in the hell had just happened. The fact that Drew had defended me so fiercely makes my heart melt a little. He is such a good man and I'm so lucky to have him in my life. *But if I wasn't so fucking screwed up, he wouldn't have had to stand up for me in the first place.*

I rub my temples and give Link an apologetic look.

"I...I can't do it. I'm sorry. Go ahead without me." He looks so lost and torn. I know he feels helpless with all this stuff. He *does* help, more than he could ever know, but I know it still kills him that he can't fix it, can't take this hurt and pain from me. I know he's about to say he's going to stay with me so I cut him off. "No, you are not missing this. Colin is one of your best friends and mine now, too. You go for both of us. Give them my love and tell them I'm sorry. FaceTime me from the reception, ok?" I force the tears not to fall though I know my eyes are glassy. I don't *want* this to beat me. I don't *want* to be broken. But I tried, and I can't win. Not today. *Maybe not ever.*

I give him a quick goodbye kiss and meet Drew's gaze, mouthing *thank you.* He nods and goes off to talk with a dark-haired woman who looks to be in charge. I vaguely make out the words "crash" "sole survivor" and "husband and child," and see the woman's shock and sorrow before she turns a furious gaze at Jay as the door to the office opens again.

"Are you sure?" Link asks softly, searching my face.

I try to give him a reassuring smile. "I am. Go. Have fun. Maybe next time." I hike a shoulder. I know deep down that I'll never be able to do it. I usually think of myself as pretty damn strong, but I'm not strong enough for that. I'll never be able to fully get past what I've experienced, what I've lost. Panic threatens me once more as I think about Link and Drew on that plane, of what could happen to *them*, but I rein it in before Link sees. He doesn't need one more thing to worry about, one more reason to doubt that I'm worth all of this hassle. I give him another kiss and grab my weekender bag, quickly hauling it out to the car before he can offer to do it.

"Bye!" I call over my shoulder, lest he try to come after me. He looks defeated and worried, but doesn't follow. Panic is threatening to strangle me, but I somehow manage to keep it in check long enough to toss my bag in the back, give a jaunty double honk goodbye while waving out the window, and speed out of the parking area. I make it half a mile before I have to pull over.

I gasp for air and sweat breaks out over my forehead and neck. A strangled cry bursts from my lips, so forcefully it actually hurts. I can't see past the tears and can barely breathe. I squeeze the wheel so hard my fingers ache.

I somehow manage to get my phone and call Dr. Forrester. She answers on the first ring, probably expecting the call, knowing deep down that I wouldn't be able to get on the plane and escape a meltdown. I can only imagine what I look like on the FaceTime video.

"Savannah," she says calmly, "I need you to breathe."

"C-can't," I manage to rasp. I clutch and claw at my chest, desperate to ease the ache, desperate to get air into my lungs.

"Savvy, you're alright. Focus. Five things you can see," she says, gentle but demanding. It's one reason I love her so much, why she is such a damned good doctor. She has the perfect balance of gentle coddling aunt and no-bullshit drill sergeant. "Tell me the five things, Savvy." Five things? I...I can't! I can't focus on anything! *Fuck, fuck, fuck.* Flashes of the crash start to bombard me, but then they morph, Link now mixed up in the memories somehow. *His* eyes meeting mine as the plane goes down, *his* blood on my hands, *his* body among the wreckage. *No, no, no. Can't lose him too. Please.*

I bite my lip so hard I taste blood.

"Come on, Savannah. You can do this. Breathe. Focus. Five things."

I gasp and dark spots dot my vision, but I somehow suck in a ragged breath, then another. *Ok. Ok. I can do this. Five things.*

"T-the bottle of water. The necklace on my rearview. The frayed edges of my shorts."

"Two more. Come on."

A little more air. A little less pressure in my chest and head.

"The hair tie on my wrist. And the Captain Ultra keychain." I almost smile. *Lincoln.* I picture his face, imagine he's here beside me, and I calm a bit more. Breathing gets a little easier, tears start slowing. *He's ok. He's alive and well. He'll be fine.*

"Good. That's good. Now, three things you can hear."

I take another broken breath and force myself to focus, to listen. The screams and alarms in my head are quieting, but still there. I strain to hear over them, clenching my fists. Again, I picture Link and pretend he's resting his hand on my shoulder, pulling me back from the brink, and the sounds fade. Now I can hear—

"The AC blowing through my vents. Music from the bar across the street." I roll my window down and look over the bar in question and hear the unmistakable sounds. "And someone puking in the parking lot of the same bar." I actually manage a shaky laugh and Dr. Forrester smiles.

"There you are." She's in her late forties, with short chestnut hair, light brown eyes, and a kind smile. "Want to talk about it?"

I exhale roughly and lean back in my seat, wiping sweat from my neck. "I made it into the hangar and tried to visualize, like we talked about, but I just...couldn't." My shoulders slump. I feel like I failed.

Reading me so easily, Dr. Forrester says, "You did not fail at anything, Savannah Riley. Do you know how impressive it is that you even tried to get on that plane? I am beyond proud of you. This is a soul deep wound for you, Savvy. No one expects you to ignore it or pretend it doesn't exist. And if you *can't* get past it, that's ok too. There is no right or wrong here. No test to be passed or failed."

I know she's right, but I can't stop feeling utterly defeated. Still, I give her a reluctant nod. "I just...I hate feeling broken for him," I say quietly.

"I know that isn't how he sees you."

"I know, I just...I don't know." I run my hands through my hair and grimace. I need a shower. I set the phone in the holder on the dash for a second while I toss my mane up into a messy bun. "I just...want better for him, I guess."

"Such is love," she says, wistfully, before eyeing me seriously. "Are you alright?"

I nod, feeling much better. "I'm alright now. Thank you."

"Any time, Savvy, you know that." We've become close over these years. She's a trusted friend, not just a doctor. We say our goodbyes and I feel silly for how I reacted. Though a thread of worry still lingers, I know that statistically speaking, Link and Drew are safe on that plane. Panic isn't flaring up again like before, but I do feel a heavy weight on my chest that I know won't ease up until they're wheels down in Cali. I rub the center of my chest, trying to ease the strain there, and my phone buzzes. I actually smile, despite feeling like a clusterfuck of epic proportions.

Link: About to take off. Miss you already.

Savvy: Miss you too. I'm sorry I'm such a headcase.

I add a silly face emoji, though I'm only about ten percent kidding. Will he get tired of it all one day? Will he finally decide that all my baggage is just too heavy for him to help cart around? The thought makes my chest ache. *God, I hope not.* I know he deserves someone less screwed up than me, someone who doesn't come with all the history and issues. I grit my teeth. *Someone who can get on a fucking plane without having a panic attack for crying out loud.* But I can't deny that I'm selfish enough that I hope he never agrees.

Link: Shush. I love you.

Link: Drew says he loves you more.

I giggle.

Savvy: I love you both. Safe flight.

I scrunch my nose. Was that a weird thing for me of all people to say?

I call Tiff and ask for an emergency bestie dinner and drinks. She calls me an idiot for even asking, and tells me to meet her at The Crab House in thirty.

Please don't give up on me, Link, I think as I pull back out onto the small highway. *Please stick with me.*

CHAPTER 19

Lincoln

Long-distance relationships suck balls. We're making it work, but the last five months have been less than ideal. Any events that were within reasonable driving distance, Savvy attended with me. Each one was amazing, but saying goodbye at the end was getting harder and harder. I guess I'd gotten so used to having her close by during my time in Sandlapper Cove, that now that I'm gone, I feel like I'm missing one of my limbs. I know that sounds dramatic, but whatever. It's the truth. Of course, long-distance is better than the alternative of losing her completely. My heart had stopped for a second when she'd even mentioned the possibility of ending things when filming wound up and it came time for me to leave.

"Is that what you want?" I'd asked, stunned and barely able to breathe.

"No!" she'd all but yelled. "Not at all!" I'd relaxed and pulled her into my chest. As long as her chips were still all in the ring, then we were ok, we could make it through anything. She'd survived paparazzi and bombarding fans, gossip magazine covers and horrendous comments on social media posts. Hell, she'd dealt with me filming a sex scene for the movie so much better than I would have imagined. When I'd broached the subject, running a hand over the back of my neck, telling her that there was a scene coming up on the schedule, I'd been a wreck. So nervous, I'd talked a mile a minute as I tried to explain that it wasn't actually sexy at all and there were a million people around and it didn't mean anything and I even threw out that I'd be thinking of her the whole time before cringing—and she'd *laughed* at me.

"Link, calm down. It's a sex scene. Who cares?" I'd frowned. Audrey had lost her ever loving mind on me when I'd had to do one in the past, railing at me that I was all but cheating on her—which was really rich since she was *actually* cheating on me at the time.

"You...it doesn't bother you?" I'd asked, confused. She'd hiked a shoulder.

"Not really, no. It's part of your job and it isn't like you're actually having sex with her." She laughed when I'd studied her, waiting to see if she was joking. "Link, I've never been a jealous person, it's just not part of my DNA. So, I'm definitely not going to be jealous over something that you are doing for your job. I've met Shreya and she's amazing." She'd leaned in to kiss me, nipping my bottom lip. "I actually look forward to seeing the finished product. A scene between the two of you is sure to be hot as hell."

She'd survived meeting my parents and sister, and, not to anyone's surprise, they'd all loved her. They'd all come to spend a week and celebrate mom's birthday. Savvy insisted on hosting a dinner for mom at her place, setting up a beautiful outdoor dinner by the lake, twinkle lights in all the trees and my mom's favorite cake made to order from the best bakery in town. She'd even printed out one of the shots she'd gotten of me down at the beach and framed it for mom as a gift. Mom had teared up at the thoughtfulness of it and had gushed for what felt like hours about how brilliant the photo was.

Mom, Juliet and Savvy all stood together and laughed as they watched Sami play with Griffey. It had been amazing to watch Savvy with Sami, the two fast friends. I knew without a doubt that Savannah had been an amazing mom and my heart clenched at the thought of her feeling like she failed her daughter.

Watching them together had given me a glimpse of a future I wasn't sure I'd ever have, but it didn't stop me from letting myself imagine it for a few minutes: Savvy running around the yard with *our* daughter, a beautiful little fiend with Savvy's blonde hair and mischievous smile, and my green eyes, who liked horses and mud puddles and princess dresses. I could see it so damn clearly that I clenched my jaw at the sudden wanting. I knew it wasn't the future we would have, at least not in the conventional way. Savvy couldn't have kids, not after all the injuries she'd sustained in the crash, but maybe we could still have a family one day. I know that it might be too much to ask her to become a mother again, and I'm ok with whatever decision she makes, but I can't deny that I want it.

Dad and I looked on from the dock, smoking cigars. I wasn't a huge cigar guy by any means, but dad and I always had one together on every trip. Tradition and all that.

"She is something else," dad said, glancing towards the girls and smiling as Savvy said something that had mom and Juliet throwing their heads back laughing. He turned back to me and caught me still staring at Savvy. "And my God, son, I've never seen you look so happy."

"I haven't been," I admitted easily. "I can't explain it, dad, she's just...she's..."

He'd grinned, tan skin crinkling by his green eyes, so similar to my own. "The one?" he finished for me.

I let out a long exhale. "That about sums it up."

Before they left, Juliet had vowed that if I didn't marry Savvy, she was officially petitioning to kick me out of the family. With the way mom hugged Savvy goodbye, I had a feeling that she and dad might be on board with Juliet's plan.

Savvy had survived her first small red carpet with me at a charity event up in D.C., looking absolutely flawless and blowing everyone away, including me. I'd been speechless when I'd seen her in her fitted scarlet gown and soft curls, reminding me of an old Hollywood starlet. She'd posed for photos, smiled indulgently when I'd answered questions, and had even given a huge donation to the cause before the night was out. She'd been perfect...and we'd barely made it back to the hotel room before I had her up against the wall, kissing her like my life depended on it. There was something intensely arousing about getting her out of that dress, slowly unclasping and unzipping and removing each item slowly and carefully—but not the heels. Those babies stayed on for the duration. The sight of her standing in her heels—*only her heels*—as I sank to my knees in front of her and hitched one leg over my shoulder will forever be branded in my mind.

She'd nearly been trampled by fans and photographers outside of a hotel once and merely laughed, shrugging it off.

So, yeah, Savannah had taken to navigating all aspects of my crazy life like a fish to water. If she could handle all of that, we could handle a few months apart while we figured everything out. I'm traveling like crazy right now anyway, doing press stuff and events for the *Shadowlands* fifteen-year anniversary and surprise reunion season that had just been announced, plus all of the promotion circuits starting for the new movie. So, even if we *did* actually live together full time, I'd be gone all the time right now anyway. I tell myself that, but it doesn't really make it any better.

Of course, if she was ok flying, she could easily come with me to all of this stuff, but I would never pressure her to do that. I long to have her by my side, for her to experience this stuff with me, but I can't ask her to push herself into something she isn't ready for. She may never be ready for it and that's ok. We'll deal. I know she worries I'll get tired of her "metric fuck-ton of emotional baggage" as she likes to call it, but I'm still trying to figure out how to convince her that that could never happen.

"Missing our girl?" Drew asks me as we head out to a press event, handing me a cup of coffee.

"Bless you." I take a sip and sigh in relief. "And yes, I'm missing *my* girl."

He gives me a dry look and enunciates slowly, "*Ours.* Get over it, mate." I chuckle and he grins. "What's the plan then? You can't do this forever."

I sigh, knowing how right he is. We're making it work but it isn't enough. I don't want to settle for "making it work" with Savvy. I want her in my life, completely. I want to fall asleep with her in my arms and wake up with her hogging the covers. I want to cook her dinner and hear the adorable noises she makes while she eats. I want to kiss every inch of her, want to worship her like she deserves. I just want...her. Simple as that.

"I don't know yet. We've still gotta figure it all out." I can't ask her to leave her home, to leave the connection she has with her husband and child there. Could *I* move there? Would she even want me to move there with her, to have us all in the same space? Would the past and the present be too much for her all together? I suppose I could get my own place nearby, like the beach house I'd stayed in while we were filming. I'd be willing to do just about anything to be closer to her right about now.

"Do you think she'll get tired of all this?" He motions to the giant line of screaming fans waiting outside the venue as we pull up.

I worry about that every damn day.

"Let's hope not," I mutter as we step out of the car and wave, and the screams ratchet up even louder.

***

"I miss you."

"I miss you more," she replies. I sigh, running a hand through my hair while I lounge in yet another hotel bed. It feels like the hundredth one this week. I'd forgotten how crazy promotion tours can be. Her eyes dip down on the screen, taking in my bare chest. When she glances up again, she bites her lip, her pupils expanding. Heat flushes through my body and my cock responds, hardening just at her hungry gaze. We became quick studies in sexting, phone sex, and FaceTime sex as soon as I left Sandlapper Cove, though I miss her actual touch so much I can barely stand it.

As if reading my thoughts she says, "Just a couple more weeks. You and Drew are still coming for my birthday, right?"

"Of course. But I don't want to talk about Drew right now..." I lick my lips and arch a brow at her, wondering why her shirt is still on.

"Dang, really? You know how he gets me going..." I narrow my eyes and she digs her teeth into her bottom lip, eyes alight with that sensual mischief. She loves to tease me about Drew, to rile me up like that. Loves even more when I *retaliate.*

"Top off. Now, Savannah," I command. Her cheeks flush and her gaze turns even more heated. She obeys, pulling her tank over her head, revealing those luscious breasts. I groan and scrub a hand over my mouth. I want my tongue on those harden peaks so fucking bad. My cock pulses beneath the sheet, desperate for her. Her breaths grow shallow, her breasts quivering. God, have I ever wanted anyone this badly? No, not even close. When I see her again, all bets are off. The house may not survive.

I grin at the thought as I slip my hand beneath the sheet and tell her exactly what I want her to do.

***

"We're about fifteen minutes out," I tell Savannah as we head towards her place. Drew and I just got to town to spend a few days here for her birthday and I'm thrumming with excitement. This distance really has been killing me. I'm ready to quit acting all together if it means I can just spend every second of every day with Savvy. It's coming up on exactly one year since I met her, and I'm working on planning something special for it. Maybe...a ring? Would that be cliché or ridiculous? Probably but I honestly don't care.

"He won't stop grinning like a lunatic!" Drew calls. I roll my eyes and put the phone on speaker. "Savvvvyyyyy! I've missed you, love."

"I've missed you too." I can hear the smile in her voice and my own grin widens. I probably really do look like a lunatic. I hear what sounds like her engine cutting off and her keys jangling in the background.

"You home, babe?"

"Yep, just pulled up. I grabbed us some take out for dinner and some beer."

"Please say it's from Ruby's. Please, please, please..." Drew literally clasps his hands to his chest as he pleads with her, as if she can see him.

"I know what my boys like." I can see her in my mind's eye, phone resting on her shoulder while she carries bags up the wide front porch, golden hair framing her face, that brilliant smile lighting up her face as she calls us *her boys*. "Speaking of what my boys like: Tiff will be here in a bit too, Drew."

They had an interesting friends-with-benefits thing going on, both of them swearing up and down that there wasn't anything more to it than that. I know Drew well enough to know that he's telling me the truth, that he likes Tiff immensely as a friend and likes hooking up with her even more immensely, but there wouldn't be anything more. So long as Tiff was on board with that—and I'd made him *swear* that they'd discussed it at length and were both on the same page, and then gotten confirmation from Savvy of the same directly from Tiff's lips—then I'm happy for them to do whatever they want.

Drew grins at the news, waggling his blonde brows at me.

"And here I thought it was *your* birthday, Sav, but you're the one giving me gifts."

She chuckles. "Well, my birthday isn't technically until tomorrow, so...happy Tuesday I guess. Oh hang on, I gotta toss you in the bag with the fried chicken for a second so I can get the door open."

Drew inhales dreamily. "It's almost like I can smell that fried heaven through the phone." I can hear the door open and close behind her, though the sounds are a bit muted since the phone is in the take-out bag. I'm surprised I don't hear Griffey barking in greeting. He's normally right there, tail wagging, tennis ball at the ready.

A few seconds later, I hear a scream and the shattering of glass. My spine stiffens and my blood goes cold.

"Savvy? Savvy, what happened? Are you alright?" I share a look with Drew when she doesn't answer, his dreamy look gone in an instant, his body tight with alert and his blue eyes filled with worry.

"Wh-what do you want?" I hear her say, though her voice sounds far away. My blood turns to ice. *Is somebody in Savvy's fucking house??*

"Savannah!" I yell, fear nearly taking my breath.

CHAPTER 20

Savannah

"Savannah! Savannah, answer me!"

I barely hear Link's voice on the other end of the phone, still inside the bag with all the food. I'd dropped the beer, and glass and amber liquid cover the floor around me. I grip the take-out bag like a life raft, my knuckles turning white. A woman stands across the living room—with a pistol in her hand, pointed directly at me.

She's tall, maybe five-nine, and slim, but with what look to be some surgically enhanced curves. She's pretty, with jet black hair that shines in the sunlight streaming through the back wall of windows, dark brown eyes, high cheekbones and bow-shaped lips. I've always envied girls who had that perfect shape. Why am I even thinking about that right now? My thoughts are fuzzy, a faint ringing in my ears. *Focus. Focus. Dear God, focus.*

"Put the bag down," she says, voice cold and steady. I swallow hard and slowly take the few steps to the set the food on the large island, keeping my eyes on her as I move. I turn my back to put the bag down and quickly reach inside to turn the volume down on the phone. Link and Drew are both yelling, but I don't want her to know a call is connected right now. Hopefully they can still hear everything that's going on and get help. My hands shake like crazy as I try to surreptitiously shift the phone so it's at the top of the bag.

"Hey!" I jump when she yells, spinning to face her. She motions impatiently with the gun, directing me to move back from the counter. I obey, but now there is nothing between us, nothing that I could possibly hide behind if she decides to pull that trigger. My fight-or-flight impulses are warring inside me, part of my mind searching for a weapon of some kind, the other part wondering if I can make it down the hallway before she gets a shot off. However, I don't listen to either. Instead, I do the third F option no one talks about and simply freeze. I just stand there like a deer in headlights, staring at this stranger with a gun pointed at my chest.

"Wh-what do you want?" I ask, voice shaking. Everything has taken on that weird dream like quality, just like the moments before the crash had. I'm fighting through the haze, desperately trying to think and reason out what was happening without panic overtaking me. It takes way too long for my brain to catch up. Something is nagging at me, something I need to figure out. *I'm missing something...*

Griffey! He's sweet, but protective of me and our home. He never would have let her in here, unless...

My blood turns cold and my stomach lurches when I see the golden bundle of fur on the floor on the other side of the room near the windows. My fear momentarily subsides, rage taking its place.

"What did you do to him?" I scream, hot tears scalding my eyes. *No. Can't lose him! Can't have failed him too. No, no, no!*

She looks offended by my accusation. "Nothing! I would never hurt an animal, I'm not a monster." I want to laugh in her face at how ridiculous that is, but I don't think laughing at the crazy lady with the gun is a good move. "I just gave him a sedative so I could get into the house. He's fine." She tranquilized my freaking dog? That means that this was premeditated. She *planned* this, has probably been watching me and this house, figuring out my routines and how to best get in. This is like an episode of *Criminal Minds* or some shit. *What the fuck??*

I've always felt safe out here despite the somewhat solitude of it. Now that's been violated and I feel both sick and enraged. This home is more than just four walls. This home is a part of me, a part of my family that I can never get back—and she has tainted it. I clench my fists at my sides and try to focus on surviving first. *Then*, I'll make her pay for it.

"Can..." I swallow hard. "Can I check on him?" She seems irritated but waves the gun towards Griffey, making me so nervous I think I'm going to puke. I don't dare turn my back to her as I ease towards my fur baby, keeping as much distance between us in the large living room as possible. I keep my eyes on her as I ease down to my knees beside Griffey. I place my hand on his warm body and nearly sob when I feel the steady rise and fall of his chest. Just sleeping. I close my eyes in relief for a moment, but her voice cuts into my short reverie and they flash open again.

"See, I told you." She sounds *annoyed* with me and again I have the hysterical urge to laugh at the situation. *She* broke into my house, drugged my dog, and is holding me hostage...but she's annoyed that *I* didn't believe she wouldn't hurt Griffey. *And I thought* I *had mental issues...*

I stand on shaky legs, keeping my hands in front of me because that's what people always do in movies when they're confronting an armed maniac, and I quite frankly don't know what else to do. Maybe if I can figure out what she wants, she'll just go away, or if I can at least keep her talking, it will give Link and Drew enough time to get help. Can they even hear me?

"Why are you here?" I ask, pitching my voice a little louder than usual and hoping she doesn't think anything of it. My voice is shaking but I can't make it stop. "Is it about money? I have cash in the safe, but I can get you more, as much as you want." Is that what this is about? Robbery? It's fairly public knowledge that I'm beyond loaded, so I guess it makes as much sense as any other possibility.

She curls her lip. "I don't want your money," she sneers. She studies me, tilting her head this way and that, but never lowering her gun. "You're pretty, I'll give you that. Even prettier in person." *Huh?* What does that have to do with a damn thing? My mind races, trying to figure out what the hell to do. Do I run for it? Will she really shoot me? Am I going to die? Once upon a time, I'd wanted that very thing, had nearly done it myself to end my pain and join my family, but now I wanted to live. I wanted this life with Link more than anything in the world.

To have that taken away now, when we're just getting started? We've barely had a chance! This isn't fair. *Life* isn't fair. And I'm so fucking sick of it! Tears well again, but this time they're from anger, not fear. I'm officially saying fuck you to the universe. I'm sick of it, sick of being put through hell and tested over and over again. Haven't I passed yet? What more do I have to do??

She continues, bursting into my raging thoughts. "But he still deserves someone better. Someone who understands his life.

Someone not covered in disgusting scars." She curls her lip again as her eyes flicker across the numerous places where my skin is disfigured. I frown. *They're all covered right now. And who is* he? What is she talking about?

I'm about to ask her what she could possibly be talking about when realization finally sinks through the fog in my brain.

"Link. You're here because of Link." She'd seen my scars online, in all of the pictures that have been posted of Link and I in swimsuits from the yacht and other times when we were caught on the beach together.

A dreamy smile pulls at her lips. "He's *perfect*," she sighs. "We're soul mates, you know. He's always so nice when we see each other at events, always accepting my gifts with a smile and a hug and telling me how he's missed me in between our meetings. The last time was just a misunderstanding," she says, sounding both annoyed and also like she's trying to convince me of something, though of course I have no idea what. *Last time?* "We have so much in common and I know *everything* about him. Do *you* know what his favorite dog's name was? Do *you* know that he broke his leg when he was twelve falling out of the hayloft on his family's farm? Have *you* seen all of his movies?" She gets louder and louder with each question, until she's shrieking at me.

She's a delusional fan. I've seen stories like this before, about fans who can't differentiate fantasy from reality, but I never thought it could really happen. The gun shakes wildly in her hand as her emotions escalate. My throat goes dry. Was Link hearing all of this? Had he called the police? Were they on their way? I think maybe I hear wheels on the drive outside, but I can't be sure.

She glares at me again. "And yet, he's with *you*." She spits that word, like it tastes bad on her tongue. "A little small town, nobody *freak*! I understand his world, I'm part of it—you never will be! You'll never be good enough for him."

"You're right," I say, trying to placate her. Is that the right move? Or will she think I'm patronizing her and pull the trigger? Fuck, I don't know the right answer! Her eyes narrow suspiciously, but the rage seems to have dimmed a tiny bit. I decide to push my luck on this route. "You're completely right. I don't know why he picked me. He deserves someone better, someone whole and beautiful. I've told him that a million times."

She nods and a small smile ghosts over her lips. "Yes, see. You understand." She sounds so earnest, actually hitting me with a full smile like we're old friends agreeing on gossip about some boy. "You *know* that you can't be with him."

I nod, hoping that maybe she'll put the gun down now that I'm agreeing that Link shouldn't be with me. Hell, part of me really *does* agree, always has. But then her smile fades and she straights the gun once more, a cold resolve settling over her face that has my heart thundering in my ears and my whole body going cold.

"He'll grieve you for a bit, but I'll be there to comfort him and he'll understand why it had to happen, that I did it for us."

Panic flares. "Wait, just wait! Please don't do this. Please. I'll leave him, I promise. I'll never speak to him again. I'll do it right now, I'll call him and break it off."

She seems to be considering things when the front door bursts open. She turns, gun trained on the door and I can barely breathe. Lincoln stands there and I can see police cars all over the front lawn. *Man, they coordinated fast.* Or maybe it's been hours already, I have no idea. Everything is becoming a little pear-shaped. I think I hear Drew yelling outside, a distant "*what the fucking fuck, Ashmore!?*" sounding very far away.

I'm frozen in place but the woman recovers quickly enough, moving back towards the wall of windows so that she can keep both me and Link in her sights, but a wide smile pulls those perfect bow-shaped lips upward.

"Link," she breathes. "I've missed you."

"I've missed you too," he says, holding her gaze and keeping his hands raised in surrender. *Huh?* "I didn't know that you'd been released, Carolyn." Carolyn? He truly does know this crazy bitch? Released? *What in the fucking fuck, indeed.* She scowls and shakes her head, but Link adds smoothly, "If I had, I would have come to see you sooner." *He's* placating her now, trying to use her clear affection—or obsession—with him to get her to stand down. My heart beats wildly. What if she turns on him? The thought has me feeling cold all over, my chest feeling like it's going to burst.

Her smile returns and she flashes me a *told ya* look.

Link takes a slow step forward. "Now, why don't you just put the gun down and let Savannah go, so we can talk? Just the two of us."

She wavers, looking unsure, even lowering the barrel of the gun a few inches, but quickly pulls it back upward. She shakes her head hard again.

"No, I can't. She has to go. She'll stand between us because you love her so much." She flashes a hate-fueled glance my way before turning back to Link. "But once she's gone, nothing will be in our way. We'll finally be together, Link, just like we were meant to be." She edges closer to me but I know better than to move. Her trigger finger is looking mighty itchy and my instincts are doing their best to keep me alive.

Link's body goes rigid and he stops moving forward. "Carolyn, you don't need to do this," he says. Though he's hiding it well, I can hear the slight tremble in his voice, can hear the utter terror roiling beneath the surface.

"I *do* though, baby. Don't you understand?" she begs him to comprehend what she apparently sees so clearly.

I catch movement out of the corner of my eye: dark shapes moving in the backyard, just off the deck, but I don't dare turn to look fully. The police are surrounding my house...because there is a crazed woman with a gun pointed at me and Lincoln is in here unarmed and without any protection. My throat starts to close up with panic and fear and I have to fight to hear over the ringing in my ears. I'm starting to slip over the edge, but I hold on for dear life, glancing from Carolyn to Link. He's holding Carolyn's gaze and I can see him willing her to listen to reason. His jaw muscle ticks over and over. *His tell.*

Carolyn searches Link's eyes for a long moment and then seems to make a decision.

"It has to be done. You'll thank me one day." She turns to me, determination in her eyes, and raises the gun. I know deep in my bones that this is it. No more hesitating, no more talking. She's going to pull that trigger and there is absolutely nothing I can do to stop it.

She squeezes the trigger and I meet Link's gaze, whispering his name.

CHAPTER 21

Savannah

Several things seem to happen all at once:

Lincoln bellows and I've never heard anything more anguished or angry in my life; I hear the crack of the gun and glass shattering; I squeeze my eyes shut as searing pain shoots across my right shoulder and warm liquid splashes over my chest, neck, and face.

My eyes fly open as I fall to my knees. I can't move my right arm and the pain is nearly unbearable. Everything feels strange, like it's happening in slow motion or I'm watching it through a haze. All of the sounds around me are muted, like I'm hearing them from underwater. *Again. I've been here before. Can't be here again.*

I hear Link yell my name and shouting from outside. The room is suddenly swarming with people. Police officers? Link slams to his knees in front of me and I feel his hands on my face, but I can't see him clearly, can't focus. I'm slipping. I feel myself going and know somehow that if I go this time, I might not come back.

"Savannah? Savvy, are you alright? Savvy, answer me, baby." I want to, but I can't. The pain in my arm is blinding. I raise my other hand to my face, feeling like it takes years and so much energy that I sway as the room tilts violently. I swipe the back of my hand over my cheek, wondering how I've cried so much in the split second between when Carolyn pulled the trigger and now, and why my tears are so...sticky. When I pull my hand away, it's stained dark red. *Blood.* So much blood. My eyes are wide and unblinking. *Shock? Am I in shock?*

Link tries to catch my attention, tries to force me to look at him even as someone else drops beside me and starts to poke at my hurt arm. I barely feel the pain anymore. *Slipping...slipping...*

I hear someone scream my name from just outside. Tiff?

Again, Link tries to shift so that he's blocking...something. But as big as he is, he can't hide this from me. I look past him and see Carolyn's body, a gaping, ragged hole where her pretty face used to be. A sea of red surrounds her, my rug no longer white. So much blood. Everywhere. I sway when it finally hits me: the blood all over my face is *hers.*

Too much. It's all too much.

My vision tunnels and darkness engulfs me.

***

"Savvy, love, you've got to wake up. You're really starting to worry Link, and you know how much of a softy he is." Drew? I can't open my eyes. I can feel his hand in mine and can hear the steady beep of monitors, can smell the all too familiar scent of *hospital.* He sounds upset and I want to tell him that it's ok, but I can't seem to push my way past the heavy darkness pressing down on me. Meds. I've been sedated.

I don't remember anything after passing out in the living room, but I can feel the sharp ache in my shoulder, feel the bandage covering the wound. I'd been...shot. By a mad woman in my own home, before the police had blown her brains out...I force my thoughts to stop in their tracks before they pull me under again.

Another voice. "She'll be ok, she just needs time. Her shoulder was a through and through—which is the *M* world that she despises so I won't utter it." I want to smile but my face won't cooperate. "The rest..." Dr. Forrester sighs and I imagine her tucking her hair behind her ears, her tell when she's concerned. "She's in shock. Her mind is trying to protect itself by shutting everything out for a while." A while? How long have I been out?

"Will she recover from that? After...after everything else?" *Link*. God, he sounds so broken. I want to tell him I'm ok, even if that isn't the whole truth. Shock. That sounds about right. I can't think about everything that's happened. It's just too much. I don't know how much more I can take...don't know if I'll recover from this one. The trauma of losing my family to a freak accident was one thing, but being attacked in my own home, where I'm supposed to be safe...I don't know why, but it's pushed me over some edge I didn't know existed for me.

"Savvy is strong...but this is like adding a bowling ball to a house of cards." I hate that it's such an accurate description. I start to slip but then a memory of Link flashes in my mind, him telling me how strong I am, how much I amaze him.

So, no. I refuse to accept that I'm so fragile, so damn breakable. I've fought too fucking hard to be strong after everything I've been through. And if Link believes in me that much, then I'll try to be that person.

Even as my mind rebels, still trying to shield me from everything, I force myself to think about what happened. It's the only way I can move forward, right? To face the trauma. That's what I'd had to do after the crash. I could do it again...couldn't I? If it means finding my way back to Link, I'll do anything.

So, I open my mind and force myself to think about what had happened: someone broke into my home, hell bent on killing me, ready to shoot me in cold blood to take me out of Link's life. I'd cheated death time and time again with the crash and all of my injuries afterwards, but this was different. The crash had been all speed and chaos. This was...calm. Quiet. I'd had time to think about what was going to happen to me, to think about all the things I was losing while I stared down the barrel of the gun. I didn't have that when the plane went down. I agonized over it later and had had those quick thoughts in the few seconds we had, but it had all happened so fast, I didn't have time to process it fully until later. With Carolyn, I had time to think about *everything*, to be gutted by everything that was about to be taken away from me while I waited for her to make a decision.

Because I wasn't good enough to be with Link. Because I'm scarred. Because I don't belong with him. That's what Carolyn believed—and didn't a part of me believe it too?

Carolyn. Who was now dead. Whose brain had been blown to bits across my living room...the living room where my daughter had once taken her first steps, where my husband drew up plans for an epic treehouse that he would never get a chance to build while we sipped Coronas, where Link and I had made love on the day I'd told him about my past and that I loved him.

They're already closed, but I squeeze my eyes shut harder against the memories of her blood, hot and sticky all over me, bright red staining the thick white rug and the marble countertops. *Shit.* I've pushed too hard too fast. The monitors beep like crazy as my pulse races, and I feel like a weight has been placed on my chest, pressing me deeper and deeper downward. I can't breathe. I can't think. *No more, no more, no more.*

"What's happening?" Link and Drew both demand.

"Savvy!?" Link yells while doctors or nurses or both rush in and start shouting instructions. My heart is beating too fast, but I can't make it slow.

I can't...

I can't...

I...

Darkness.

***

Again, I start to swim upward from the depths. I can't open my eyes, but I can hear the low conversations around me again.

"This is my fault," Link whispers, voice low and hollow. He's sitting beside me and I want so badly to wrap my arms around him, but I'm a prisoner inside my own body. Between the meds and my own mind shutting down, I can't move.

"It's not, mate."

"It is though. Carolyn was unhinged, but *I* was the fixation of that. She only went after Savvy because of her delusional relationship with *me*. This is all on me, Drew. I almost got Savvy killed." His voice breaks at the end and so does my heart. I don't want him hurting like this. It wasn't his fault. I need to tell him, but I can't wake up, can't move my lips. Damn this! I shouldn't have pushed so hard before. I wanted so badly to be strong, but I'm not.

"But you *didn't*. She's alright, Link. She's right here, she's alive." Drew sounds exhausted and strained, miles from his typical cocky, happy-go-lucky self. "It's a bloody miracle."

"How many miracles can one person possibly get?" Link whispers. I've been wondering the same thing. My luck has to run out at some point, doesn't it?

"Link..." Drew sounds closer now, like maybe he walked to Link, probably put a hand on his shoulder and squeezed it in comfort.

"I...I can't risk putting her in this position ever again," Link whispers and he sounds so...defeated. *What does he mean?* "She was almost trampled outside of an event. They plastered her body across the tabloids and mocked her scars for all the world to see. They used her past as a gossip story. And then a psycho tried to murder her, Drew. Don't you get it? My life is causing her nothing but pain. I'm...I'm not good for her." I want to argue with him, to tell him that even though, yes, everything that comes with dating a movie star hasn't been rainbows and puppies, the good has far outweighed the bad. He has to know that, doesn't he?

I feel his lips graze my forehead. "I love you too much, Savannah. I won't let you be in danger or hurt again because of me. I have to..." He clears his throat. "I have to let you go." What? What does he mean *let me go*? God damn it, wake up! Is this even real? I've been having crazy dreams, so maybe this is just another one.

A nightmare.

He takes a ragged breath and I feel his lips press against mine. A drop of warm liquid treks down my cheek and I don't know if it's his tear or mine.

CHAPTER 22

Savannah

I finally wake who knows how long later with a heavy, cold sense of dread in my stomach. My eyes feel like they've been glued together, but I finally manage to pry them open. I wince at the light, blinding after so long in the darkness. I blink several times and the pain slowly recedes, my vision clearing. I glance around and my gaze lands on Tiff as she fiddles with flowers across the room. My eyes make another pass and I realize the room is overflowing with them. Roses and lilies and daisies, sunflowers and succulents. I spy huge bundles of peonies and my heart clenches. I know those are from Link. He knows they're my favorite and sends them to me almost every week when he's away...or he used to? Had that conversation been real?

She turns and gasps, rushing to my side. Her eyes are glassy as she brushes the hair back from my face.

"Oh my God, Sav! Don't scare me like that! I thought I was going to lose you for good that time." She wipes tears away and squeezes my hand.

"Sorry," I croak. She pours me some water from the pitcher on the table and helps me ease up to a sitting position. My throat feels raw—had I been screaming? I drink the whole cup, the cool water soothing my ravaged throat.

As many times as I've been in the hospital, Tiff knows that one of my least favorite things is waking up with that terrible fuzzy-mouth feeling and knowing that my breath could knock out an elephant. She quickly hands me a toothbrush, travel toothpaste, and an empty cup with a knowing smile.

"Bless you," I rasp. I quickly brush my teeth with probably a bit too much vigor and eventually feel slightly more human again. Well, my mouth doesn't taste like an old shoe anymore, at least. The rest of me is still undecided.

Tiff sits beside me and holds my hand, watching me like a hawk. Now that her relief from my waking is fading, I see the worry in her eyes, the sorrow. My entire body goes cold and I feel like I've been stabbed in the heart.

"He's gone, isn't he?"

She looks sad but doesn't sugarcoat things for me. One thing I love so much about her.

"Yes, he is." I close my eyes but can't stop the tears. Part of me already knew, already accepted my loss before I even woke, but the other part is shattering. "I'm so sorry, Savvy. He stayed by your side for the first week,"—first *week? How the hell long had I checked out for?*— "barely leaving even to pee. Drew and I had to physically force him to eat or shower. Colin was here too, and James. They managed to get him to change clothes and sleep a few hours here and there, but he was a complete wreck." I frown. She sounds like she feels sorry for him. Normally Tiff would be cussing him up and down for pulling a stunt like this, for ditching me—*dumping me?*—while I was unconscious and recovering from a bullet wound. So, why does it sound like she's *defending* him?

"I don't think I've ever seen a man that anguished, Sav. It was brutal. Everyone else was worried too, of course, but Link was like...I can't even explain it. He was just broken." I eye her and she understands what I'm asking. "I know, I know, I should be hating him, but..." She chews on her bottom lip for a second before continuing. "Well, I can't fault him for leaving, for not wanting you in this crazy life of his if it's going to put you in danger. It's all insane—the fans and the paparazzi and the media—but someone trying to *kill* you over him?! That's just pushing it too far!"

"You *agree* with him?" I ask incredulously, even as a part of my own mind whispers that *I* do. Hadn't a part of me always been apprehensive about this life? About being in the public eye and navigating being with a celebrity, trying to wrap my head around dealing with everything that came with that? I'd tried my best to take it all in stride and I think I did fairly well, but I'd hidden a lot of my worry and unease from Link, trying the whole fake-it-til-you-make-it route.

Truth is that it was fucking *hard*. Having my past opened wide for the world to see, having my every move scrutinized, reading horrible comments about myself online—I was too ugly, too fat, too thin, too scarred, too small-town, too much of a gold digger (guess no one had unearthed my net worth yet)—the list went on and on. It was all just a lot to deal with. It was worth it to be with Link...or at least, that's what I'd told myself. Maybe I was wrong. Maybe I was lying to myself, living in a fantasy world that couldn't possibly last.

Tiff gets that determined look on her face. "You don't get to guilt trip me here. A crazy obsessed fan broke into your house and almost *killed you*, Sav! If they hadn't gotten there in time..." She shudders and I barely stop myself from doing the same. It had been too close. "All I'm saying is that I understand where he was coming from. He wants to protect you and I can't blame him one bit for that. You've been through enough," she adds softly. Is she right? Should I just let this go, let *him* go?

"He, um, wrote you a letter." She nods towards an envelope on my bedside table. I'm starting to feel...numb. I know I'm shutting down—not checking out completely like before, but just shutting down, going on autopilot to survive. I'd done it before. I go through the motions, I do what I need to do day to day to physically survive, but everything else is just muted, hidden. Like I've shoved all my emotions in a closet and locked the door. Tiff seems to know exactly what's happening—she's seen it happen before, after all— and looks worried, but continues the conversation to try to pull me back out again.

She sniffles and wipes the last evidence of her tears away, forcing a smile. "So, I think the entire town sent you flowers," she says brightly. Overcompensating. I appreciate the effort. She gestures to various vases and baskets as she lists names. "Those are from Mr. Drake, the library sent the sunflowers, Ms. Earney of course sent the tulips right from her front yard." Her eyes sparkle. "Even *fans* sent some. You have fans, by the way, in case you didn't know. These ones here are from Michael." My lips actually curl a fraction at that.

She sits on the edge of the bed. "Griffey is fine. The vet checked him out and everything came back all clear. I've had him at my place while you've been recovering, so you know he's been spoiled rotten, but he's definitely missing you—though Lacey did help me sneak him in a few times after visiting hours." I huff out a low laugh, imagining the two of them sneaking the Golden Retriever through the hospital in the dead of night. I can absolutely guarantee that Tiff was humming the *Mission: Impossible* theme song the whole time.

After a few minutes of silence, I force myself to ask the nagging question.

"How long since..." I swallow hard as flashes of that day spring to mind and my palms start to sweat. The gun pointed at me. Searing pain. Hot blood spraying across my body from Carolyn's head. I clench my teeth and force the memories away. "How long have I been here?"

"Two weeks. Your bullet wound is basically healed, you'll just need the stitches removed in a few days. I know you hate the M word, but it was one. *You're* one—again."

"I know," I say quietly, knowing just how differently everything could have gone. I could easily be dead. Carolyn could have shot *Link.* Just thinking about him sends pain lacing through me, but...but maybe he's right. I was prepared for this to just be a summer fling when I first met him, and though things had gone wildly differently than originally planned, maybe that's for the best. Maybe we weren't meant to be something permanent. *But God, I want us to be.* I want him so badly that my entire body aches for him, my heart threatening to bleed out before I tighten that old tourniquet on once more.

"I'm going to go get the doctors, tell them you're awake. You'll probably be able to go home tomorrow if Dr. Forrester signs off on your mental state." She leans down and gives me a hug and I manage a small smile for her. Her eyes dart to the letter again before she leaves the room. I glance at it but decide not to read it yet. I'm determined to hold myself together enough that they'll let me leave. Once I'm home, I can fall apart again, but without Link there to hold the pieces together, I'm not sure what will happen.

***

Tomorrow turned into five days. The doctors were a little reluctant to let me go after such a traumatic experience and the little mental vacation I took afterward, but they finally relented. Now I stand in the middle of my living room, forcing myself to breathe. Tiff stands behind me, letting me do this, but within easy reach if I need her. Somewhere between finally leaving the damn hospital and stepping through the front door, I'd decided that Carolyn would *not* ruin my home for me. She would not destroy all the wonderful memories I have here with one terrible one. This place was my sanctuary, my dream, my haven. I refuse to let Carolyn take that away from me.

Everything's been cleaned completely, not a speck of blood remains. My rug is gone, but I let that slide off of me. If there's one thing I've learned over the years dealing with all of the things, it's that sometimes you just have to let things go. They don't matter. Let them go. The rug doesn't matter. The reason it's gone doesn't matter. Let it go. *I'm channeling my inner fucking Elsa hardcore right now.*

I force myself to remember that day, to walk through every moment. My heart rate kicks up and sweat breaks out on the back of my neck. Tiff steps up silently behind me and slides her hand into mine. I squeeze it and let the tears fall. She's always there when I need her, always saving me in one way or another.

I let the memories come: The gun. The fear in Link's eyes. The determination in Carolyn's. The blood. The pain. *Breathe. Breathe. Breathe.* After an eternity of replaying it over and over, I feel...ok. It will be a long time before I truly forget those horrific moments, all the blood, but I'll get there. I glance to the wall and my heart splinters. I'd printed one of my favorite shots of Link and placed it above the couch, just beside the portraits of Mia and Matt from years ago. I should take it down...but not yet.

I promise Tiff that I'm alright and she leaves to go pick up some groceries and bring Griffey back over. Once she's gone, I pick up my phone, pulling up my last message with Link, from that day. My eyes prick with tears again.

Link: just landed!

Savvy: hope Drew has noise-canceling headphones at the ready...

Link: dear God I love you.

Two weeks. In two short weeks my life had gone from quick, flirty texts with the man I loved to...empty. How had it all fallen apart so quickly? I ache to text him now. To tell him I love him. To tell him I miss him. To tell him to fuck off and that I hate him. *All of the above.*

My finger hovers over the keyboard, but I sigh and lock the phone screen before I do anything stupid. Maybe he was right and just cutting out clean was the right way to do this. A clean break, that's what they always say, right? I remember a doctor saying that about my arm once when I'd broken it during a soccer game: *Good news! It's a clean break. That'll make the healing process much easier and quicker.*

So, maybe it *will* be easier this way. I don't know. Some moments I think yes, others I want to scream no. I don't know what the right answer is. All I know is that this fucking hurts way more than a bullet to the shoulder.

***

It's been a month without a word from Link. A month since he left me. Or dumped me. Or whatever. I still haven't read his letter. I'd thrown it away twice, almost torched it once, and opened it to read it, only to immediately shove it back in a drawer too many times to count.

I cycle between feeling heartbroken, feeling semi-ok and believing that maybe this is for the best, and absolutely raging that he ended things the way he had, that he'd ended things at all.

Today, I'm in a rage state and I'm very tempted to yank his photo off the wall and have a bonfire. I stare at it for a few minutes, remembering the day I took it, remembering how much fun we had at the beach and all of the downright naughty things we did afterwards.

"You know what, fuck it," I say, jumping up on the couch and yanking the picture down. Griffey barks at me, putting his front paws up on the couch and staring intently. To help? Or to stop me? I'm not sure.

I stare down at the photo in my hands, wanting to destroy it, but then all of my anger drains out of me like someone's pulled the plug. I sink down on to the couch, legs curled beneath me. I know he didn't end things this way to hurt me. I know he thinks he's doing what's best, what he believes will keep me safe.

And at least part of me agrees with him, which makes this all so much harder.

I study the picture, running my fingers over the cold glass. The shot is of him down at the beach by his rental house. I'd captured him mid-laugh, so he's got this gorgeous genuine smile on his face, and he's looking down. His profile is so striking in black and white, highlighting his square jaw with that touch of stubble I love so much, and proud nose. I sigh and hang the frame back on the wall where it belongs. Whether we're together anymore or not, he's still a part of my life, forever a part of my heart, just as Mia and Matt are.

"I miss you," I whisper to all of them, leaning my forehead against the wall as tears slide down my cheeks.

CHAPTER 23

Lincoln

I hate this. I hate every second of every day without Savvy. Drew and Colin have tried to change my mind a hundred times in the past month, but I'm not going to. This is what's best for her and that's all I care about. My own heart can bleed out as long as hers is still beating. I felt like a coward essentially breaking up with her in a letter, stealing away in the dead of night while she was in a hospital bed for fuck's sake, but I knew if I'd been there when she woke, I wouldn't have been strong enough to go through with it, to do what had to be done. It's the right call.

But fuck if it doesn't hurt like hell.

When we'd been apart before, it had felt like I was missing a limb, but now it's like I'd amputated it myself, made the conscious decision to slice through it with a jagged saw. *For the best, for the best, for the best.* I have to tell myself that at least fifty times a day. I've almost called her too many times to count, but somehow stopped my finger from pressing the button each time. She deserves for me to make this clean.

She hasn't called me either, so she must agree with the choice...but I'd be lying if I said that part of me hadn't hoped that she'd call as soon as she'd woken up to scream at me, demand that

I come back immediately and stop being an idiot. That hadn't happened, so she must think she's better off without me, without being part of my chaotic life. *The life that almost got her fucking killed*, I remind myself again.

Whenever my resolve begins to crumble, I force myself to remember those moments of terror when I saw Carolyn raise that gun and pull the trigger. I hadn't been able to breathe, had never been so terrified in my life. It felt as if I were drowning and on fire all at once, and I never want to feel that way again. I would have done anything to trade places with her, to take that bullet, to shield her from all of that. I'll never be able to forget the shellshocked look on Savvy's face, Carolyn's blood splattered across her front and her own blood pouring from her shoulder, the screams that had come not long after her initial shock that nobody could stop until they'd sedated her. When I remember all of that, my resolve fortifies like a steel fucking trap. *She's better off without me.*

I'm constantly thinking about her, though, despite my best efforts. Some days are harder than others, though no day is ever easy. Today is a hard one. Today is the anniversary of the day I met her, the day that changed my life in ways I never thought possible. I stare at the little velvet-lined box on my desk. I haven't been able to bring myself to get rid of it. I let myself imagine what today would have meant if things had turned out differently. It would have been another new start, just like that day at the Fort had been one a year ago. I clench my jaw and snatch the box off of the desk, shoving it into a drawer and slamming it closed. I lay my head in my hands and, not for the first time, let myself break.

✳✳✳

Two more months pass. It's still hard. I still miss her every day. Thank God Tiff has broken the Bestie Code and texted me here and there to let me know how Savvy is doing. She'd kept me updated on Savvy's recovery and let me know when she had first gotten out of the hospital, how she forced herself to go back to the house and face everything. My lips had curled when Tiff had told me about it, told me how Sav had gritted her teeth and said "that bitch won't take my home away from me. So, I'm fucking doing this...and if I have a breakdown, well, hell, not like it hasn't happened before." My girl was so damn strong. *Not your girl anymore, idiot,* I remind myself.

Even with the updates from Tiff, I still wonder how Savvy's doing with everything. Is she hurting? Is she having nightmares?...Does she hate me? Part of me hopes she does, figures it'll make it easier for her to move on if she does. The thought of her moving on slices like a knife and makes me want to scream until my throat bleeds. But she deserves to. She deserves to move on and be happy and live her life—without me. I close my eyes and accept the pain, the churning acid in my throat, the feel of my chest constricting like a giant fist is squeezing my heart to pulp.

I've itched to talk to her about all these press events I've been having to do, to share funny stories or vent my frustrations, to just doze off with her on the phone with me because I've been so damned exhausted. I just...I miss her. I miss everything about her. I miss the way she laughs at the absolute stupidest jokes, and not just a little chuckle, like full on laughing until she snorts. I miss the way she steals all the covers and then complains that it's hot. I miss the way she somehow always knows exactly what I'm trying to say even when I can't even get close to expressing it correctly in words.

She became the love of my life and one of my very best friends all at once, and now I've lost both.

"Are you sure about this, son?" dad asks. I'd come out to the farm to get away from everything for a few days, but unfortunately have to head back to reality tomorrow. The world of movie promotions doesn't give a shit that my heart is utterly pulverized and that I'll never recover. Nope, still gotta plaster that smile on and do endless interviews and be my normal charming self.

"No," I sigh. "But yes." He seems to understand without me having to explain and nods.

"I understand, but for what it's worth, I think you're making a mistake."

I turn to look at him, feeling like I'm sixteen again, just needing my dad to make sense of the world and fix all of my problems.

"She almost died, dad. Because of *me*."

"She almost died before you came into the picture too," he reminds me. "What happened with Carolyn was tragic, but it was a freak occurrence. One in a million—just like the odds of you finding another Savannah."

I press my lips into a thin line, not liking his take...because I know he's partly right. But I just can't take the risk. I'd rather her hate me than be in danger or hurt because of me. And not just physically. The mental toll that being torn apart on social media takes is insane. I know she says it doesn't bother her, but I know it does, at least on some level. One of these days, it would have been too much for her and then she would have left me anyway.

At least this way it's a clean break and she doesn't have to get even more hurt before it happens.

I clench my jaw, feeling the muscle tic over and over. Even that reminds me of her—she'd told me more than once that it was my tell. She knew when I was upset or feeling something strongly when that muscle started to tic. I tighten my hands on the railing until my knuckles turn white.

"She deserves better," is all I say.

Dad gives me a very dad look and squeezes my shoulder before heading back into the house. I stay on the porch, leaning my forearms on the railing and staring out over the land. It's so peaceful out here. Sometimes I wish I wasn't Lincoln Ashmore, that I was just a regular guy who could live out here in the peace with the woman I love beyond all reason.

I sigh, knowing that's a dream that will never come true, and head back inside.

CHAPTER 24

Savannah

I've finally decided to read Link's letter. It's been almost four months and I know that it needs to happen. This is the last piece of the puzzle. Once I do this, the picture will be complete, the snapshot of my time with Link a beautiful memory that I can take apart and put back in the box.

I've been avoiding it all this time, knowing that this will be the end, and I haven't been ready for that until now. I mean, I'm not *actually* ready for it now, but I know that I never truly will be, so delaying it any longer isn't healthy. Dr. Forrester and I have talked about it at length, along with everything else, of course. She'd been extremely concerned that I was going to backslide drastically after the shooting. There was only so much any one person's mind and soul could handle. She wasn't saying I wasn't strong, but she'd been worried that the traumatic experience with Carolyn and losing Link afterwards was going to be my final tipping point.

I've been doing pretty well overall, all things considered, but everyone is worried about me. I'm not in the kind of dark place that I went to after the crash, despite Dr. Forrester's (completely legitimate) concerns, but I'm just...here. Auto-pilot. I haven't gone back to volunteering at all, when I hang out with Tiff, I zone out without meaning to (which of course she forgives because she's a far better friend than I deserve). I don't even take Griffey on our coffee date every morning anymore. I sigh. I may not be in the dark places, but I'm not anywhere too bright either.

The nightmares have been bad lately too, but they aren't about the crash, like usual. Instead, they're about Carolyn and Link. Sometimes it's a replay of that day, almost exactly as it happened. Others it's so much worse: I watch Carolyn shoot Link and I wake up screaming and crying and, on more than one occasion, violently ill. Those are the dreams that made me understand his decision. If roles had been reversed, I don't think I could live with myself feeling like I put Link in danger like that. So, I still don't like it, but I *get* it.

But since the universe apparently delights in my misery, I can barely turn on the TV or scroll through anything online without seeing Link's face. He's been doing non-stop promotions for the new movie and the *Shadowlands* reunion. Every time I see him, it's like a grenade explodes in my chest. He seems like he's fine, answering questions, smiling, laughing, but I know him well enough to see that he's miserable. I'm conflicted on that honestly. A small, terrible part of me is glad he's not happy, not just out there totally ok when I'm barely keeping it together.

The bigger part of me hurts that he's hurting, though. I *do* want him to be happy. He deserves that and so much more. He never gives himself enough credit for the man he is. He's so damned *good* in a world that mostly isn't, he deserves everything he wants out of life: to be himself, to be happy, to have a family. I clench the steering wheel when a sudden whip of pain lashes me, knowing that he'll have all of that some day with someone else.

I've been antsy all day knowing I was going to do this, and though I didn't really have a destination in mind when I got in the car, I end up at the Fort. I want to roll my eyes. *Of course I did.*

"Ending it the same place it began," I say to the waves. "How fucking poetic." I toss a shell into the surf as hard as I can. I take a few deep breaths and then pull the envelope out of my bag. I trace my fingers over my name and I realize they're shaking. Tears are already stinging my eyes and my pulse is racing. I feel too hot and too cold at once, but know I need to push through. *Ok, it's time. Just rip the band aid off.* I hesitate for a few seconds longer before tearing the envelope open and yanking the folded page out.

I read the letter, then read it again. A third time. The tears fall and my heart clenches. God, I still love him so much. I miss him so much. The letter is full of his love for me, and full of pain as he explains why he had to leave, why he's making the hardest decision of his life to make my own better.

I read the last sentence over and over, my eyes drawn to it as something shifts inside of my chest, an unshakable resolve rising up in me.

No.

Suddenly, everything clicks into place in an entirely new way. Just like that, the path of my life focuses with perfect clarity after months and months of an uncertain mess spread out before me. I scramble up, my heart racing. I sniffle, scrubbing away tears as my resolve hardens.

"No," I say, out loud this time. I freeze for a moment as my eyes snag on something out in the distance.

Was that a...fin?

I want to laugh. I want to cry. But a smile curls my lips. "Ok, ok. I get it, baby. I get it." I grab my bag and sprint back to my car, sand flying behind me and pelting my ankles.

CHAPTER 25

Lincoln

There's a downpour in L.A. after almost eight months of drought. We definitely need the water, but rain reminds me of Savvy—*Jesus, what* doesn't *remind me of her?*—of how much she loved the sound it made pinging against the metal roof of her house, how she loved to sit on the porch and watch storms roll through. How one had done just that when we'd made love on the floor of the living room after she told me she loved me the first time. I wince at the memory and rub my chest. I'd managed to go a whole twenty minutes today without thinking about her, but now I'm right back in it. I know it's been months and it's time to start moving on, but I just can't. I don't want to. I made the choice to end things, but that doesn't mean I'll ever stop loving Savannah Riley. I won't be with her, but she will always be with me.

My doorbell rings, rousing me from my stewing, but I frown, brows furrowing. I'm not expecting anyone and only a handful of people have the gate code. It rings again—and again. Followed by banging and more ringing.

"What the fuck?"

If someone needed something so badly, why didn't they call first? Somewhere between annoyed and pissed, I head to the door. I'm honestly not in the mood for any visitors, let alone unexpected ones who ring my doorbell fourteen times and bang on my door like a fucking jackhammer.

I yank the door open, fully prepared to demand an explanation, almost itching for a fight honestly, but my words die on my lips.

Savvy.

On my doorstep.

Drenched from the rain.

This can't be real...can it? We both just stare for what seems like ages. She's breathing hard and soaking wet, but God she looks gorgeous. Rain drops spike her long lashes, and the gold in her eyes is sparkling in the porch light. Neither of us seems able to speak, but when the car honks she manages a negligent wave goodbye. Is that...Colin's car? What is happening?

Why is she here? *How* is she here? Tiff had texted me yesterday afternoon and told me that Savvy had just had a follow up appointment with the cardiologist. So, how in the fuck did she drive across the entire country in less than a day? *Unless...*

My eyes go wide and words finally slip free, breaking the strange trance we're both in.

"You...you got on a plane?"

She shakes herself, and her eyes blaze. Her shoulders shift back and she juts her chin. Dear God I've missed seeing her like this: Strong. Stubborn. Determined.

"Of course I got on a fucking plane," she snaps, as if that isn't a huge deal. "I needed to tell you in person that this—" She yanks my letter out of her jacket pocket. The envelope is wet, the ink running on the front like black veins across the white paper. "—

is bullshit. Beautifully sweet bullshit, but bullshit all the same. And also to say that you're a coward. But mostly, the bullshit thing."

She got on a plane. She flew across the country to come here to...yell at me? *She got on a plane.* Then my brows draw down as I stare at the letter in her hand.

"You're only just now reading it?" I never imagined she wouldn't have read it in all this time, though I guess I should have. She narrows her eyes and I immediately regret saying it, but my mind is racing, my mouth not really taking orders from my brain. I hold my palms up, silently retracting my statement. "Savvy, I—"

"No. You don't get to talk now. You listen and you listen up good, Lincoln Ashmore. *I* decide what's best for me, not *you*." I remember writing the words, each stroke of the pen like a knife to my chest: *I'll love you with every breath for the rest of my life, but I can't do this to you anymore. You deserve better. You deserve the best. And what's best for you, is a life away from me.*

She swallows hard and stares into my eyes for an endless moment and everything seems to freeze around us, as if the entire world is holding its breath.

"And what's best for me, *is you*."

My chest cracks and my breath hitches. Before I can think, I have her in my arms, one hand tangled in her hair and the other cupping her cheek, pulling her face to mine. My lips crash against hers.

Contact.

Heaven.

How had I survived without this? Never again. I slant my head and deepen the kiss as she clutches at the front of my shirt, fingers tearing into the fabric. Our tongues tangle in a familiar, desperate dance. She manages to pull free after what seems like an eternity. She places both hands on my face and holds my gaze. Her eyes are fierce and determined.

"I love you. I need to be with you. You are it for me, do you understand? We can figure out this crazy life of yours—because it's *my* crazy life now too."

"But...you almost died..." She silences me with a kiss.

"That was a *fluke*. How often does any celebrity have fans that go off the rails like that?" Just as my dad had pointed out. "Exactly," she says with a smile when she sees I'm on the brink of admitting she's right. "Link, if I have learned anything in this life, it's that anything can happen to anyone at any time. There's no rhyme or reason. You can't protect me from it and I don't expect you to. But *I* get to decide how I spend whatever time I have left on this roulette wheel, not you. So much of my life has been out of my control—my parents' deaths, the crash, losing Matt and Mia—but this? Choosing how I spend my life? *That* is mine to control, and I plan to from now on."

A smile spreads across my face and a sense of rightness settles over me. Everything shifts in my mind in that instant. I know we can do this. We can navigate everything, can make our life what *we* want it to be, despite my career. It won't always be easy, but I know that we can handle it—together. She's right: the letter was bullshit and I was a coward. I really thought I was doing the right thing, but now I see that being apart isn't right for either of us. We're stronger together, better together.

From the very beginning, I knew we were meant to be together. She makes me *me* in a way no one else ever could. I need her in my life or it will never be a full one. If she didn't want this,

I would be strong enough to let her go, but she does. By some fucking miracle, she wants and needs me as much as I want and need her. I've loved her since the minute I saw her, and I don't care how cliché that sounds. It's the truth. She is my truth. She is my home. She is my everything.

"So, if you still want this with me, then I want this with you. My chips are still all in the ring, Link."

"That's not the saying," I mutter as I pull her into another kiss. She smiles against my lips, laughing as tears slide down her cheeks. "Link," she says, and the desperate plea in her voice breaks something inside me.

A heartbeat later, she's in my arms, legs wrapped around my hips. God, I've missed the feel of her, the taste of her. I walk us back inside as she yanks her sodden shirt off, quickly followed by her bra. I'm already dropping to my knees in the foyer, knowing that I can't make it any further. She seems to agree, hands flying to my jeans while I pull my own shirt off. I need her so badly, need to reassure myself that she's actually here, to show her how sorry I am, how much I love her. I make quick work of her jeans and she shimmies her hips to help me get them off. *Dear God why is wet denim the worst thing on the planet!?* She laughs at my frustrated grunts and the sound is like coming home.

"Who knew the Captain's downfall was wet jeans," she teases breathlessly. I grin before leaning down to give her a kiss and soft bite on her hip, and her soft moan drives me wild. I swear to God I'm about to find a knife and cut the damned things off of her, but they finally slide the rest of the way off of her legs. I toss the cursed things away, a soggy *plop* sounding from the other end of the foyer. I lay beside her, pulling her body tight against mine and kissing her hard, reveling in the feel of her lips on mine, the feel of her tongue against mine. I tunnel my hand into her lace panties and groan when I find her wet already. I quickly slip two fingers inside her and she gasps against my mouth.

"Missed you. Missed this. Need more," she pants as I pump my fingers in and out, in and out. She rolls her hips in time with my thrusts, mindless. My cock pulses as she rides my hand, and I'm desperate to bury myself deep inside her. As if reading my mind, she yanks at my boxer-briefs. I pull away long enough to remove her panties and shift between her thighs. She holds my gaze as I slide inside until her eyes finally flutter close, a gasp of pleasure breaking free from her lips.

"Fuckkkk," I rasp when I settle myself as far as I can go. She grips my hips, fingers digging into the small of my back as she urges me to move. I do. Long, deep thrusts while I kiss her until she's breathless. I pull back to look at her as I move and I've never seen anything so beautiful.

"I love you, Savannah. God, I love you."

She arches up and kisses me before pushing at my chest with both hands. I know her well enough to understand exactly what she wants. I shift so that I'm sitting and she settles herself in my lap, wrapping her legs around me. She rocks her hips and a ragged moan bursts from my chest. I grip her waist as she rides me, our sweat-slicked chests rubbing against each other as she moves.

"I love you, Link," she whispers before slanting her mouth over mine once more. Our tongues dance as our bodies writhe. She grips my neck and leans her body backward and the new angle has us both moaning and cursing and praying. I've replayed memories of her over and over since the day I left her, but they pale in comparison to the real thing. She's gorgeous. She's sexy. She's *mine.*

Soon, we both careen over the edge of bliss. She drapes her arms around my neck and rests her head in the crook of my neck as we try to slow our breathing. I wrap my arms around her, holding her so tightly to me that I'm afraid I might hurt her, but I can't stop. I thought I'd never have this again and I let out a long shuddering breath as everything hits me. All of the emotions I've been bottling up over the last four months come pouring out, and she squeezes me tightly as I let them. I let myself break, and this time, she's the one holding all of *my* broken pieces together.

That's what we do. We put each other back together again. We always will.

At last, I get a handle on myself and pull back. I brush strands of damp golden hair back from her beautiful face, tucking the locks behind her ears and softly stroking her cheekbones with my thumbs. I lean my forehead against hers, eyes sliding closed.

"You got on a plane," I whisper.

I can hear the smile in her voice when she responds.

"I got on a plane."

Savannah

Two years later

"Drew's pulling up now."

Link leans in to give me a quick kiss. He pulls back, and then thinks better of it, coming back into kiss me deeply. I'm breathless by the time he pulls away again.

"You keep that up and Drew is going to walk in on something dirty."

Link snorts. "As if that's never happened before." I giggle. Drew had, in fact, walked in on Link and I in compromising positions a time or two over the past few years. He'd playfully asked if he could join in each time. One of these days, I'm going to say yes just to see his reaction.

I glance out the window and sigh at the view. Horse pastures for miles, crystalline lake beyond that, thick forest on all sides. Link and I had agreed that while we knew life would always have some bit of crazy involved, we didn't want to be in the heart of it. So, he'd sold his place in L.A. and found us a beautiful piece of land in Oklahoma, not far from where he'd grown up actually, and we'd built our dream house together. We kept my house in

Sandlapper Cove and visit as often as we can. That house would always have a piece of my heart and would always be special to me, but it isn't my home anymore. Here, with Link, *that's* my home. Always will be.

I'd survived my first premiere for the movie that brought us together, and even if it hadn't been a worldwide success, winning a few awards along the way, it would forever be my favorite Ashmore flick. Even topping Captain Ultra, which was really saying something. After that, I'd gotten used to red carpets and interviews, though I still like to stay out of the spotlight and let Link shine for the both of us more often than not.

Overall, the life of a movie star's wife isn't quite as crazy as I'd been expecting. I glance down at the ring on my left hand now and smile, still not quite believing that Link and I are married, that I'm this lucky. After the crash, I never imagined my life would continue, let alone that I'd be happy again. I meet Link's gaze and his smile makes my stomach flip and my toes curl. Because of him, I've learned to be happy again. Because of him, I finally learned that moving on doesn't mean forgetting, it just means making more room in your heart for the past and the future to exist together. I still think of Mia and Matt, still miss them every day and stop every so often to watch a few scenes before letting them fade to background noise again, but I know that they'd want this for me.

I still wear my first wedding band around my neck, and even now, my fingers reach up to stroke the cool metal. I'd decided to take it off one night, feeling like it was time, like I owed it to my new husband to stop being so attached to my old one. My hand had been shaking, but Link had placed his over it, stopping me. He'd smiled and without a word, told me that keeping a part of

Matt with me was right. If I hadn't known before that moment how good of a man Lincoln Ashmore was, that would have been all the proof I needed.

I grin as Link bends down to scoop the baby up from the bed.

A daughter named Riley.

It had been Link's idea to use my former married name as her first name, a way to honor what had come before and keep Matt and Mia in our lives in a way. I swear, every time I think I can't possibly love him more, he pulls stunts like that and makes me realize that the well of love I have for him is truly depthless. He kisses her chubby cheek and my heart feels like it's going to burst.

"Are you ready to meet your uncle Drew?" Link asks, bouncing Riley on his hip and making her giggle. She's got my blonde hair, but Link's green eyes and though I am probably biased, I believe she's the prettiest baby in the world. It had killed Drew that he hadn't been able to be there for her birth and then had to wait almost six months before officially meeting her in person because of his filming schedule and an unexpected blizzard canceling all flights the first time he'd tried to come visit.

He'd insisted on FaceTiming with her almost every day though, which was utterly adorable, but it still chapped him that Tiff had met Riley before him—which of course, she continually threw in his face. Their friends-with-occasional-benefits situation has remained over the years. According to Tiff: *sometimes when we're around each other, I get the itch and he is a damn fine scratcher.*

They both loved their de-facto niece so much I could barely stand it. She'd been the surprise of all surprises to say the least. Looking at her now, cooing and grabbing Link's hair with her little fingers, I can't help but think back to that fateful doctor's visit.

"You're pregnant," Dr. Melton said, eyes dancing with delight and that look all doctors get when anything related to the M word happens in the medical field. Because of my injuries in the crash, I'd been told over and over that the chance of me ever conceiving again was slim to none. Slimmer than none. So much slimmer than none, in fact, that I hadn't even bothered with birth control.

He smiled. "It's a Mir—"

"Don't. Say. It," I said, eyes closed, trying to breathe through the onslaught of emotions. Guilt. Joy. Love. Hope. Fear. No, not just fear: utter terror. I couldn't have another child, couldn't survive...losing another child. That familiar feeling of my ribs tightening and making it hard to breathe started, shocking me. I hadn't had a panic attack in almost a year, Link helping to make my path of grief easier and easier to navigate with each passing day.

"I'm...I'm sorry," he said, confused. "It's just that given your history..."

"I know," I sighed, trying to push past the panic. "I know. It's a...miracle." I said the word with a grimace, as I usually did, but this time, it didn't feel right. The emotions still warred within me, but the one that was becoming louder and louder was hope.

A baby with Link. He'd always wanted a child, a family, and though he'd all but given up those hopes with me, I knew he would be ecstatic. Beyond ecstatic. He'd be over the fucking moon. And...I was too? Or starting to be anyway.

A whole new future opened up before my eyes. The same way it had that day on the beach when I'd read Link's letter and my path shifted, becoming something new and completely set. I could see it so clearly: Link with our baby in his arms; me rocking my son or daughter to sleep; Link teaching him or her to ride horses like he had growing up and to fish like he so loved to do; me taking a million pictures of them all together. I wanted it.

I suddenly wanted it so badly my hands clenched into fists. I knew in that moment that I would fight like hell for it. I would fight for this future, for this baby. I knew that a big part of that fight was going to be against myself *and all of my baggage, but I would do it. And I would fucking win.*

Because I wanted this baby. I wanted a family with Link.

I smiled at Dr. Melton and tears filled my eyes. "It's a miracle," I breathed.

I'd gotten a Captain Ultra onesie and added "Jr." to the name as my way of breaking the news to Link. He'd looked at it in confusion for a few long moments before he turned a stunned, teary-eyed gaze to me.

"But I thought..." He trailed off and shook himself. "Seriously?" he'd croaked. When I'd nodded, holding back tears of my own, he'd bolted up from the couch, nearly tackling me. The end of the video was the phone flying through the air and my scream-turned-giggle as he picked me up and twirled me around and around. The audio had actually caught what we'd done next on the living room floor, but we'd edited that part out before sharing video with family and friends, and, eventually, the world.

We're still fairly private when it comes to our lives compared to most people in Link's position, but we both really care about his fans—the ones who don't want to murder me anyway—and do share a bit of our lives with them.

I'd gained a semi-huge following of my own once I'd finally reactivated my social media pages, partly because of being Link's girlfriend, then fiancé, then wife, but also because of my reputation after that very first Gatorcon with Michael and everything I'd done piggy-backing off of that since. I'd started a foundation that paid ASL interpreters to be available at comicons across the country for anyone who might need it. It had struck me that not every deaf person would have a brother to attend things with them like Michael had. So, now, when purchasing tickets for any major con event, anyone who might need it could sign up to have an interpreter available to them at no extra cost. Michael had been a big part of the process and the foundation was in his name. He now gets an all-access to pass to any con he wants and we meet up at as many as possible.

I'd started up my photography again too, but it's all pro bono these days. I do a lot of shoots at cons and events, and of Link as Captain Ultra visiting children's hospitals and things like that. I've mostly mastered my fear of flying after that first rip-the-band-aid-right-the-fuck-off trip when I'd gone to tell Link he was an idiot. I still can't believe I'd actually done it sometimes. Looking back, I remember the phone call with Colin.

"I'm coming to L.A.," I'd blurted as soon as he'd answered.

A slight pause, then a whoosh of a relieved breath. "Oh thank God. You're both complete idiots. What can I do?"

"Tell me where I need to fly in to and come pick me up when I get there." I started shoving clothes and toiletries into a weekender bag that Link had gotten me before one of our road trips. It had almost ended up in the dumpster in the weeks after he'd left, but thankfully I'd thought better of that plan.

"Fly? Like...on a plane?"

"No, on a fucking goose. Yes, on a plane," I'd snapped before quickly adding. "Sorry. I'm amped up right now. Big life-altering revelations and all that."

"Apology accepted," he said quickly, and I could hear the smile in his voice. "Ok, give me twenty minutes and I'll have everything lined up. I'll text you the details."

"Thanks, Col."

"Savvy."

"Yes?"

"Are you...well, I just mean..."

"I'll be ok. I can do this." I was eighty percent sure I could, anyway. I zipped my bag and closed my eyes. "I *need* to do this," I corrected.

"Ok, I'm on it. Text you soon."

"Thanks, Colin. Love you."

"Love you too, Sav."

I'd laughed when I heard James in the background yell, "Oh my God, is that Savan—" before Colin hung up.

The drive to the airport with Tiff was honestly a blur. She was also worried, but happy I was going to get my life back.

"Bout damn time," she'd said when I called her and explained what was going on, grinning like a Cheshire cat on the FaceTime video.

"I would like to point out that *you* were the one that said you agreed with the decision!" I accused as I ran around, trying to find my phone charger.

She rolled her eyes. "At first, yes, but I didn't *really* think it was right, and I honestly never imagined either of you would actually stick to it. I figured one of you would have broken down long before now," she shrugged. "You two belong together. It's disgustingly romantic, actually."

Somehow when we got to the hangar, I didn't completely freak out. I mean, my stomach had knotted and I was a sweaty mess when it was all said and done, but I got on the plane and didn't pass out, so I call that a huge win. I think in that moment, my raw determination outweighed everything else and kept all of the other thoughts locked out. I had a goal—getting to Link, and I had an obstacle in my way—a flight. This time, the goal was too important to let the obstacle win.

After about an hour into the flight, I felt much better, even relaxed enough to watch a movie, though I didn't really pay much attention to it. I still white knuckled my arm rest most of the trip, and downed a whole mini bottle of Jack Daniels to help dull the edge of panic, but overall, I was remarkably proud of myself.

Now, flying is just a part of our lives. Sometimes it's harder to make myself get on the plane than others, memories flaring up for whatever reason, but usually Link is right there to squeeze my hand and get me through it. We've been able to explore the world together now that I'd gotten past my fear, gotten to see and do things I never could have imagined.

We head out of Riley's nursery, Griffey following close on Link's heels, ever the protective big brother. I sigh in pure contentment as I watch them go. I smile when I hear Drew bust in the front door, bellowing, "Where is my bloody niece!?" I laugh when I realize for the millionth time that this is *actually* my life.

I'm still far from "fixed." I still have bad days, but the good ones far outnumber them. I still miss the family I lost, but am soaking up every second with the new one that I've been blessed with. Things aren't always perfect, but the imperfections make it all the better. It would be so boring if things were perfect all the time...and the makeup sex makes pretty much every fight worth it in the end.

My road trip of grief and healing is smoother now, but every so often I still hit a pothole or wind up on a detour through rougher terrain.

And that's ok.

When I see Link holding our daughter, when I see the absolute unyielding love in his eyes every time he looks at me, when I think of everything we've built together and how full my heart is, I understand that every bump in the road led me here. It hasn't always been easy, and I've wanted to give up more than once, but in the end, it's all been worth it. Life is more beautiful than I ever thought possible, and it's all because of three little words:

Carpe Fucking Diem.

ACKNOWLEDGMENTS:

- To my family and friends: thank you for always supporting this strange little hobby.
- To my awesome PA, Laura, who rocks my socks on a daily basis.
- To my fantastic ARC team for always being up for reading and reviewing my nonsense.
- To Kayleigh and Lexie for putting up with my endless second-guessing and opinion-seeking on this one. From title, to cover, to opening lines: y'all have these two fabulous ladies to thank for this one (or to blame, if you hated it...)

More books by K.D. Miller:

(ALL available on Amazon and included for FREE with Kindle Unlimited subscriptions!)

New Adult Sci-Fi:

Titan Rising

Titan Unleashed

Titan Reckoning

New Adult Fantasy:

Evansfire

Adult Paranormal Romance:

Dark Burning (Veracity of the Gods, Book 1)

Sweet Tempest (Veracity of the Gods, Book 2)

Red

www.kdmillerbooks.com

www.ingramcontent.com/pod-product-compliance
Lightning Source LLC
Chambersburg PA
CBHW020101310726
48970CB00002B/423